DEATH TO IMMORTALS!

Before anyone could react, a 7.9mm bullet took Milo in the pit of the arm. The bullet bored completely through his chest before exiting in the left-frontal quadrant and going through the biceps, skewering both lungs and his heart along the way. The lancing agony had been exquisite, unbearable, and Milo had screamed. He drew in a deep agonizing breath to scream once again and that second scream choked away as he coughed up a boiling rush of blood. . . .

HORSECLANS #14

ROBERT ADAMS

A MAN CALLED MILO MORAI

A SIGNET BOOK

NEW AMERICAN LIBRARY

NAL BOOKS ARE AVAILABLE AT QUANTITY DISCOUNTS
WHEN USED TO PROMOTE PRODUCTS OR SERVICES. FOR
INFORMATION PLEASE WRITE TO PREMIUM MARKETING
DIVISION, NEW AMERICAN LIBRARY, 1633 BROADWAY,
NEW YORK, NEW YORK 10019.

SIGNET TRADEMARK REG.U.S.PAT.OFF. AND FOREIGN COUNTRIES
REGISTERED TRADEMARK—MARCA REGISTRADA
HECHO EN CHICAGO, U.S.A.

SIGNET, SIGNET CLASSIC, MENTOR, PLUME, MERIDIAN and NAL BOOKS
are published by New American Library,
1633 Broadway, New York, New York 10019

First Printing, February, 1986

1 2 3 4 5 6 7 8 9

PRINTED IN THE UNITED STATES OF AMERICA

This, the fourteenth volume of HORSECLANS, is
dedicated to:

Mr. Gary Massey, gentleman-attorney;
Mr. Scott Wasmund, gentleman-CPA;
Dr. Bill Brown, gentleman-cardiologist;
Mr. Richard Evans, gentleman-editor;
Mr. Ed Hayes, gentleman-journalist;
Mr. Ken Kelly, gentleman-cover artist; and to
Mr. Bernhard Goetz, gentleman-at-arms.

PROLOGUE

The day of hunting, trapping, seining and foraging for wild plants, fruits, nuts and tubers had gone well in this rich, not often hunted slice of the great prairie. Fillets of fish and thin slices of venison now had been added to others already in the process of curing over slow, smoky beds of fire scattered about the camp of the hunters.

All of the daylight hours, those who had not ridden forth with the hunting and foraging parties or fished the small river had been hard at the tasks of tending the fires and the meat and fish that hung above them, had scraped and stretched and salted and rolled the skins and hides, rendered fish offal for glue, and performed the countless other tasks necessary to maintain the camp and its temporary inhabitants—human, feline and equine.

Between chores, certain of the camp detail cared for and saw to the needs of an injured boy. His intemperate insubordination of the preceding night had resulted in his chief flinging him into the still-live coals of a large firepit —a regrettable but very necessary cost of survival in the often-harsh environment was instant and savage punishment for failure to obey leaders, for repeated instances of such undisciplined conduct might well one day cost lives, his own and many another also.

As Sacred Sun declined in the western sky, the parties began to return to the camp with the spoils of their forays on the countryside and waters. Having less distance to travel and being also blessed with the faster, easier road, the fishing party was the first back at the campsite, where they drew their small boats of hide and wood through the shallows and up upon the shelving beach before unloading their catches of assorted fish, then, with flashing knives, all set about the cleaning, scaling or skinning and filleting of the feebly flopping creatures. The larger of the fillets went to the racks above the smoky fires, while the smaller went into piles and pots for the evening meal.

The foragers were next to return, offloading hampers of assorted plant materials from led horses to be sorted, dried and repacked to bear back to the clans or used immediately for their own sustenance. Then this party divided, and while some saw to the horses or the sorting, others remounted and rode out to check lines of traps, snares, pits and logfalls.

The first of two hunting groups rode in with a spirited whooping, laden with no less than three good-sized deer —two of them ordinary whitetails, a buck and a big doe, but the third a rare and much-prized spotted buck with palmate antlers—a smallish wapiti buck, some near-dozen long-legged hares and an assortment of other small game and birds.

While still this first party of the hunters, with the more than enthusiastic assistance of those already in camp, were hard at the messy jobs of flaying and butchering, the sometime-foragers came back, having emptied and reset traps or rebaited those they had found empty. They bore some cottontails, squirrels, one big and three smaller raccoons, a black fox, a mink, a woodchuck, two skunks—one striped, one spotted—half a dozen muskrats and four thrashing feet of thick-bodied, now-headless watersnake which had been a chance acquisition of a muskrat trapper.

The lower edge of Sacred Sun was skirting very close to the western horizon and the pots and pans above the scattered cookfires were already beginning to emit fragrant steam before the second party of hunters was sighted across the grassy expanse that lay above the narrow, winding, flood-carved river valley in a wider portion of which lay the campsite.

So slowly did this party move that it seemed clear they must ride heavy-laden with game. But as they came closer, those gifted with the keenest sight could see that although there was game strapped to several horses, two others bore between them a makeshift litter, and at the tail of the party limped an injured horse—its head hung low, dried blood streaking its barrel, stripped of all gear and encumbrances save only a rawhide halter, bloody froth surrounding its distended nostrils and slowly dripping from muzzle and lips.

"Sun and Wind," muttered Hunt Chief Tchuk Skaht to no one in particular, "I thought today's hunting went too well to be true or to last. Wind grant that that's not a Skaht in that litter, yonder . . . but that baldfaced redbay looks much like one of our herd. And if the horse was hurt, then what of its rider?"

As the column wound down the path from above and into camp, the form on the litter could be seen to lie unmoving, very, very still, its eyelids closed, its sunbrowned hands folded across its chest. Tchuk's heart plummeted to the depths of his felt and leather boots when he recognized the face—Myrah Skaht, daughter of his cousin, Chief Gaib Skaht; a pretty girl of only fourteen summers, a girl with the promise of becoming one of the best archers in her clan.

He walked heavily in the direction of the cleared space wherein returning parties usually offloaded, his mood as heavy and dragging as his steps. "It's always the young," he brooded silently to himself, "the best, the brightest, that hunting and raids and simple accidents cost us. At least six or eight boys and girls who likely will never contribute much to our clan, whose loss would have soon been clean forgot, but, no, we here lose Myrah . . . and probably her fine, well-trained hunting mare, as well, from the looks of it. Poor Gaib will be bitter for long and long, I fear me, with this painful loss of so fine and so promising a daughter; I hope that he doesn't blame me for it."

As the leader of the hunting party wearily dismounted from his stallion and set about removing saddle and gear from the mount, Tchuk came close and asked the question he had to ask.

"Did she die well, Uncle Milo? Our bard is certain to ask me . . . and her grieving father, too."

Looking up from where he had bent to unbuckle the

cinches of the hunting kak, the man thus addressed smiled and replied, "Be not so pessimistic, Tchuk Skaht. The unfortunate mare will probably have to be put down this evening, from the looks of her, but young Myrah was not hurt badly, only knocked giddy and shaken up. I had her put in a litter only because she seemed to have trouble sitting a horse, then I gave her a draft of sleep-root to spare her discomfort on the journey. She's only asleep, you see, not dead."

"What happened, Uncle Milo? No mere fall would have torn the mare up that way."

While continuing to work, the man called Uncle Milo used their shared telepathy to answer the question. "We hunted this day that wide strip of forest over by the big river of which this one is a tributary, bagging six of the small straighthorns, among other beasts, this morning. After the nooning, we all fanned out to see what else we could add to our take for the day. Our first intimation of trouble was when we heard the mare's screams.

"It would appear that Myrah arrowed a yearling pig, but for some reason, her loosing did not fly with her usual trueness and the wounded beastlet fled into an area of heavy brush with Myrah in full pursuit of it."

Tchuk Skaht, an experienced and widely respected hunter, blanched. "Oh, no, a sow . . . or worse, a boar. And her without a spear."

"Just so," agreed Uncle Milo, adding, "In her pain and hysteria, I couldn't get much out of the mind of the mare, so this is a reconstruction based on educated guesses and what I found when I got to the scene.

"Apparently, the old boar came out of the dense cover and tushed the mare just behind the off foreleg. Myrah may not even have had time to see him. The mare reared, of course, slamming the rider's head against a thick over-hanging branch so hard that the impact cracked the boiled-leather helmet clean across, though there would appear to be no damage to the head within.

"Half-mad with pain, the mare of course lashed out at the boar as the savage beast pressed his attack, but ac-complished little damage to him, hampered as she was by the thick brush and nowhere near as fast as him, anyway.

"Matters stood thus when two of the boys came riding up. That Gy Linsee is big for his age was a rare blessing, at that place and time. Realizing at once that a horse was a detriment there, he rolled out of his saddle, after putting a brace of rapidly loosed shafts into the boar—fletchings-deep, he drove them, too—got the stubborn beast's attention and took him on his spear . . . where he was holding him when I and most of the rest of the hunt came up and dispatched him."

Nodding solemnly, Tchuk said, "Would that so brave a young man were a Skaht, but I honor him nonetheless. Young Karee has rare insight, it would seem. If she openly announces and he does the same, I will speak Gy Linsee's part to my chief and her father and hope that he elects to live among the Clan of Skaht. If he so desires, I would be honored to have him as guest at the Skaht cooking fire, this night."

Milo went about the rest of his work with a sense of satisfaction. The first real break had finally occurred. A Skaht had invited a Linsee to guest at his evening meal, and Milo could rest assured that, taking into account the event that had precipitated the offer and the exalted rank of the man who had made it, there would be nothing save sweetness and light (even if some of it was forced and grudging, at first) toward Gy Linsee from his hosts. It was, at least, a start.

Clans Linsee and Skaht were both Kindred clans of long standing and ancient lineage. However, within the last couple of generations, the two had developed a senseless enmity. The clans had taken to insult, thievery and pilferage, assaults and the occasional killing and, at last, riding on raids against each other, not only meetings of warrior against warrior in open, prearranged battle—which would have been bad enough—but striking at encampments, as well.

At length, the Council of Chiefs of the tribe, that loose confederation of Kindred clans known as the Horseclans, had decided that enough was enough. The vendetta had gone far enough and they were upon the point of riding down in overwhelming force upon the two clans, stripping them of all arms and possessions and, after disenfranchising them, declaring them to be not of Horseclans stock, driving them out onto the prairie, afoot, unarmed and maimed, to die or live.

But Milo Morai had good memories of both of the errant clans, and he prevailed upon the Council to allow him to try just once to show them the error of their current ways and teach them to live once more in peace and in brotherhood, one with the other, as did all the rest of the Kindred clans.

So disgusted and dead-set were the chiefs of the Council that it is likely that no normal man, no ordinary chief, could have swayed them. But then Chief Milo of Morai was no mere man, no ordinary chief. For as long as there had been Horseclans upon the plains and prairies, there had been Uncle Milo. This same, ageless, unchanging man had succored, lived among, guided the Sacred Ancestors from whom most of the present clans held descent since the hideous War and the Great Dyings had extirpated most of mankind from all the lands. Unlike every other man and woman of the clans, he alone never aged; the same Uncle Milo who might have merrily jounced upon his knee a new boy-child of the clans might stand in the throng, unchanged in any way, as the husk of the old great-grandfather that that boy-child had, over the long years, become was sent decently to Wind on a pyre.

Therefore, when Uncle Milo had ridden in—unexpected and unannounced—with the Tribal Bard and made his request of the assembled chiefs, none of them had even thought—no matter the intensity of their emotions, their fears and the resolve to which they had but just come—of saying nay to this man compounded of equal parts myth and stark reality.

So, rather than riding down upon the erring clans with fire and thirsty swords, the Council had sent riders summoning the chiefs of Linsee and Skaht to the place whereat they sat in formal sessions. Arrived, the chiefs and subchiefs were informed of the decision that the Council had made, then, before any could protest, they also were informed of the request of Uncle Milo and the agreement of Council to grant his request. But it was impressed upon them that this was at best a brief reprieve and that only clear proof of a resolution of their ongoing feud would or could bring about a full reversal of Council's earlier ruling and resolution. This meant that full cooperation with the schemes of Uncle Milo were of paramount importance to both Linsees and Skahts, did they harbor any hopes of surviving into another generation as Kindred clans.

Autumnal hunting parties traditionally ate very well, and this one was no exception. While still Sacred Sun was nudging the western horizon, the stewpots had been set aside so their contents could cool enough to be eaten and the coals of the firepits were put to the task of cooking other foods for the weary but ravenous men, boys and girls.

The contents of those lazily steaming pots were hearty, nutritious fare, indeed. To a stock made by boiling cracked bones had been added those bits and pieces of meat and fish too small or otherwise unsuited for the curing racks, edible roots of various kinds, wild greens and herbs and a bit of precious and hoarded salt, then the mixtures had been thickened by additions of toasted, late-sprouting wild grain, seeds and nutmeats.

The second and last course of the meal would be spit-roasted rabbits, hares, squirrels and birds. If anyone remained hungry after that, they could always gnaw at a hunk of the hard, strong-flavored cheese they'd brought along on this hunt, though generally it and the gut tubes of greasy pemmican were held back for a possible emergency.

When the carcasses on the spits were nearing an edible degree of doneness and the horses were all cared for and other needful tasks accomplished, the Skaht boys and girls began to gather about the cookfire pit. Then Hunt Chief Tchuk Skaht called for their attention, addressed them, speaking aloud for the benefit of that minority who were possessed of little or no telepathic ability.

"Kindred, mine, a guest will share our fire and our food on this night, a brave young man, who will be honored by us all for his act of selfless courage in defense of one of us Skahts during the course of Uncle Milo's

hunt, earlier today. I will bring him amongst us, but he
will be a clan guest, not mine only.

"He is a Linsee-born, but he cannot help that regrettable fact, for none of us have the option of choosing the
clan of our parents, and I'll be expecting each and every
one of you to show him true Skaht hospitality as well as
the deference and the honor due a young man who saved
a Skaht girl from death or serious injury at no little risk to
himself.

"Be you all well warned: I'll brook no misbehavior toward our honored guest—no ragging, no name-calling,
no insults, no challenges. If anyone does not understand
all that I have just spoken, tell me now. Well?"

A stripling stepped from out the throng on the other
side of the firepit. His pale-blond hair cascaded loose
upon his shoulders, dripping water onto the shirt and
trousers that clung to a body still damp from his evening
dip in the riverlet. A look of sullen near-defiance smoldered in the depths of his blue-green eyes.

"Hunt Chief, with all due respect to you, I think you
try to go too far. Working with the damned Linsees, riding alongside of the scum, hunting or fishing or gathering
with them . . . I—we—have debased ourselves to do all
these things because you and our chief and Uncle Milo
said to. I shared herd guard with one of them today, but I
can see no reason why I should have to ruin my meal with
the stench of one of them in my nose. No, hunt chief or no
hunt chief, you go too far, demand too much of us, this
evening. I'll not sit still for it, whether others do or not.
What did he do, anyway—stop some silly girl from
squatting in a stand of poison oak?"

It was a hoary joke amongst the clans, but still a few
hesitant laughs came from here and there, and the boy
preened himself, half-sneering at Tchuk the while.

Tchuk was on the verge of making his way around the
firepit and giving the impertinent whelp physical cause
to respect his betters when a hard little hand grasped the
boy's arm and spun him about to face the combined
wrath of two of his clanswomen.

Karee and Myrah Skaht, both of them about as damp
as was the boy, Buhd, having but just laved themselves

and their garments in the riverlet, were clearly hopping mad.

"How dare you speak so to Hunt Chief Tchuk, you puling snotnose!" snarled Karee, striking him with some force in the chest with the flat of one calloused little hand.

With the boy's attention thus distracted from her, Myrah took the opportunity to kick his shin, hard, with the toe of her fine leather riding boot, snapping, "Look at your clan chief's daughter, you insubordinate puppy! It was my father gave the rule to Tchuk Skaht for this hunt, therefore, it's my father's—your chief's—orders you would disobey. I should let the hunt chief kill you as you deserve, but I, myself, came close enough to my death today to relish life . . . even so worthless a life as yours."

She kicked him again, on the other shin, then raised her voice. "Know you all, on the hunt today, I arrowed a shoat and, failing to kill it outright, foolishly pursued it into heavy brush. The shoat's squeals brought out a monstrous old long-tushed boar. He charged my mare, savaged her, and she reared suddenly, casting me from the saddle. Then that hellish boar made for me, and you would all be building me a pyre and sending me home to Wind, this night, save for the heroism and strength of Gy Linsee. He rode up, arrowed the boar twice, then came in afoot to take a beast that outweighed him by hundreds of pounds on his spear and hold him there until more hunters came up to kill the creature.

"*That* is why he is to be our guest at food, on this evening. And any who offer him less than he deserves, than he has earned in full this day, will assuredly find the blade of my knife in his flesh."

After a single, slow-moving, grim-faced sweep of her glance completely around the circle, she suddenly smiled and added, "Who knows, Kindred? Perhaps Uncle Milo will honor our fire and food, as well, with his presence. Then, maybe, he'll tell us all more of his tales of the olden days as he did last night."

If there was any one thing in particular that Horse-clansfolk instinctively honored, it was proven bravery, even in an enemy . . . *especially* in an enemy. With the tale of Gy Linsee's courageous feat in succoring their chief's daughter become common knowledge, the big young man was received and feted in time-hoary Horse-clans tradition, for all his un-Horseclanslike size and height, his un-Kindredlike dark hair and eyes and his Linsee lineage. And, as all had hoped, Uncle Milo readily accepted the invitation of Hunt Chief Tchuk Skaht and dined around their firepit on the thick stew, the baked tubers, the roasted meats and the oddments of nuts and late fruits.

The meal concluded, those who had done the day's cooking repaired to the riverbank to scour the precious metal pots with sand and cold water, then filled them with fresh water and brought them back to fireside for the preparation of the morning draft of herb and root tea, which, with a few bites of hard cheese, was the breakfast of most Horseclansfolk.

The rest of the diners sat ringed about the firepit. They picked their teeth with splinters of firewood, cleaned their knives, wiped at greasy hands and faces. They chatted, both aloud and telepathically, or brought out uncompleted handicraft projects to work at by the fire-light. One group of boys and girls set a small pot of cold, congealed fish glue to heat in a nestlet of coals, laying a bundle of presmoothed, prerounded dowels by, along with sharp knives, collected feathers and preshaped hunting points of bone and threads of soaked, supple sinew, all for arrow-making.

One of the older boys began to carefully remove the bark from a six-foot length of tough hornbeam—the best part of a sapling killed through some natural cause a year or so before and then cured where it stood by the winds and sun. The boy had recognized it for the rare prize that it was—such made for fine spear shafts or the hafts of war axes—and he meant to finish it as much as possible before they rode back to the clan camp, where he would make of it a gift to his father.

Slowly, carefully, using a belt knife for the drawknife he lacked, helped by a cousin who steadied the sapling, the boy took off the bark in long, even strips, which he flicked into the firepit and out of his way. With the last of the horny outer bark gone, he sheathed his knife, took the two-inch-thick length of wood upon his lap and began to sand it with a coarse-grained, fist-sized river rock, keeping a finer-grained pebble of equal size close to hand for semifinal finishing.

Two different youngsters—a boy and a girl—squatted and braided thin strips of rawhide and sinew into strong riatas. Others honed the edges of various types of knives, spearheads and axes, or the points of fishhooks, gaffhooks and hunting darts. Yet another young Skaht was industriously knapping a lucky find of ancient glass—shards of a bottle broken long centuries before and rendered a deep purple by hundreds of years of unremitting sun—into projectile points, such points being much favored for hunting, since they needed no fire-hardening as did bone and their points and edges were sharper and more penetrating than even honed steel; he already had knapped and fitted to a hardwood hilt a larger, triangular piece of the glass to be used for the splitting of sinews.

With a speed born of manual dexterity and much practice, Myrah Skaht was converting a length of antler into a barbed head for a fish spear, her knifeblade flashing in the firelight. All the while, she engaged in silent converse with Gy Linsee, where he sat between Hunt Chief Tchuk Skaht and Uncle Milo, both she and Gy being gifted with better than average telepathic abilities (that trait called "mindspeak" by the folk of the Horse-clans).

The boy and girl conversed on a tight, personal beaming, and such was the very way that Milo "bespoke" Tchuk Skaht. "They are fine young people, Tchuk, all of them I've seen, this night; those who have the good fortune to live to maturity will bring great honor to Skaht, of that you may be sure."

The hunt chief beamed his sincere thanks for the compliment to his clan and young clansfolk, but then sighed audibly and shook his head, setting his still-damp braids asway. "But so few will be still alive in ten years, fewer still in twenty, and it seems that always the very best are they who first go to Wind. They die in war, in the hunt, in herding, they succumb to wounds, to fevers and other illnesses. The girls, many of them, will die during or just

after childbirth, and both boys and girls will be swept off
and drowned in river crossings, will fail to outrun prairie
fires or will be done to death in stupid, pointless, singular
accidents. We two sit amongst a bare twoscore or so only
half of whom will ever live to even my age, yet I know of
Kindred clans that number more than twice as many
younkers, warriors and maiden archers."

He sighed even more deeply and again shook his head.
"It would just seem that Clan Skaht is intended by Sacred
Sun and by Wind to remain small and weak upon the
land. And ever fewer Kindred of other clans seem of a
mind to wed into Clan Skaht, to accept our boys and girls
as spouses for their own clansfolk or even to host our
wandering hunters as befits true Kindred. And this great
mystery is not of my mind alone, Uncle Milo. Right often
have my chief and the subchiefs and bard in council discussed these very topics . . . vainly."

Milo frowned. "Oh, come now, Tchuk, you are an intelligent man, and so too are they, else they would not be
leaders of their clan, but you and they have chosen first
and foremost to think only within narrow limits. Open
your mind, man, loose your thoughts, and you quickly
will see the basic reason for all . . . well, for most of the
afflictions of not only your clan but of Clan Linsee, as
well.

"Well?" he prodded after a moment. "Think of it,
man, unfetter your mind and think. You posed questions
—now give me the answers to them, as you can and
will."

It did not take long. "The . . . the feud . . . the feud
with Clan Linsee . . . is that it, Uncle Milo?"

Milo smiled briefly. "You have a cigar coming, but I
don't have one, so how about a pipeful of my tobacco
instead, Hunt Chief Tchuk? Precisely! This damnable,
idiotic feud is at the bottom of all the tribulations of both
Clan Skaht and Clan Linsee. Nomad clan versus nomad
clan is a flatly murderous type of warfare . . . but you
know that fact well, don't you? Raidings of Dirtmen
steadings are one thing—the element of surprise holds
down the number of casualties amongst the raiders, as
too does the fact that the modes of thinking are very
different when you compare settled farmers and nomad

herders and hunters. And, also, the prairiecats and our strain of horses with their telepathic abilities give us a distinct edge over our prey. Yes, there are losses sustained in raiding Dirtmen, but mostly they are but piddling compared to the loot, livestock and slaves gained for the clans. Why, the hunt results in as many or more deaths and serious injuries for a far more paltry return in benefits, but you know that, too.

"On the other hand, when you ride to raid or war against men just like yourselves, you can expect the butcher's bill to be high, almost insupportably high. How in hell are you going to surprise a camp the perimeter of which is patrolled by farspeaking telepathic cats and horses? And if you choose to set your own cats on the guard cats, the resultant din of feline battle is going to be heard for miles. Though I understand that the cat chiefs, both yours and Clan Linsee's, past and present, wisely refused to engage in active warfare and raiding against any Kindred clan, only fighting defensively.

"Had your clans been allowed to keep up this senseless round of raidings and ambushes and duelings and battles, the time would soon have come when neither of you would have had sufficient strength remaining to even hold your own against the natural adversaries that beset us all our lives on the prairies and plains. The only reason, indeed, that you two weakened clans have survived this long is that almost all of the non-Kindred nomads have been killed off, driven off or melded into our tribe over the last few generations. Had such fearsome fighters as Clans Staiklee, Duhglisz, Kahr, Lebohn and their ilk still roamed in enmity to the Kindred, you had all been rendered corpses or slaves.

"All of the other Kindred clans face precisely the same attrition from natural causes and from riding the raid against Dirtmen as do Skaht and Linsee. That they manage—barring the rare disaster—to maintain a constant strength of numbers in spite of certain losses results from the fact that they live by, adhere to, The Law and the ancient customs proven from the days of the Sacred Ancestors to the present.

"First and foremost of the Law is that Kinship is holy, Tchuk. Had clan not helped Kindred clan in times of need or danger over the years, there would today be no tribe, no clans. In union there is strength for all of our confederation of interrelated clans and families. Such disunity and enmity as your two clans have practiced can lead only to chaos and death for you, your descendants and, eventually, your clans.

"Unfortunately, there are a certain number of hotheads, greedy, suicidal and homicidal types, in every generation of every clan. Clans Skaht and Linsee have, over the more recent years, set a bad example, and other, more sober and Law-fearing Kindred clans have avoided mixing with them because they feared the bad influence upon their own few fire-eaters. Looked at from their viewpoints, no man could blame them for being somewhat less than Kindred toward you. Prove only to the Council of Kindred Chiefs that Skaht and Linsee can live harmoniously, one with the other in peace and true brotherhood, and you will see how quickly there are offers of Kinship from your Kindred of all the other clans."

He seemed on the verge of beaming more to the receptive hunt chief, but his mind was just then smitten by a beaming of the combined power of Myrah Skaht, Karee Skaht and Gy Linsee. "Uncle Milo, please, won't you do as you did last night? Please tell us all more of the olden days, of your life before the Great Dyings and of how you formed the Sacred Ancestors into our clans of today."

"If I do, it will have to be, as last night, told to all, Linsees as well as Skahts. Will you welcome them among you if I agree to open my mind and memories again to you?"

Chapter 1

Although radios and gramophones blared out songs of coins falling from the skies, the only thing that the skies over depression-racked Chicago seemed to be producing were rain, snow, sleet and windborne stenches from the stockyards this winter of the Year of Our Lord 1936.

Or, at least, so thought Police Officer Bob Murphey as he squatted, back to a wall, keeping watch over the unfortunate gent who lay unconscious before him on the damp, slimy, gritty stones of the alleyway. Bob was certain that this one was a real gent—his clothing was too fine, too obviously expensive, for him to be aught else than a gent or a hood, and it was too conservative of cut and color to be the latter. That expensive clothing had likely gotten him into this sorry pickle, Murphey silently reflected. Why, his shoes alone represented a week's pay for the average working Joe these dark days . . . if said Joe was lucky enough to be working at all.

Bob had been walking his beat, huddled into his uniform coat against the chill and the thick, cloying mist, when he had passed the alley mouth and sighted in his peripheral vision a flicker of movement too large to have been a mere rat or alley cat or gaunt scavenger dog. He had turned back then, taken his best grip on his billy club and demanded, "Now what in hell's goin' on back there?"

There was scuttling movement, then footfalls rapidly receding down the alleyway. Murphey had proceeded cautiously on until he had suddenly tripped over and almost fallen onto a recumbent body. A brief examina-

tion had revealed that the victim was not dead yet,
though from the amount of blood clotting the dark hair,
he might soon be. After he had carefully, as gently as
possible, dragged the body closer to the alley mouth, he
had trotted the half-block or so to the callbox and
reported the need for an ambulance at this location.

He had returned in time to find two miscreants—likely
the same ones who had slugged the gent's head and
robbed him to begin with—engaged in trying to get off
the man's shoes and greatcoat. One of them had gotten
away, but the other now sat handcuffed and groaning
from the beating Bob had inflicted with his billy club.

"I'm getting old," thought the shivering policeman,
clenching his jaws to stop his teeth from chattering.
"Twenty years ago, it's the both of the bastards I'd've
got, not just this one. When I come back from France
back in '18, all full of piss and vinegar, it looked like the
world was my oyster for sure. What in hell happened to
all those plans, all those chances I knew was just sitting
out there waiting for Big Bob Murphey to come along?"

After glancing at his prisoner and assuring himself that
the clubbed and moaning man offered no further threat,
Murphey let his billy dangle from his wrist by the thong
and tucked his numbed hands under his armpits. "I
wonder if that poor gent there was in the Great War,
too? Likely he was—he looks about of an age with me.
'Course, he prob'ly was an officer—he looks the type. He
sure got his breaks after the war, else he wouldn't be
laying there in a greatcoat that cost a hunnerd dollars if it
cost one red cent. I dunno—things would prob'ly have
fell in place better for me if I hadn't gone and married
Kate as soon as I did. Hell, she'd've waited for me to
make my pile, and we both and the kids too would've
been a sight better off if I had. But then, I'd prob'ly've
lost it all back in '29 like the rest of the high-rollers did
and ended up dead or riding boxcars or in jail or sweeping up horse biscuits with the WPA. At least I got me a
steady job and three squares a day for me and Kate and
the kids and a roof over our heads and coal to burn in the
Arcola, and all that is a whole helluva lot more than most
folks can say these days."

His hands thawed a bit, Bob Murphey delved into his coat pocket and brought out the billfold he had taken from his handcuffed captive. Leaning toward the dim light out of the street beyond the alley mouth, he opened the butter-soft calfskin and riffled the sharp new bills contained therein. Sinking back onto his haunches, he whistled between his teeth. At least six hundred, maybe a *thousand* dollars, between one and two years' pay for the likes of him, if you didn't include the piddling amounts of cash and merchandise that he accepted now and then from certain cautiously selected persons on his beat for the casting of a blind eye on victimless activities.

"Well, Mr. Milo Moray," he muttered to himself, reading the name stamped in gold leaf inside the billfold, "sure and you're bound to have a sight more where this came from. And you do owe me something for saving your life tonight, after all."

He stood up then and emptied the billfold, folded the bills into two wads, then stuffed one down each sock to come to rest under the arches of his feet. He then stalked over to stand looming over the prisoner.

"What did you and your partner do with this man's money?" he demanded of the battered, manacled criminal.

Snuffling, the slumped, bleeding man half-whined, "Didn' have time to do nuthin' with it. It's still in his billfold, hones' to God, it is."

Bob Murphey sighed. "Wrong answer, feller." Leaning down, he unlocked and removed the handcuffs, returned them to their place, then took a two-handed grip on the billy club and brought it down with all of his strength upon the prisoner's head. Bob was a beefy man, a very strong man, and the one blow of the lead-weighted baton was all that was necessary to cave in the gaunt prisoner's skull. Then he tucked the empty billfold back in the pocket from which he had taken it when first he had searched the man.

Of course, the initial victim of attack was apprised of none of these events until much later.

He awakened in a bed. The bed was hard, and the

small pillow under his head had the consistency of a brick. He had no idea where he might be, why he was where he was, or exactly who he was.

A woman of medium height was making one of two beds on the other side of the room, moving swiftly and surely, tucking up the sheets in smooth motions that left tight corners. It was when she turned to do the same for the other bed that she noticed that he was awake. Smiling warmly, she left the rumpled bed and bustled over to crank up the head of his bed.

"Oh, Mr. Moray, doctor will be so glad to hear that we're finally conscious. How do we feel? Any headache, hmm? Would we like a drink of nice, cool water? An aspirin?"

"Yes," he finally got out, wondering if that croak was his normal speaking voice. "Water. Please, water."

The white-clad woman eased him a little more erect with an arm that proved surprisingly strong, then bore a glass with a bent-glass tube to his lips and allowed him to drain it before lowering his body back down. He was again asleep before his head touched the stone-hard pillow.

When he once more awakened, the wan light that had come earlier through the window on his right was gone, replaced by the bright glare of the electric lamp in the ceiling above him. The two beds across the room sat crisply empty, and the white-clad woman who had given him water was nowhere to be seen. However, another woman, also wearing white—shoes, stockings, dress and odd-shaped cap atop her dark-blond, pulled-back hair— sat in a chair near his bedside reading a book.

He tried to amass enough saliva to moisten his mouth and bone-dry throat but, failing in the effort, croaked, "Wa . . . water."

Obviously startled, the seated woman dropped her book and sprang to her feet. "Certainly, Mr. Moray, of course you may have water, all the water you want. But you've got to try to stay awake for a little while, too. Poor Dr. Guiscarde is dead on his feet, but he insisted that he be called as soon as you woke up again. He needs to examine you and talk with you about something he thinks important."

While speaking, she had pushed a button, and, when another woman in white opened the door, she said, "Miss Pollak, please get word to Dr. Guiscarde that Mr. Moray is conscious now."

Although she had promised him all the water he wanted, she actually allowed him only small sips from the glass tube and carried on a nonstop monologue for the ten minutes before a spare, gangly young man entered and took her place at the bedside, signaling her to raise the head of the bed. From his black bag he removed a stethoscope, a reflector mounted on a headband and several other instruments, with which he proceeded to subject the patient to a brief examination. Then, bidding the woman to leave the room, he took her chair, slumping into it with a deep sigh.

"Do you recall anything of what happened to you night before last, Mr. Moray? No? Well, a beat cop interrupted a pair of men who had slugged you, knocked you down and were in the process of robbing you. When he went to the callbox to get an ambulance down there, the two came back, but that was when their luck ran out; one ran again but the other fought, and the cop killed him with his baton, I hear tell. Officer Robert Emmett Murphey is as strong as the proverbial ox, so I find it entirely believable that he bashed the robber just a little too hard.

"The hoodlum who got away must have had the money from your billfold, that and your watch and chain, which were ripped from your vest to the severe detriment of the pocket and buttonhole, I fear me. But they never had time or leisure to get your vest open, much less the shirt, so your moneybelt and all within it are laid away in the hospital safe in an envelope that I personally sealed before turning it over to the administrator. But, man, don't you know that it's been illegal to hold gold for more than two years now? If the federal government knew you were walking around with six or seven pounds of double eagles, they'd roast you over a slow fire.

"Not that I necessarily agree with Roosevelt's policies, you understand, for they don't seem to be working out all that well for the vast majority of the people who have elected him twice, now. About the only good thing he's done was to make it legal to sell good booze again, in place of those poisonous bootleg slops.

"When you are ready to convert some of those gold pieces to cash, let me know. I think my father would buy them from you at a premium, since they look to be brand-new, unworn coins. He's a well-known numismatist, so he can buy and hold them legally, which is one way to get around Roosevelt and his socialism.

"Strange thing about you, though. When they brought you in here, your hair was a sticky mat of blood, yet I could find no wound or even an abrasion anywhere on your head to account for that blood. Your hat was crushed, which might mean that the thick, stiff furfelt absorbed most of the blow you were dealt, but that still doesn't account for the blood. My theory is that blood from the man the cop killed ran down to the center of the alley and pooled under your head. Gruesome, heh? But it's as reasonable a theory as any other, I think.

"I'm going to have you moved upstairs to a nicer room, a real private room. I'd like to observe you for a few days —head injuries can be tricky. You can easily afford private nurses and these days most of the nurses are in dire need of patients who can pay for their services. Mrs. Jennings, who was here when you woke a few minutes ago, will be your night nurse, and I have another in mind for your day nurse, too. Should you not care for what the hospital kitchen calls food, and not many do, there are several restaurants hereabouts that can cater your meals for reasonable costs.

"Whom should we contact about you, Mr. Moray? Family? Friends? Business associates?"

It took some little time, days of repetitive questioning, the bringing in of other doctors, specialists, before the man called Milo Moray was able to finally convince them all that he truly lacked any memory of his name and his life prior to the assault on him by the two thugs.

The room was bright, cheery, furnished fully, and had attached a private toilet and bath to justify its steep rate of five dollars a day. The patient found the food provided bland but palatable and only rarely had meals fetched in to him from outside sources. Mrs. Jennings and Miss Duncan, his nurses, cared for him competently, brought him books from the nearby public library and helped him pass the time with conversations. As he could remember nothing of his past life, they told him of themselves and, in Mrs. Jennings' case, of her husband and child.

Not that he ever seemed to lack for conversation. His status as something of a mystery man seemed to bring the oddballs out of the woodwork, as Dr. Gerald Guiscarde put it. He himself spent as much time as his busy schedule would allow with his patient, conversing with him as an equal, and he also continued to set various tests to the man he called Milo Moray.

Among other things, he was able to determine that although his patient's English was accentless, non-regional American, he also was more than merely fluent in High German and French, as well as Latin and Classical Greek. Dr. Sam Osterreich, the psychiatrist, was able to add to the list of accomplishments the facts that the memoryless man was also well grounded in Yiddish, Hebrew, several dialects of Plattdeutsch, Hungarian, Polish and Russian. Through assorted visitors, it was established that the man called Moray could converse in such other tongues as Slovak, Croatian, Italian, Spanish, Arabic, Turkish, Armenian and Basque.

But he proved unable to understand Cantonese, Sioux, Hindi, Tamil or Welsh, though he was proved to be fluent in Irish Gaelic, Scots Gaelic and Dutch. It was the consensus of opinion among the linguists that Guiscarde filtered in that, although probably a university graduate, certainly well educated, Moray had not learned most of his vast array of tongues in an academic setting, but rather through living among and conversing with the people whose native languages he had learned so well and in such depth.

Dr. Osterreich was a stooped little gnome of a man whose English was sometimes halting and always heavily accented. He had studied under fellow Austrian Dr. Sigmund Freud. In his mid-fifties, he was a very recent immigrant and had been a widower since his wife had died of influenza while he had been serving as a medical officer of the Imperial Austro-Hungarian Army in the Great War.

One early evening after his office hours, he showed up

at the mystery patient's room with a large chess set and board, a commodious flask of fine brandy and a brace of crystal snifters. He had been prepared to teach the game to his host, but it proved unnecessary, in the end, for the man called Moray was sufficiently adept to make their games long and slow, and the psychiatrist was to return many times for chess, brandy and rambling chats in English, German and Yiddish.

After a signal defeat one night, the doctor tipped over his king and regarded his host for a long moment. "Whatefer you war, *mein freund*, goot, solid gold I vould lay that a military man you vunce war. The firm principles of strategy and tactics most naturally to you seem to come. You ponder, you efery aspect weigh, but then mofe mit alacrity and resolution. Too young you look to have been in the late unpleasantness, but to know all that you seem to know, I also feel that older than you look you must assuredly to be. Efen mit a true ear for languages, for instance, more years than you seem to have vould have required been for you to have mastered so fery many as you haf. Most truly a puzzle you are, *mein freund*, Milo."

Some month after first awakening in the hospital, the patient had just breakfasted one morning when Dr. Gerald Guiscarde arrived with a large, thick manila envelope under one arm.

"Milo, I've conferred with Sam, and we agree that there's nothing we can do for you, in the hospital or out, so it's just a useless waste of your money to stay here any longer, I feel.

"Now, I took the liberty of sending your gold to my father, and he bought it all, as I was certain he would, for thirty-four dollars per coin, which came to two thousand, eight hundred and fifty-six dollars. There's an accounting in the envelope along with your moneybelt, but I'll tell you now that with the hospital, the nurses, Sam, me, and the specialists all paid, you still have two thousand and twenty-two dollars and eighteen cents.

"Have you plans after you leave here? You don't intend to leave the area, do you? Sam and I still would like to see you regularly, keep up with your progress, as it were."

The patient smiled sadly. "Where would I go? What

would I do? I seem to have lost not only my past but, with it, any roots I might have had. No, I suppose I'll find a residence hotel somewhere, then try to find a job of some description."

But his day nurse, Fanny Duncan, would not hear of such a thing, and that was how he wound up a boarder in the same house in which she lived. His ten dollars per week brought him a comfortable room, three plain but good meals per day, bath and toilet down the hall, clean bed linens once a week and a familial atmosphere.

In 1914, Staff Sergeant Patrick O'Shea had left the Army he had so dearly loved behind him to take over the management of the brewery following the calamitous deaths of his father and all three of his elder brothers in a boating accident. He had also married his eldest brother's widow, Maggie, a new bride become suddenly a new widow, and they had moved into the big, rambling family house. With a staff of well-trained servants, they lived comfortably and happily, their first, Michael Gilbert O'Shea, being born in 1916. Patrick himself seemed to be adapting well to his executive position, but then the first dim tattoo of the war drums began to be heard and the warhorse in him began to champ at the bit.

By the time the twins, Sally and Joseph, came along, their father was in the trenches. He returned to a business ruined by Prohibition. He returned crippled and nearly blind from being gassed. That was when Maggie, perforce, took over the house and the family.

Regretfully, she let most of the servants go, retaining only the cook, the children's nurse and a single house-maid. After conferring with Patrick's attorney, she sold the brewery—lock, stock, barrels and land—for the best price she could get, paid the workers a generous sever-ance and then followed the attorney's advice in investing what was left. Thanks to the income derived from those shrewd investments, she was soon able to hire back all of the former servants and go back to the kind of life into which she had married. And thus they lived for more than ten years.

Then, overnight, their fortune was wiped out along with many another on Black Friday. Her attorney and financial adviser, who had been on that Thursday a multimillionare, shot himself in the head with a shotgun. Maggie's butler did the same with a German pistol. With a rare prescience, she went down the following Monday and emptied what money lay still in her accounts out of the banks which soon were closed.

By this time, the children were really too old to have need of a nurse, so she retained only the cook and Nellie, the maid. She firmly insisted that her elder daughter, Sally, and her younger, Kathleen, spend most of their free time in learning the arts of housekeeping and cooking, for she anticipated and feared the day when there would be too little money left to pay for any servants at all. Herself, she dusted off her only marketable skill and secured a nursing job in the nearby hospital; it was not much money, true, but it was steady and far better than nothing.

With two guest rooms and two more rooms of former servants sitting vacant and useless, Maggie O'Shea got the idea of taking in boarders, nurses, all of them. When, in 1934, Michael's appointment to the United States Military Academy emptied yet another room, she had no difficulty in promptly filling it with another nurse, Miss Fanny Duncan.

In 1936, two more rooms became vacant. Joseph enlisted in the Navy and his twin, Sally, moved into the hospital residence hall to begin her nurse's training. This meant that Maggie had to hire on a second maid, but there was space for another in the quarters that had once been the chauffeur's over the garage, and with the combination of her salary, her husband's pension and seventy dollars each week in paid rents, she could easily afford the extra employee. And so there were presently two more nurses in the house that certain of the more affluent neighbors were beginning to call "the Convent of Saint Maggie," not that Maggie cared a fig. She had kept her house, kept her family together, adequately fed and clothed and even provided gainful employment for non-family household members, which was more than many another could say in these hard, bitter times.

Even crippled as he was, a living testament to the horrors of modern warfare, to the inherent dangers of a soldier's life, Maggie often felt that the government should be paying Patrick far more than his pension for, if nothing else, his recruiting activities. He had gotten his eldest an appointment to the USMA, persuaded his youngest to enter the military, along with many another man and boy with whom he had come in contact over the years. The old soldier had even gone after the nurses resident in his home and, at length, blarneyed one of them, Jane Sullivan, into entering the Army Nurse Corps.

Jane Sullivan's room became vacant while Fanny Duncan was still nursing the mystery man, and it was Fanny who first got the idea, broached it to Dr. Guiscarde and, with his not inconsiderable help, convinced first Maggie O'Shea, then the man called Milo Moray.

"Look, Maggie," Guiscarde had said, "we want to keep the patient in a sheltered environment for as long as necessary, and we want that environment to be as close as possible to the hospital. And it's not as if he were some deadbeat or bum, anyway. No, he's not employed yet, but in confidence I'll tell you this: he paid a staggering bill for his hospital room, round-the-clock nursing and the bills of several doctors in full and in cash, to the tune of well over eight hundred dollars, and he's still well heeled even after the outlay. His resources would allow him to pay your going rent for going on four years even if he never got a job.

"Although he still can't remember his past life or even his own name, he's a proven brain—brilliant. He speaks a score of languages at the least, fluently, too. Dr. Samuel Osterreich says that he has met darned few men who were as good at chess as is this patient. . . ." He let that last dangle enticingly, having been coached on that particular by Fanny Duncan.

"Well," Maggie pondered aloud, "I've never taken in a man for a boarder before, but this man sounds like he . . . and poor Pat has had nobody living in to play chess with since the boys left. All right, doctor, I'll take him on a trial basis. If he works out, fine. If it looks like he won't fit in, I'll have to heave him out. Okay?"

After his first meeting with Mr. Milo Moray, Pat O'Shea told him bluntly, "Mister, whatever else you was, you was a soldier, once, prob'ly a of'ser. You just carry yourself that way, and b'lieve me, I knows. Most likely, the bestest way for you to get your mem'ry back is to re-up. 'Course, with you not rememb'ring and all, you prob'ly won't get your commission back right away, but when you ready to enlist, you just let me know. I'll get you back in—I knows some guys, local."

Milo—he was finally beginning to think of himself as Milo Moray, since that was what everyone called him, for all that the name evoked not even the faint ghost of a memory within him—tramped the streets for over two weeks, searching in vain for some variety of employment. There just were no jobs available, it seemed.

Pat O'Shea pointed out that the frustration would be every bit as bad or worse in another area. "It's the same all over thishere country, Milo. A few folks thinks and says it's bettern it was five, six years ago, but don't look that way to me, no way. Bestest thing a man could do, I think, is to enlist. The Army's a good life. Oh, yeah, it's hard sometimes and a man don't get paid much, but he gets his clothes and three squares a day, regular, and he don't have to pay doctors or dentists nothin', and once he gets him a few stripes, he's in like Flynn, less he fucks up or suthin'."

Dr. Sam Osterreich arrived at the O'Shea house shortly after dinner of a night. After a few games of chess with O'Shea, he took Milo aside and opened the briefcase he had brought along.

Shoving a wad of newsprint toward Milo, he said, "Read, if read you can, please."

Two of the sheets were German newspapers, one was Russian, one French and one Italian. To his surprise, Milo discovered that he could comprehend all of them, and he began to read them to the psychiatrist, but was interrupted by a wave of the hand.

"*Nein, nein,* you do not understand. Translate them to me, please, if you can."

When Milo had done so, had translated the gist of short articles from four of the five papers, Osterreich nodded brusquely and took back the papers.

"Enough. *Gut, gut, sehr gut.* A job you now haf, if still you need of one haf, *mein freund.* You may vork here, in your home, or in an office downtown from where you must in any case go to be gifen the papers each week and to return the completed translations of the indicated articles. One penny per word will be paid for each accurate translation returned, and to be accurate, they all must, this very important is, Milo.

"The bulk of the papers will in German be, but some will in Russian be, or in French, Spanish, Italian, various of the Slavic and Scandinavian languages, Finnish, sometimes, Yiddish, Dutch, Portuguese and even Slovakian."

Pat O'Shea had been shamelessly eavesdropping, and he now demanded, "Now, just a minute, doctor, what in hell you getting Milo mixed up in, anyhow? Some of this-here Bolshevik mess? I heard you just say some them papers was going to be in Russian!"

Osterreich shook his balding head vigorously. "Nothing of the sort, Mr. O'Shea. To a group of recent immgrants I have the honor to belong, to be an officer. Convinced we all are that in Europe a very bloodbath approaching is, a holocaust of such proportions as nefer seen in the world before has been. To alert the citizens and officials of this, our new homeland, we are now trying through means of issuing a monthly digest of signs culled from European newspapers. We do this at our own expense, for most imperative it is that our new, free, vonderful homeland be warned, be prepared and secure when starts does this conflagration, for in this war, coming, there no neutrals will be, we fear; all nations combatants will be and only the strongest vill survive it."

O'Shea snorted. "Bejabbers and you're talkin' nonsense, doctor, pure nonsense. It won't be no more wars, not big ones, anyway. We got us the League of Nations and the World Court to settle diff'rences in Europe. Pres'dent Woodrow Wilson—"

"Your pardon, Mr. O'Shea," Osterreich courteously interrupted, "but I must say that your vaunted President-of-the-United-States-of-America a true naif was, and used shamelessly by France and Great Britain was to their own, most selfish ends. Nothing his supposed-great deeds accomplished but to sow the seeds of discord and misery and future war for Europe and the world. The so-called Treaty of Versailles was nothing of the sort, Mr. O'Shea, rather was it the ultimate revenge of France for the defeat she in the Franco-Prussian War suffered. Not only did the provisions of that hellish document leave France as the sole large, united, strong and vealthy nation upon the continent of Europe, it sundered, impoverished and thoroughly humiliated two of her historic rivals for hegemony—the German Empire and the Austro-Hungarian Empire. She had no fear of her other two historic rivals, for Britain had been her ally and took her part in all the negotiations, while Russia in utter turmoil was not to be a threat.

"Legally robbed of eferything of value—ofersea colonies, merchant ships, naval ships, most of the bullion that their monies backed, their heafy industries und mining, denied credit universally und with their monies worthless—the defeated were left with only starvation and despair on national scales. Und just as the despair of millions of Russians bred Bolshevism, Mr. O'Shea, so the soul-deep despair of the cruelly used Germanic peoples has bred its own brand of fanaticism, a variety efery bit as dangerous to individuals and to nations as is the Russian variety.

"But the true horror of our group, Mr. O'Shea, is that Americans like you seem blissfully unaware of just how close to worldwide war we coming are. This is why the dissemination of our digest so important is, for very few Americans speak any of the languages but English, so necessary it is to translate the other important languages into English, hoping that what they read in our digest will cause them to take from the sand their heads in time."

Milo's first day of work at the office of Dr. Osterreich's group revealed to him and the others there that he spoke at least two other languages, Ukrainian and Modern Greek, at least six regional dialects of German, three of French and the variant of the Dutch language known as Afrikaans and still spoken only in the Union of South Africa. But that first day also revealed to him that was he to get any meaningful amount of work done each day, it would have to be at someplace other than in that office.

All of the other eleven men and women in the office had immigrated within the last decade from various

European lands. One man and two women were White
Russians and were jokingly called "the old non-nobility"
because they had been in America longest. In addition,
there were an Austrian, two Germans, a Pole, two
French ladies, a Hollander and a Neapolitan Italian.
Milo had met a few of them before when Osterreich had
brought them to his hospital room to try to determine just
how well he spoke certain foreign languages with which
the psychiatrist, himself, was no more than peripherally
familiar, and of course those whom he had not met had
heard of him from their coworkers and from Dr. Osterreich.

The staff all were bubblingly curious, and none of
them seemed to believe that he truly could recall none of
his past life. The two Russian ladies seemed to firmly
believe him to be a Russian nobleman of some degree
who had found it prudent to bury his past lest agents of
Josef Stalin find and kill him; the Russian man, on the
other hand, was working under the firm assumption that
Milo was a Trotskyite on the run or possibly a Cossack
officer who had left Russia with his regiment's payroll in
gold.

All of the others had their own opinions as to Milo's
true identity, most of them wildly speculative if not
downright romantic, and they constantly harassed him
with questions to the point that he elected to do all future
work either at the boardinghouse or in the enforced tran-
quillity of the public library.

He soon found the library a good choice, for frequently
he came across words in various languages of which he
did not know the exact meaning. Reference books and
dictionaries available at the library gave him not only the
meanings he sought but also seemed to give him something else of a puzzling nature to ponder.

Chapter II

"*Ach, mein freund* Milo, I do not at all odd find this matter," Osterreich said, shaking his head and smiling. "Most of these words and phrases of general conversation are not." He flicked away the list that Milo had meticulously written out. "If, as suspect I strongly do, you mastered your multiplicity of tongues through living amongst people of those tongues rather than more formally, it fully understandable is that many modern words and technical terms of narrow usage you would not have learned. Do not to further trouble yourself with regard to such trifles.

"You are doing good work, very good work, incidentally. The translations are most precise, yet without meaning of the original languages losing. Where do you work? At the O'Shea house?"

"No," replied Milo, "at the public library. It's always quiet, and there's reference books available there, as well. I tried to do it all at your office, but decided after one day that I'd never get the first article finished in less than a week, not with all the interruptions.

"What did you tell these people about me, Sam? The Russians think I'm Russian, the French and the Germans seem to think I'm German, and everyone there is clearly of the opinion that I'm lying about my inability to recall my past, that I'm on the run from one government or another, a spy or an international crook."

Osterreich sighed. "I know, I know, Milo. Of these fanciful suppositions some of them haf broached to me, too. I told them only the truth, that an amnesiac you are following probable neural damage which from a blow to the skull resulted. More recently, of their consummate silliness I haf chided them; how much good my vords to them did, I know not, howefer."

He sighed again. "I had had hopes that to work around so many people to jog your memories to the surface it might. But this work you do so well is of great importance, and if you do it best alone, so be it.

"But to other matters: how goes your life at the O'Shea domicile?"

"The Convent of Saint Maggie?" answered Milo. "That's what the neighbors called it before I moved in, I hear."

Osterreich wrinkled his brows in puzzlement. "She is so religious, then?"

Milo laughed. "No, Sam, she had all females in the house, with the sole exception of Pat—two daughters, two or three female servants and five to seven female boarders in residence. The neighbors don't appear to like the idea of a boardinghouse in their neighborhood. I guess they would all have preferred that Maggie sink into genteel poverty rather than manage to survive and hold her own the way she did. She's a fighter, that woman. I admire her."

"And what of the others, there, Milo? What of them do you think, eh?"

"Pat O'Shea," Milo chuckled, "if he had his way, would long since have had me and everybody else in the house—excepting only Maggie, his daughters and the servants—in some branch of the armed services, having already gotten both of his sons and one of Maggie's former boarders so persuaded. He keeps working on me, of course, using every excuse he can think of to get me to enlist in the Army of the United States of America. Were you twenty years younger, no doubt he'd have been after you, too.

"As for the rest of the household, I see most of them only at dinner and, sometimes, at breakfast. Those nurses who work the night shift sleep during a good part of the day, and those who work the day shift, as does Maggie, have to be on the floor at seven a.m. and so leave at a godawful hour of the morning. Fanny Duncan hasn't been around for two weeks now, or nearly that; she's on private duty at the home of some wealthy people up near Evanston, living there to be near the patient at all times.

"The cook is a widow about sixty, and Irish, like Maggie herself. I've been polishing my Irish Gaelic on her, learning new words . . . and that brings us back to my list there, Sam. She, the cook, Rosaleen O'Farrell, says that I speak an Irish dialect that she's not heard since she was a child, in Ireland, and then only from her rather aged grandmother."

"I had thought that to settle that matter we had, Milo," said Osterreich with very mild reproof in his voice. "Now, what of the other persons with whom you reside?"

Milo shrugged. "I've met Sally O'Shea but once, and that very briefly; she's living at the hospital, in nurse's training. The few conversations I've had with Maggie's youngest, Kathleen, have been mostly her monologue on a hash of something concerning the subjects she's studying at the University of Chicago. The elder of the two maids is a friendly sort, Canadienne; we chat in French. The other maid hasn't been with Maggie too long, a colored girl from somewhere down South; I don't talk much with her because I have great difficulty in understanding her—they must speak a very odd dialect of English where she comes from."

Milo's job was better than no job at all, but the income he derived from it fluctuated from two or three dollars a week to, occasionally, as much as twenty or thirty dollars a week, so that all too often he found it necessary to dip into his dwindling hoard of cash from the sale of his gold coins. This would have been bad enough, but he discovered through countings that someone else apparently was dipping in, as well; there never was a large amount missing, no more than ten dollars at a time, but after the third or fourth such occurrence, he invested in a small steel lockbox with a key, a length of log chain, a padlock and a neckchain on which to carry the keys.

He had bought a well-made box with a good lock of heavy construction, and he was glad he had when he found deep scratches on the face of the lock and marks

along the edges of the box resulting clearly from vain
attempts to pry open the lid. A few days later, he
returned to his room from the library to find the box
pulled out from under the iron bedstead to which it was
chained and with a few millimeters of nailfile tip broken
off in the lock. The removal of this required no little
effort and the necessity of borrowing a pair of tweezers
from one of his co-boarders, Nurse Irunę Thorsdottar.
But a week later, he had to borrow them again to extract
a short piece of stiff wire from the lock. On that occasion,
he confided in Irunn about the problem of the thefts and
attempted thefts, and between them they devised a plan
to apprehend the thief in the act.

The tall, broad-shouldered and -hipped woman shook
her blond head, her pale-blue eyes above her wide-
spreading cheekbones mirroring disgust and anger.
"Nothing lower, Mr. Moray, than a sneakthief. I'm not
rich, precious few folks are these days, but if a body here
was in real need, I'd loan them what I could and I judge
you would too, so it can't be no excuse for them to steal or
try to steal from one of us. We'll catch the snake, though,
count on it."

Milo and Irunn had, however, to bring one additional
person in on their plot, and Rosaleen O'Farrell, upon
being apprised of the cause for the scheme, was more
than willing. So, on the day Milo left the house at this
usual time, bound in the direction of the library, battered
secondhand briefcase in hand; and Irunn long since
having departed to begin her shift at the hospital, the
second floor lay deserted as soon as the maids had
finished sweeping and dusting it and moved on to the
third floor, whereon two night-shift nurses lay sleeping.

Cautiously, Milo returned by way of the service
entrance and Rosaleen let him up the back stairs,
relocking the door behind him, then returning to her
work. Safely out of sight behind the closed door of
Irunn's room—it being directly across the hall from his
own—Milo opened the wooden slats of the venetian
window blind just enough to allow light for reading and
settled himself in a chair with a library book to wait and
read and listen. Nothing happened on that day, nor on
the following two days, and he was beginning to think he

was needlessly wasting time better spent elsewhere, but on the Friday, about midafternoon, he heard footsteps, two sets of them, and a whispered mutter of voices from the hall outside Irunn's door. One of the voices sounded vaguely familiar; the other, deeper one did not.

Laying the book down soundlessly and gingerly easing out of the now-familiar chair, he tiptoed over to take a stance hard against the wall behind the door to Irunn's spotless, scrupulously tidy room. He was glad that he had positioned himself just where he had when the door was slowly opened enough for some unseen person to survey the room from the hallway, then ease it shut again before passing on to open and view the other rooms on the second floor.

Only by straining his hearing was he aware of when his own room's door was opened, then almost soundlessly shut. There was another dim, unintelligible muttering of two voices, then a brief rattling as his strongbox was dragged out from under his bed on its chain. He gave the thieves a good ten minutes, during which time there were a couple of almost-loud clanks, half-whispered cursing in a man's voice, another clank, then the commencement of a scraping-rasping noise which went on and on.

Opening Irunn's room door and then his own on the hinges that they two had carefully oiled at the beginning of this scheme, Milo entered the room to find Kathleen O'Shea, daughter of Maggie, kneeling beside his bed, watching while a black-haired, sharp-featured young man plied a hacksaw against one link of the logchain; the blade had already bitten a couple of millimeters deep into the metal.

When Kathleen looked up and saw Milo, she shrieked a piercing scream, which caused her companion to start, look up himself and heedlessly gash open a thumb and a forefinger with the blade of the saw. But he seemed to ignore the injury, and, dropping the handle of the saw, he delved his right hand into his pocket, brought out a spring knife and, all in one movement, flicked upon the shiny five inches of blade, rose to his small feet and lunged at Milo's belly.

Milo never could recall clearly just what happened then or in what order events occurred, but when the blur of motion and activity once more jelled, his assailant sat propped against the neatly made bed, his eyes near-glazed with agony. The young man was gasping loudly, tears dribbling down his bluish cheeks, his right arm cradled in his lap with white shards of shattered bone standing out through flesh and shirt and suit coat, which coat was beginning to soak through with dark blood from that injury as well as from the doubly gashed left hand that supported the injured arm.

Milo's own shirt was sliced cleanly a bit below his rib cage on the left side of his body, sliced about the length of an inch, and there was blood on his shirt around and below that opening, but he had no time at that moment to examine himself for injuries or wounds, for Kathleen still knelt unmoving in the identical spot she had occupied when first he had entered and apprehended her and her companion in the commission of their crime, and she was still screaming. Peal after peal had been ringing out without cessation, and agitated movement could be heard from the floors above and below, as well as on the stairs.

Rosaleen O'Farrell was the first to arrive, and her initial action was to take Kathleen by the hair and slap her, *hard,* with palm and backhand on both cheeks, twice over. That effectively stopped the screaming. The cook's muddy-brown eyes took in the strongbox chained to the wrought-iron bedstead, the hacksaw, the slightly damaged link and the massive padlock from the keyhole of which an ineffective wire pick still protruded.

"Caught them, did you?" she stated to Milo in Irish Gaelic. "I knew, I did, it's telling herself I was that no good would come of them dirty furriner boys Kathleen has been bringing into this house. I think that one's the Dutch Jewboy, Jaan what's-his-name, a godless Bolshevik."

At the shaken Pat O'Shea's insistence, Maggie was rung up at the hospital and summoned home. She was advised, also, that it might be wise to bring a doctor along who was prepared to handle a compound fracture of the lower arm, as well as dislocations of both elbow and shoulder joints, not to mention a case of shock. The two night nurses from the third floor, both wakened by the screams of Kathleen, which had been of a timbre to wake a corpse, had raised the slight, fainting young would-be burglar and would-be knifer onto Milo's bed, removed his shoes and tie, unbuckled his belt, ascertained the full extent of his injuries, then set about trying to slow his loss of blood, while keeping his feet elevated and his body warm.

By the time Maggie came puffing across the lawn from Dr. Gerald Guiscarde's motorcar, her plump face nearly as white as her uniform, a few more judiciously applied slaps of Rosaleen's hard hands and a stiff belt of neat whiskey pressed on her by her father had brought Kathleen out of her hysterics to a stage of red-eyed, moist-cheeked snuffling interspersed with shudders, gaspings and swallowings and the occasional horrified stare at the man called Milo Moray.

But when Maggie entered, Kathleen sprang up and flung herself into the stout woman's arms. "Oh, Mama, Mama, he *killed* him! He did! Right in *front* of me! I *saw* him do it."

"Stuff and nonsense, Mrs. O'Shea," snapped Rosaleen from where she stood in the archway between front and rear parlors. "The Jewboy ain't dead . . . yetaways. But it's I'm thinkin' he should be. The little bugtit, he's been sneakin' out money from Mr. Moray's room for weeks, he has, either him or Kathleen, more's the pity. Mr. Moray bought him a lockbox and chained it to the bedstead, he did too, but somebody"—she stared hard at Kathleen as she paused, and the girl flushed and refused to return the stare—"has been tryin' to pick the locks.

"Mr. Moray and Miss Thorsdottar got together to catch the thief, and fin'ly, today, he did. When he went into his room this afternoon, he found Kathleen and that Jewboy takin' a hacksaw to the chain, set to carry the box away, I'd say, I would, so's they could bash it opened. And when they come to see him, Kathleen comminceted a caterwaulin', while the Jewboy went at poor Mr. Moray with a switchblade jackknife, he did.

"Poor Mr. Moray, he should ought to've kilt him, but he didn', just busted his arm a wee bit and unjointed his shoulther and elbow, is all. He—"

"*God Almighty damn, Milo!*" burst out Dr. Gerald

Guiscarde from the foyer, which he just had entered after parking his SSKL 1931 Mercedes-Benz in the parking area off the driveway. "For the love of Christ, man, sit down! How deep did the stab go, do you know? Do you feel pain, weakness or giddiness? Any nausea?"

Not until the doctor had had up Milo's bloody shirt and undervest to see what looked like a minor and closing scratch on the skin of the abdomen beneath would he believe his prized mystery man to be unhurt. Only then did he leave for the upstairs, guided by Michelle, the maid.

Maggie pushed her daughter from off her bounteous breasts and said, "Kathleen . . . ?" When the girl did not answer, merely stood snuffling, with downcast eyes, the older woman gave her a shake that rattled her teeth.

"*Answer your mother* when she speaks to you! If you think you're too old for me to take down your knickers and paddle you, you've got another think coming, young lady!"

"Oh, Mama, he . . . he *killed* him. He just tore poor Jaan apart *with his bare hands*!" Kathleen's voice had risen to a higher pitch with each succeeding syllable, and so the last four words came out as a near-scream.

Rosaleen resignedly took a step or two forward, her intent to administer a few more wallops of her sovereign Old Country cure for hysteria. But Maggie had her own brand of cure. She once more shook her slender daughter, a shaking that was painful to watch and revealed just how much power lay underneath the adipose tissue.

She nodded. "It's true, then, isn't it, Kathleen? You've been letting in hoodlums to steal from my boarders, haven't you? Well, you shameless hussy, answer me?" She gave the girl another shake, of shorter duration but just as powerful if not more so. "Haven't you?"

"Bububu . . ." Kathleen blubbered, her tears once more at full flow. "But, M-Mama, it . . . it wasn't really stealing. Jaan ex—explained it all to me . . . to us all. Lenin said that—"

"Lenin, is it?" Pat O'Shea sprang up from his chair. "Is this what that damned university teaches you? I'll not see *you* go back to learn more godless Boshevism, daughter.

It's to the nursing school, with your sister, you'll be going, by God, there or as a novice with the Holy Sisters of Saint Agnes.

"Mrs. O'Shea, we should be ringing up the police to come and fetch that Dutch Jew up abovestairs. I'll not be having a heathen Bolshevik longer under my roof!"

"Aye!" Rosaleen O'Farrell nodded her firm approval. "It's doing it now, I'll be. The jail's the best place for the likes of that one. Corruptin' young, witless, Christian girls!"

But Maggie O'Shea would not have the police summoned. Instead, when Dr. Gerald Guiscarde had done all that he could immediately do for Jaan Brettmann, he drove into the business area and brought back from his tailor shop old Josef Brettmann and his eldest son.

When the three men entered the parlor, Milo immediately recognized the youngest, not simply because of the strong familial resemblance to the injured knifeman, but because he recalled him from the office from which he received the papers and to which he returned the translations.

He walked forward, his hand extended, "Sol, what are you doing here?" he asked in Dutch.

The newcomer was slow to take Milo's hand, took it only gingerly then, and quickly took back his own hand. Not meeting Milo's gaze, he said softly, Mijnheer Moray, this is my father, whom you had not yet met. The boy, he who robbed you and tried to kill you like some commom thug, that is . . . is my younger brother, Jaan. The medical doctor explained all that happened while we rode here in his auto. Jaan has humiliated me, our father, all of our family before with his wild, radical ideas and schemes, but never to this extent, never housebreaking and attempted murder.

"I do not, cannot understand him and his university friends. America has been so good to him, to us all, has given us so much that we never would have had in Amsterdam or anywhere else. How could he have done, have even thought to do, such a horribleness?

"I do not know what your losses have been, but we— my father and I—will assuredly repay them. It may take time, but you will be fully repaid by the Brettmann family."

He turned, *"Papa, dit is Mijnheer Moray."* Then, switching languages, he added, "Mr. Moray speaks also Yiddish and Hebreish, Papa."

The little old man was tiny. Shorter than either son, neither of whom was of average height, shorter even than the girl, Kathleen. He wore thick-lensed, wire-framed spectacles high on the bridge of a Roman nose, was clean-shaven and utterly bald. He was slightly hunchbacked and peered up at Milo from dark eyes full of tears, and a lump of pity blocked Milo's throat.

With the agreement of all concerned parties, the police were never summoned or even notified of the incident. When, a few days later, Jaan Brettmann emerged from the hospital, he was met by Sol, who gave him a packed suitcase, a one-way railroad ticket to Philadelphia, Pennsylvania, and the address of his father's first cousin by marriage, Isaak Sobelsky, a jeweler. True to his word, Pat O'Shea saw Kathleen yanked from out the university and ensconced in the hospital nursing school, the only other option offered by her furious parents being Holy Orders. A week or so after his erring, youngest son had been sent off to well-earned exile in the East, old Mr. Brettmann suffered a stroke, which, though it did not quite kill him, left his entire right side paralyzed, useless, making Sol the sole support of his father, his aged mother and his two younger sisters.

As for Milo, he and Nurse Irunn Thorsdottar began to enjoy occasional days or evenings—dependent entirely on which shift she was working—out. After confiding to him her passion for the works of the musical masters, many of their sojourns were to the opera or the symphony, and he soon became familiar with the soul-stirring music of Wagner, Grieg, Beethoven and Sibelius.

The translating work really took up little time, and he made use of the rest of each day and of his work locale to voraciously read of past, of present, of imagined or projected futures of the world in which he lived, hoping against hope that some word or group of words, some photograph or painting reproduction in some book would trigger his memory that he might regain his lost past. He learned vast amounts about the world, about its history and accomplishments, but he could never remember any more of what he had done, had been, before his clubbing than he had on that morning in the hospital, in the depths of the winter now past.

On each succeeding visit to the office of Osterreich's group, Milo noted that Sol Brettmann looked more worn with exhaustion and care and worry. In order to pay the medical costs, to keep food on the table, clothes on the family's backs, his sisters in public high school and the rent paid on the family flat above the sometime tailor shop, Sol had dropped out of his almost-completed law-school program and taken a second job, a night job selling—or, rather, trying to sell—life insurance.

One day, on the day when he was scheduled to collect his pay for translations completed, young Brettmann took Milo aside and pressed a wrinkled and stained envelope into his hand. Inside it, Milo found a sheaf of crisp new ten-dollar bills, ten of them in all.

"This will, I hope, recompense you for the money my brother induced the O'Shea girl to steal of you."

"Now, damn it all, Sol," expostulated Milo, "you can't afford to part with this money, you know it and I know it. How the hell did you get so much together so soon, anyway?"

Brettmann flushed darkly, hung his head and replied, "I . . . I knew that I . . . that we, the family, would be years, maybe, in getting that much . . . now, with Papa and all. I borrowed it from . . . from Mijnheer Doktor Osterreich. And he wouldn't even talk of any interest on the loan. He is a truly good man."

"Then you just give it back to Sam Osterreich, Sol. You do or I will. You owe me nothing, hear? You and your family aren't in any way responsible, so far as I'm concerned, for what your nutty, deluded brother did or tried to do."

Brettmann's thin lips trembled. "But . . . but you *must* take the money, Mijnheer Moray! You must! This is a matter of honor, of family pride, and it preys so on poor Papa's mind. I . . . I must ease at least that burden from him. It is my duty."

Nor would Osterreich take the money from Milo. *"Mein freund,* Josef an old and dear acquaintance is and much more than this I vould do for him and his family, vould they allow such of me. The vord 'loan' I used only for young Sol's pride and for Josef's. Whatefer he pays back to me I vill manage into his pay envelopes to place back to him.

"Such a shame it was, too, that from university he withdrew. A mind that boy has, a brilliant attorney he vould haf made, too. But a real *mensch* he is, it is there for all of the vorld to see!" He sighed, then, and added plaintively, wistfully, "If only to help them more they vould allow me . . . if only they vould . . ."

The spring of 1937 slowly became summer, and on the Fourth of July of that summer, Milo accompanied Irunn on a picnic outing sponsored by a Scandinavian-American society of which she was a member. Milo mixed in well with the merry, hard-eating, hard-drinking men and women, conversing easily with them in only German, at first, then, upon hearing and discovering that he knew the languages, in Danish, Swedish and Norwegian. Even as he ate and drank, mingled and walked and talked, he wondered just what was the total of languages he knew, how many of them lay somewhere in his mind, just below the surface, awaiting only the right stimulus to prod them to his consciousness.

It was while he was chatting with a Danish friend of Irunn's that the scholarly man remarked, "Your languages all are very well spoken, Herr Moray, Danish, German, Norwegian and Swedish, too; your accent is flawless in all of them. But I cannot but wonder where and when and from whom you might have learned them, for the dialects you speak are very old. Your Danish, for instance, sounds like I assume the Danish speech of two hundred years ago sounded."

Milo was trying to think just how to respond to the probe when Irunn saved the day, half-pouting mockingly, "Oh, Dr. Hans, I will bring Herr Moray to a meeting one Wednesday, soon, and you two may sit and drink and talk that night away. But now, today, he is my man and there are things to do here in God's green,

beautiful world. Come, Milo, let us get a boat and row
out on the lake."

But as they rowed around the lake, Irunn said, "You
should not have withheld from me that you spoke Norwegian, too, Milo. I don't speak it too good myself. I was
born in this country, in Wisconsin, and Papa and Mama
insisted that all of us children talk in English most of the
time. But both of my parents speak it, and . . . and soon I
must take you up to meet them . . . if you so wish, of
course."

Stroking easily and evenly—unaware of how much
practice was required to learn to handle a small rowboat
that way—Milo nodded and smiled. "Sure, Irunn, I'd
like to meet your folks."

As they two plodded tiredly up the walk to Maggie
O'Shea's boardinghouse that night, Irunn stopped suddenly, faced Milo and laid her palms on his cheeks, then
pressed her opened lips onto his. "Milo Moray," she whispered after the long kiss was done, "I love you, Milo
Moray. I am yours and you will be mine. You *will* be
mine."

Milo liked Irunn, but that was all. Besides that, he had
no intention of marrying her or anyone else, not for a
while, for a long while, possibly. But he quickly found
out that attempting to reason with the woman was
equivalent to batting his head against a brick wall.

"Irunn, can't you see that I can't marry anyone now?"

"Why?"

"Well, for one thing, I still have no slightest idea who I
am . . . or was. I could be . . . have been a criminal of
some kind, you know."

"You? You could never have been a criminal, my Milo,
you are too good, too kind. And as for who you are, you
are Milo Moray, the man I love. You are a good man, a
strong man, a man who makes a good living, a man who
my Papa will be proud to name his son-in-law and the
father of his grandchildren, when they come."

He considered packing up his few effects and leaving
the Chicago area entirely, but he had the presentiment
that that would only bring the stubborn, strong-willed
woman dogging his trail wherever he went, however far
he went.

He made an appointment and visited Dr. Osterreich in the psychiatrist's office, seeking advice and help in extricating himself from the situation. But Sam Osterreich just laughed.

"*Ach, mein gut, gut freund* Milo, marriage the lot of most men is, do not to fight it so hard. Fräulein Thorsdottar I haf at the hospital seen and talked with. A *gut* voman she is, *und* a *gut Frau* vill she for you make. Basic, Teutonic peasant stock, she is—strong, sturdy, with much vitality und not prone to easily sicken, und they little difficulties usually haf in the birthings, either.

"No, no, there no charge is for you, *mein freund*, nefer any charge for you. Just name one of your sons, Samuel, eh?"

Milo could still hear the little psychiatrist laughing as he closed the door to the outer office.

Dr. Gerald Guiscarde was of no more help. "Look, Milo, I know a little bit about Irunn and her family. They own a big, a really big, dairy farm up in Wisconsin, you know, and for these times, they're doing damned well. So you could do a hell of a sight worse, say I."

Finally, he went to Pat O'Shea. The old soldier showed his teeth in a grimace that was as close as he could any longer come to a real smile. Then he sobered and said bluntly, "Milo, time was when I felt just like you do, but I knows different, now; indeed I do. If I hadn't had my Maggie when I come home like I am from the war, God alone knows what would've become of me. And a man never knows whatall is going to happen to him, Milo, peace or war, day or night, one minute to the next, so I say when you got the chance to get hitched up to a good, strong woman like that, even if looks ain't her best suit, do it afore she changes her mind. Marry her, Milo."

After a long pause, he added, "But if you really are dead set against the institution of marriage in gen'rul and you want to get somewheres where she can't come after you and fetch you back to the altar, let me know and I'll have you enlisted in the Army and on a train out of Illinois in two shakes of a lamb's tail."

Chapter III

On the 12th of August, Maggie O'Shea received a telegram the receipt of which was to change the course of Milo's life for good and all. Taking both of her daughters out of nursing school, she and they hurriedly packed and entrained for Boston, Massachusetts, and the bedside of her last living relative, a deathly ill aunt. Pat O'Shea, who studiously avoided any public appearance at which he could not hide his hideously disfigured face, stayed behind.

Irunn had been badgering Milo for weeks concerning just exactly when he would accompany her to Wisconsin to meet her family—and, he was certain, while there, be maneuvered into asking for her hand . . . or at least give the appearance of having so done. He had been elusive and vague at best, blaming heavy commitments in his work, which was no lie, the recent volume of Western and Central European periodicals having so increased that he now lacked the time at the library to get very much of his history and current-events reading done, spending whole days from opening to closing of the facility translating and writing out the articles in American English. With the swollen volume and a limited budget, the per-word rate had had to be halved, but still Milo was assured of a very good, well-stuffed envelope each week.

Irunn *had* been badgering Milo, but on the Sunday following Maggie's abrupt departure for points east, the big woman ceased to do so, becoming again all sweetness and light and snugglings in private and caresses in passing, and Milo breathed a silent sigh of relief, the week ahead promising to be full enough, if the thick stack of assorted publications the office staff had handed over to him on Friday was any indication.

By the time the library closed on Monday afternoon, he had—even at the rate of half a cent per word—done work to the tune of more than ten dollars and made a healthy dent in the stack of papers. But this had been accomplished only by keeping his nose pressed firmly to the grindstone, staying glued to the chair, not even taking time to leave for lunch. And so when he returned to the cool dimness of Maggie O'Shea's boardinghouse just a few minutes before Rosaleen O'Farrell called for the dinner assembly, Milo was tired, ravenously hungry and a little edgy.

To this last and to the tiredness, he ascribed his seeming foreboding of imminent doom as he hurriedly washed up and put on clean undervest and shirt. But the all-pervasive aroma of Rosaleen's corned beef and cabbage and carrots and boiled potatoes set his salivary glands into full flow and sped his pace down the stairs toward the waiting dinner table.

He was not surprised to see most of the household already seated around the long oaken table when he entered the dining room, the cloud of steam rising from the platters and serving dishes that lined the center of that table until it rose high enough to be dispersed by the air wafted lazily by the mahogany blades of the ceiling fan.

He was, however, surprised to see Irunn presiding at the head of the table—the absent chatelaine's normal place—and the master of the house, Pat, occupying a side chair rather than his accustomed spot at the other end, the foot of the board. Milo's look of wonderment at Pat was answered by a chuckle and a twisted grimace-smile.

"It's time, Milo, that you began to learn your place at table."

Milo's second surprise came when Irunn did not, as usual, eat hurriedly, then rush upstairs long enough to brush her teeth and hair and immediately hurry out in the direction of the hospital and her seven-to-seven night shift.

As the tall woman continued to dawdle and chat with various of the others over coffee and deep-dish dried-apple pie and an old, very strong cheddar cheese, Milo finally drew his watch from his vest pocket, opened the hunter case and remarked, "Irunn, you're going to be late to work, you know."

Irunn laughed throatily. "Oh, no, my love, for this week I'll be working days, not nights. It was necessary to make some rearrangements at the hospital in the absence of Mrs. O'Shea, and so what could I do but cooperate? But I am very glad, Milo, for this week we two will have so much more time together, won't we? And we can go, on Wednesday night, to the club meeting, too."

Even more rested now, a bit more relaxed, his belly now pleasantly full, Milo felt the ominous presentiment return full force. Something deep within him was screaming out, *"Danger! Be wary! Danger!"*

Excusing himself from the usual round of chess and chat and a nip of whiskey with Pat O'Shea after dinner, Milo ascended the stairs to his room, turned on the ceiling light, spread out papers on the bed and pushed his forebodings into the back of his consciousness as he applied himself to his translating chores. And there he worked steadily until his eyes were gritty with fatigue and he caught himself in the umpteeth mistake of the night. That was when he undressed, padded down to the communal bath in dressing robe and slippers, bathed, brushed his teeth, voided his bladder, then returned to his room and crawled under the cool, muslin sheet with a sigh of utter weariness. In seconds, he was asleep.

He never knew just how long he had slept, but he woke suddenly, with the certain knowledge that there was someone else in his room, somewhere in the stygian darkness of the cloudy, moonless, starless late-summer night.

When he stopped breathing, he could hear the respiration of the other entity somewhere between the closed door to the hall and the side of his bed. For a brief moment, there was also a soft, slithery rustling sound, then a series of slow, shuffling noises, akin to someone moving forward cautiously, unsure of the footing and endeavoring to raise no creaking from the floorboards that underlay the faded, worn carpet.

He made no sound either, lying in perfect stillness, though wound wire-taut, his body flooded with adrenaline, his eyes slitted so that to a casual glance they might look closed in slumber, yet straining through the slitted openings to discern just who or what this unannounced and unexpected visitor might be. Unable to longer go without air, he took several slow, measured breaths, striving to make them sound as regular as possible.

Something touched the side of his mattress ever so gently, he heard a sharp intake of a deep, deep breath, and then . . .

Irunn was upon him. She kissed blindly at his face until she finally found his mouth and glued her own wet, hot one to his. His first, instinctive effort to push the rather heavy woman off him revealed to his fingers and hands the bare fact that she was nude.

What happened after that was thoroughly instinctive, the mere course of nature. When he awakened the second time, however, in the bright light of morning, Irunn was gone from his arms, his bed, his room, and she had already left for the hospital's day shift when he dressed and came downstairs for breakfast.

The same thing happened on Tuesday night. On Wednesday night, he locked his door, but either Pat O'Shea was in collusion with Irunn or, more likely, felt Milo, her room key worked as easily as did his own in the simple old-fashioned spring locks with which the doors were fitted. On the Thursday, he considered wedging the back of a chair under the doorknob, but then mentally shrugged and gave up trying to fight her and her amorous nighttime forrays. After all, he enjoyed sex, he had discovered, just as much as she obviously did, and to create any sort of a noisy ruckus in the O'Shea house would likely get them both expelled from it on moral grounds, for friends or no, Pat and Maggie could do nothing else were they to maintain a necessary sense of respectability for the house and the other boarders. At least that was how he rationalized his continued enjoyment of the for-

bidden fruit with which Irunn was so generously serving
him each night.

If anyone in the house did hear nighttime noises, they
attended to their own business, and in any case, Maggie
O'Shea and her daughters returned after an absence of
two weeks and, with her again in the house of nights,
Irunn ceased her after-dark activities with Milo and
recommenced the night shift at the hospital.

She also recommenced harassing Milo about making a
trip with her to Wisconsin, and he, perforce, recommenced his near-lies and evasive actions.

One thing about which he had no need to lie was the
press of his work, for on the 28th of September, Germany
had been given the bulk of what had been, prior to the
Great War, Prussian Silesia, and the European press was
full of this nearly unprecedented action and speculated
frequently and at great length upon its possible
consequences. Because of these events, Milo and the rest
of the translators were terribly overworked. He now was
burdened with assignments two and three times each
week—being given more every two or three days than he
formerly had received for an entire week—and he was
working all day, every day, and generally long into the
nights, as well. The sole good thing about it was the
money. He now was earning as much as twenty-five to
thirty-five dollars a week, and despite board and room,
laundry, outside lunches when he could find the time and
remembered to eat, toiletries and odds and ends of
clothing, he still was adding substantially each week to
the contents of his strong box.

It went on and on and on. The work did not abate, nor
did Irunn's increasingly urgent demands that he meet her
family in Wisconsin. Then, overnight and inexplicably,
she again became all sweetness and light, seemingly
having forgotten her demands that Milo go north with
her immediately if not sooner. He was relieved, in a way,
though he still felt the nagging notion that it was not
over, that the willful woman had not really given up on
him, but simply had changed her mode and direction of
attack.

He came back to the O'Shea house after the library
closed of a night in mid-October to be met by Pat. "Milo,

Irunn, she had to take off for her home place in Wisconsin real sudden-like and she left thishere for you." He proffered a sealed plain white envelope.

"Milo, my own love," the note inside read, "My brother, Sven, has been taken suddenly ill, and I have gone up to be of assistance to my mother and sisters. I will be gone one week, no more, I hope. A claim ticket is enclosed. It is for a ring on which I have made the deposit and it is being made bigger for me by the shopkeeper. Please to pick it up for me on next Monday and pay the man the rest of the money for it.and I will pay you back when I come back to Chicago. With all my undying love, Your Irunn. (P.S. Please burn this note for no one but you must read it. I.)"

When Milo went downtown to the jewelry-pawnshop of a Mr. Plotkin, he was impressed by Irunn's taste. The ring was stunning, a full carat, at least, of blue-white diamond in a setting of reddish gold, antique European, or so the jeweler, Plotkin, averred. He knew Milo's name, and Milo assumed that Irunn must have telephoned him before she left for home. Back at the boardinghouse, he deposited the ring in its velvet box in his strongbox and got back to work on his translations. But something told him not to burn Irunn's note. That too went into the steel lockbox and the time was soon to come when he would be glad that he had heeded his feeling.

Things began to close in on him even before Irunn's return. First was a letter that was awaiting him when he returned to the O'Shea house one night. The postmark was a Wisconsin one, but the handwriting was not Irunn's. The writer had been a man and, from the style of the letters and numbers, a man of European education.

"My dear Herr Moray, Our Irunn has told me of your many languages, so I pen this in my native Norwegian. This is a very good thing, for although I speak and read English well enough, I never have been able to well express my thoughts in its written version, and it is very necessary that I fully express myself in this letter.

"For all that no one of us has met or even seen you, we know much of you from your letter and from our Irunn. She has made your excuses for not coming to our farm to properly ask her hand according to ancient custom, and it is true, as you so well wrote, this is a new country with new customs and we older ones must learn to live by the ways of our new land, forgetting many of the old ways of Norway.

"Irunn has spoken well and often of you, of your goodness, your gentleness, your strength and your bravery in facing and defeating the evil man with the knife. She has spoken, too, of how long and hard you work at your job and of how very much money it pays you. To make even a decent income is, I well know, no easy task in the best of times, and these are not the best of times.

"Therefore, here is your answer, my son. I will be most pleased to give you the hand of my fine daughter, Irunn, in the bonds of holy, Christian wedlock, forgoing the meeting of your person until your so-important work allows you leave to visit me at my steading. Thor Kristiansson."

Milo's second shock came the very next day in the person of a youngster who sought him out at his library table and gave him a rich-looking, parchment-bond envelope containing on heavy, embossed stationery a request to immediately come to the residence of one Father Alfonse Rüstung beside Saint Germanus' Church. After a brisk half-hour walk, Milo arrived and was greeted at the door by a young, rather effeminate-looking man wearing a cassock who bade him be seated in a fair-sized, well-furnished room.

The man who presently entered was also wearing a cassock, but there was nothing effeminate about him; his face looked to be roughly carven out of craggy granite, and his handshake indicated crushing strength. He looked to be of late-middle years, his hair was sparse and receding, his hands were big and square and thickly furred with dark-blond hairs.

After a plain, matronly-looking woman had brought in a tea tray, poured and departed without a single word, Father Alfonse got down to his reason for summoning Milo.

"Mr. Moray, I have heard so much about you that I almost feel to have known you for years." He smiled fleetingly, then went on to say, "Although, at the first, I must admit that I was concerned to hear that you were working for that Dr. Osterreich and his nest of Jewish troublemakers . . ."

"Troublemakers, Father Rüstung?" Milo interjected.

"Yes, troublemakers, Mr. Moray. People who are doing everything that they can—from a safe distance, of course—to poison the minds of the American people against Germany and the current government of Germany. You did not know that this was the purpose of their digest for which you do translations? Well, that last is yet another mark in your favor.

"But that is not why I asked you to come visit me, Mr. Moray. How you make your money is your business, as is for whom you choose to work in these times of few job opportunities, and besides, if all that you do is make accurate translations of European newspapers, I cannot see how you, at least, are doing harm to Germany. You do not try to do more than translate, then?"

Milo shook his head. "No, Father Rüstung, that's all I'm supposed to do, paid to do. But I can't see . . ."

"Fine, fine." The priest smiled almost warmly. "No, what I need to know is when you and your intended wish to schedule your wedding mass, for you both will need to meet with me several times. There are the banns to be read, and as you are not a Catholic, there will be some papers that you must sign, of course."

Milo felt for the second time in two days as if he had been clubbed down with a baseball hat. He just sat mute for a long moment, his mouth gaping open.

"Well, Mr. Moray?" probed the priest. "I must have a date today."

"*What the bloody hell are you talking about?*" he finally got out. "I'm not about to get married, not to anybody, no matter what that stubborn, pigheaded, wedding-crazy Norwegian may have told you."

Rüstung's pale-blue eyes became as cold as glacial ice, and he stared at Milo as if at some loathsome thing that had crawled from under a boulder. His voice, too, was become frigid, his words curt and clipped.

"You have taken your suit rather far, Mr. Moray, to now change your mind. I know—I am Irunn Thorsdottar's confessor. I also am not without influence in this city and state, and I here warn you, unless you do the

honorable thing by the poor girl you callously led on and
seduced into mortal sin, I *will* see you laid in the Cook
County Jail, if not in the state prison. You were well
advised to heed me, Mr. Moray—if that is truly your
name!—for I do not indulge in the making of idle threats,
and I feel most strongly in this matter.

"If I do not hear from you of your planned wedding
date in . . . ten days, I shall act to have you jailed and
tried for criminal fornication and breach of promise to
marry.

"Good day, Mr. Moray."

"Another light this all puts onto the issue, *mein freund*
Milo," said Sam Osterreich soberly. "And to underesti-
mate this Nazi-loving priest, do not, either, for he is,
unfortunately, very powerful politically in this city,
county and state."

"What has the arrogant bastard got against you,
Sam?" asked Milo. "And against your group's digest of
foreign news?"

Grimly, Osterreich replied, "Against me as one person
only, nothing of which I know, save simply that I am a
Jew, an Austrian Jew. As for his fear and hatred of our
group and the digest . . .

"You have heard of, read of, the Deutsche-American
Bund, perhaps. Yes, well, this Pomeranian priest, this
Father Alfonse Rüstung, is both an officer and organizer
of the Bund. The Bund would have eferyone to think that
they promote just only a spirit of friendship between
Germany and America combined with the same sort of
love and respect for the homeland as one sees in efery
other ethnic club of immgrants.

"But, Milo, what they to project to Americans vould
and what is their real *raison d'etre* vastly at odds are. It
true is that the majority of the Bund members and
supporters only poor, beguiled dupes and deluded fools
are, but the leaders and the organizers, these all very evil
men are, scheming together to efentually set up in this
beautiful, free country nothing less than a murderous,
fascistic government along the lines of—indeed, allied
with—the Nazis of Germany, the *Fascisti* of Italy, the

Iron Guard of Rumania and the Falange española of General Francisco Franco.

"They at great length carry on about the aims of Herr Hitler. They say that he but wishes to reunify to Germany and Austria the lands and the territories and the German-speaking persons so shamefully stripped from Germany in the vake of the Great War, to reunite all into a *Deutsches Reich*, a single nation all Germans . . . and did they truth tell, efen I could with them agree.

"But as I know, and as you must by now know from your work at translations, the truth in the Bund does not lie, which why it is that they and my group at great odds are and must always be. To silence us all they vould, Milo, to nullify our so important mission and vork, and they must not, they cannot, be allowed to defeat us— rather to defeat them we must.

"But back to your so personal danger, Milo. *Mein freund*, I and the group cannot to you offer much real protection from the priest, Rüstung. He is just too well connected to vealthy and powerful men who now occupy high places in the city of Chicago, in the County of Cook and in the State of Illinois.

"Therefore, you only two options haf. Either to marry the nurse, Irunn Thorsdottar, you must or to leaf the state and go far away. One hears that the State of California a most congenial climate has. . . . But the choice of destination must yours be, and please to not of it tell me, for then if by the police I am questioned I to lie to them would not need.

"All of the help and advice I can to give you, I haf, *mein freund*, Milo. You what, ten days haf to the expiration of the Nazi priest's ultimatum? Then your preparations make quickly and quietly. It well were that you tell no one of just when you leaving are or where you going are. Do not to sell personal possessions try, rather is to pawn them much better, demanding detailed receipts and guarantees that you may soon buy them back. When go you do, travel light—only your money, small valuables and clothes in no more than a single small case. To travel first-class, do not, and tell no one your real name, from where you come or to where you go. *Gott sie*

dankt, travel papers not required are in all this great, free
country, so to purchase forgeries you have no need. If you
need of money haf . . ."

The psychiatrist opened a drawer of his desk with a key
from his watchchain and brought out several sheafs of
bills of as many denominations. But Milo waved his hand
and shook his head in negation.

"Thank you so much, Sam, you're a true friend, but
no. I have enough money, now, to get clear out of the
country, should I choose to do so."

Osterreich smiled slightly and nodded briskly. "*Gut,
gut,* that last is just what the police I vill tell if asked by
them, that to leaf America entirely, you spoke today. No
matter how serious the charges of which the priest and
the nurse accuse you, hardly it is to be thought that to so
much trouble and expense they or the authorities would
go as to try to hunt you down beyond the borders of
America."

Milo stalked through the O'Shea house, going directly
from the front door to the sideboard on which Pat kept
his whiskey, filled a tumbler and drained it off, neat,
then refilled it.

"Saints preserve us, Mr. Moray," came the voice of the
cook, Rosaleen, from the kitchen doorway, behind him,
"it's gettin' pie-eyed you'll be in nothin' flat, swillin' of
the craytchur like that! What's befallen you, this lovely
day?"

With her on one side of the bare dining table, him on
the other, Milo sat and drank and told her all of it, from
start to the immediate present. She heard him out in
silence, only pursing her lips and frowning when he spoke
of his nights of unhallowed copulation with Irunn and
again on the occasion when he roundly cursed the priest,
for his meddling and his threats. Not until he was done
did the old woman speak.

"Och, poor Mr. Moray, it's pitying you I am. That
Miss Irunn, why she must be daft, clear off her knob.
What kind of a married life could she expect to have with
a man she had so shamefully trapped into it with lies and
all? Bad enough it is that she lied to you and to her poor
parents and forged your name to a letter of proposal,

then gave it to her father, but to lie and all to a holy priest of God, och, how terrible a woman she is who always gave the appearance of being good and so very proper. Herself will have thirteen kittens with plush tails when it's hearing of it she is."

Even as Milo opened his mouth to speak in protest at this planned violation of his impulsive confidence, Rosaleen raised her hand.

"She must know, soon or late, Mr. Moray, sure and you can see that? It's better, I'm thinkin', that she hear it from first me and then you than from Miss Irunn or this Jerry priest or . . . or others. As for the rest, it was good advice that the Jew doctor was givin' you, I thinks, I do. But just take all the time you find yourself needin' to get ready to leave; when she's heard it all, herself won't be heavin' *you* out, though she may well throw that Miss Irunn onto the streets, where the schemin', connivin' strumpet belongs. To be sneakin' around of nights and crawl naked into the bed of a decent, sleepin' man to try to make him marry her, Holy Mither save us, that's scandlous, it is, I say!

"And don't you be worryin' none about the police comin' here and haulin' you in unawares, Mr. Moray. My late husband, Jimmy O'Farrell, God bless his soul, was a sergeant on the force. Twenty-four years in harness, he was, and I still have more nor a few of the boyos as friends. I'll just be puttin' out the word and I'll know wheniver a warrant comes out for you, and you'll be knowin' as soon as I do, too."

Some hour and a half after that night's dinner, there was a knock on Milo's door and he opened it to see Maggie O'Shea, still in her white uniform, lacking only her cap. "Mr. Moray, we two must talk of the matter you discussed with Rosaleen this afternoon. Now, while the others are down in the parlor listening to the radio, is a good time. I have just hung up the telephone after ringing up and talking with Father Rüstung, and I want your version of these shocking events from your lips. I feel that as the worst happened under my roof, I have that right, at least."

Maggie seated herself in the single chair and let him tell it in his words, in his order of events and at his own pace of speech. As he fell finally silent, the stout woman sighed and shook her graying head.

"I don't really know just whom to believe in this story matter, Mr. Moray. I've known Irunn Thorsdottar much longer, of course, since she was in training, in fact, but you have always seemed an honest, decent, truthful man to me . . . and clearly to dear Rosaleen, too. She's carrying on like your sworn champion, and she's a proven good judge of character.

"Your story of this mess and how it developed exactly contradicts many parts of Father Rüstung's version of the same events, but then, of course, he got his facts or fables from Irunn.

"You swear to me that you never, at any time, under even the most intimate of circumstances, drunk or sober, asked her to be your wife, Mr. Moray?"

"Yes, I certainly do, Mrs. O'Shea. She was the first and the only one who ever discussed marriage, and I've told her until I was blue in the face that I just am in no position or frame of mind to marry her or anyone else, now. But still, she kept harping on that same tired subject, trying to get me to go with her to Wisconsin to meet her folks."

Maggie frowned then, her lips thinning and her eyes narrowing. "And yet, Mr. Moray, both Father Rüstung and the jeweler whose name he gave me, Izaak Plotkin, confirm that you bought for Irunn a diamond engagement ring. Had you forgotten that?"

Milo's voice rose in exasperation. "Now, damn it, Mrs. O'Shea, Irunn picked out that ring herself, put a deposit on it and left it with that jeweler for enlargement of the band. When she left for Wisconsin so suddenly, she gave your husband, Pat, a note asking me to pick it up for her and promising to pay me back for the cost of it. I did pick it up; it's here, in my lockbox. Engagement ring, hell— I'll wring the neck of that bitch when I get my hands on her!"

"Oh, no you won't, not in my house, Mr. Moray," said Maggie bluntly, in hard, no-nonsense tones. Then she asked, "Can you prove any of what you just told me, Mr. Moray? Everyone but you—Father Rüstung, Izaak Plotkin, my husband, Pat, and most of the rest of the household and Irunn's family's—is under the impression that she is your intended bride."

Milo sighed, hearing disbelief of him in the woman's tone. "The only scrap of evidence I have in regard to my verity, Mrs. O'Shea, is the note that Irunn left with your husband when she left here, last week. She said in a postscript that I should burn it. Now I can see why she wanted it burned, and I'm damned glad I didn't. Here, I'll show you."

When he had dragged the strongbox from its place beneath his bed and unlocked it, he handed the satin ring box and the envelope containing the handwritten note to Maggie, along with the receipt for monies paid and the dated record of the transaction on which he had insisted.

After reading everything thoroughly, opening the box, removing the ring and examining the bauble critically, it was Maggie who this time sighed and shook her head.

"Please accept my full and complete apology, Mr. Moray," she said slowly, soberly and contritely. "Knowing Rosaleen and her intuition as well as I do of old, knowing that she instantly believed you with no shred of evidence in your favor presented her, I should have believed her and you, too. It's a devilish web that the young woman has woven about you, and Dr. Osterreich may well be right that your only choices are either to do what she wants, marry her, or leave the state.

"Knowing, as we do now, of the enormity of the evil and the soul-damning sin of which she has proved herself capable, were I a man, I'd want no part of her; you seem to feel just that way, too. So I guess you must leave Illinois, for even if you are innocent of the breach-of-promise charge, you admit to being guilty of fornication, which is a mortal sin and a legal crime, as well, though not often invoked, I must admit, in these modern times, anyway. If they tried to lock up everyone guilty of fornication and adultery, I doubt they could build reformatories fast enough to put them all in.

"So, have you decided yet where you're going to go? No, wait, don't tell me, I don't really think I should know."

Chapter IV

As he slumped in his train seat on his way to Indianapolis, Indiana, Milo looked to be asleep, but he was not. Rather was he thinking back to the night of Irunn Thorsdottar's return to the O'Shea house from Wisconsin, when all pure hell broke loose and some hard truths were finally voiced.

A taxicab had deposited Irunn at the front door at about eight p.m., while Maggie and those of the household not working night shift were seated around the radio console in the parlor and Pat was facing Milo over the chessboard. Aware that Maggie disliked being disturbed when a favorite program was being broadcast, the returnee had climbed the stairs with her bag after only the briefest of greetings to the household in general.

She had no way of knowing, of course, that immediately she could be heard walking down the second-floor hallway, Maggie pushed herself up out of her chair and made for the telephone in its nook under the stairs.

When at last Irunn came back down to the parlor, walked across to the chessplayers and said sweetly, "Milo, love, please come upstairs. We need to talk, don't you think?"

At the words, a sound that could have passed for a bestial growl or snarl came from Rosaleen O'Farrell, but Maggie O'Shea laid a hand on the cook's tensed arm, then turned off the radio set and came up out of the chair once more.

"I agree, Miss Thorsdottar, there is talking to do, but it all will be done here, where as many witnesses as there are at home tonight can hear and remember. There have been more than enough lies and prevarications from you concerning Mr. Milo Moray and what he was supposed to have done or not done. I, who have known you and worked with you and lived with you for years, would never have thought you capable of such terrible wickedness had the evidence not been placed in my hands. Now, tonight, I will have the full and unvarnished truth out of you, if truth can ever come out of the mouth of a lying harlot such as you. I also have summoned your priest, Father Rustung, and the deputy administrator of the hospital, Dr. Guiscarde, along with a policeman friend of Mrs. O'Farrell's, so that all of them can hear the truth and know the immensity of your crimes against this poor man."

As Maggie had spoken, Irunn had turned first red, then white, her face seemingly drained of blood. She never spoke a word, but immediately Maggie had ceased to speak, the woman spun about and dashed up the stairs and down the hallway. A minute or so later, everyone heard her hurried descent of the rear stairs and a rattling and banging at the door at the foot of those same stairs, a few shrieked curses in both English and Norwegian, then a rapid reascent of those same rear stairs.

Rosaleen showed a set of worn yellow teeth in a grin. "It was thinkin', I was, that she might try to skedaddle when faced down she was, Mrs. O'Shea. Beware, now the front she'll be tryin'."

With her still-packed bag in hand, a purse in the other and a bundle of uniforms and dresses under one arm, Irunn came pouring down the stairs like a spring freshet in flood, to not halt or even slow until she abruptly became aware that Maggie O'Shea's not inconsiderable hulk loomed between her and the door that led to freedom.

"Get . . . get out of my way!" she gasped, fear and anger plain on her face and in her voice. "You got no right . . . no right at all not to let me out."

"If any of us needed any further proof of Milo's innocence in this sorry matter, you've just supplied it, you brazen hussy. You're not going out this door until I say so!" snapped Maggie.

"The hell I'm not!" Irunn screamed, dropping her travel case and armful of clothes to swing a powerful roundhouse right at Maggie's head.

But Maggie O'Shea was ready. She caught Irunn's telegraphed buffet easily on her left forearm even as she sank a paralyzing punch into the younger woman's solar plexus. A ready follow-up was not necessary. Irunn staggered back across the foyer, wide-eyed, gasping for breath, clutching with both her big hands at the point of impact, until her heels struck the first step of the staircase and she lost her balance and landed hard on her rump on the lower landing.

Between the two of them, Maggie and Rosaleen got the woman up and into a chair in the parlor to await the priest, the doctor and the policeman. As soon as she could breathe almost normally and talk again, Maggie and Pat and the cook began to throw hard questions at her, intuitively recognizing the lies she attempted and continuing their relentless probings until they got the truth out of her.

The three were merciless. When once they had what they took to be the truth or near to it, they drilled her, asking the same questions over and over in slightly differing forms. By the time Dr. Gerald Guiscarde arrived to be ushered into the parlor, Irunn was in tears, sobbing, all the defiance and fight drained out of her.

Coldly, efficiently, Maggie took her through the whole of the sordid story for the benefit of the physician, ending by asking, "Doctor, is this the kind of woman that we want nursing at the hospital?"

"Good Lord, no!" was his immediate reply. "It's . . . it was diabolical . . . almost unbelievable. And all of this misery and trouble and sorrow simply so that she could get her greedy hands on Milo's couple of thousand dollars? And knowing Milo as Sam—Dr. Osterreich—and I have come to know him, he would probably have given, or at least made her a long-term loan of the money, had she been truthful with him at the start.

"No, the hospital wants no part of a woman like this . . . and I doubt that the Board of Examiners of Nurses will look with any degree of favor upon this evidence, either. Let her go back to Wisconsin or somewhere else—

anywhere else, and nurse there if she can. She's a disgrace to a fine and noble profession."

A police lieutenant and a sergeant were next to arrive. They were greeted warmly by Rosaleen, had whiskey pressed upon them by Pat O'Shea, and Maggie put Irunn through her paces once more for their benefit. Then Rosaleen brought out trays of cupcakes and little chess pies.

By the time the priest and his effeminate subordinate drove up to park their ornate Daimler beside the doctor's Mercedes-Benz and the plain black city-owned Ford, leaving their chauffeur outside to keep warm any way that he could, Irunn was well drilled and resigned to the utter ruination of her nefarious schemes, her professional career, her life. She went through the recitation of her multiple misdeeds with but little prompting from Maggie. Irunn did not once raise her gaze from her lap and the hands clasped there.

Looking even grimmer than Milo remembered him, Father Rustung spoke not one word until the tale was completely told, then he said, "And you told all of these lies to me and to others, you defiled your chastity and forged a letter simply in order to gain for your family a sum of money owned by Mr. Moray, Irunn Thorsdottar?"

In tones of dull apathy, she answered, "Papa has said so often that if only he had a thousand or two dollars he could do so much with the farm and the barns and the herd and have a bequest of real value to leave to my dear brother, Sven. And besides," she went on, a degree of animation returning to her voice and manner, "Milo had no need of the money—it was just lying useless in his lockbox under his bed. The Jews were paying him more each week than even I, a graduate nurse, make in a week."

With a curt nod, the priest said, "Yes, my child, another instance of the fierce love of family that is but a hallmark of the Aryan race and folk. I, of all here assembled, can fully understand why you did what you did, the lies and the . . . the far more heinous sins, the mortal sin of fornication, even. But mere understanding and even a degree of sympathy does not in any way justify your transgressions. The penance I shall lay upon you will be heavy, child, awesomely heavy, and as hard or harder to bear than what the hospital and secular authorities will likely do . . . although I shall strive to afford you as much protection from them as my office permits, of course, when once I am certain that you truly repent your sins.

"It were probably better that you depart with me, this night, for after all of this, I doubt that you would be happy or even welcome for any longer under this roof. I will take you to the home of a good German family for the night, and tomorrow you can first make a true confession, receive penance and absolution, then I will do what I can to help you out of these difficulties."

He turned to the younger man. "Father Karl, please fetch Fritz and have him take this child's things out to the auto."

Then Rüstung stood up and, pointing a forefinger at Milo, demanded, "You *did* use this child's body, you *did* take her flower, you *did* have carnal knowledge of her?" His voice quivered slightly with the intensity of his emotion, his cold blue eyes fairly spitting sparks.

Milo had not liked the man from minute one of their meeting and now could think of no reason to dissemble or mask that dislike. "You know damned well that I did, priest! Yes, I slept with her, but it was she that came to *my* bed, night after night, despite a locked door on one occasion. And she was no virgin from before the first night!"

Father Rüstung nodded another of his curt, grim-faced nods and turned to the police lieutenant. "Well, lieutenant, you heard him damn himself out of his own mouth. Where are your handcuffs? I want him arrested this instant for criminal carnal knowledge and fornication.

"You should also know that he is a dangerous radical who will divulge nothing of his past life to anyone. He may well be a Bolshevik, for I am reliably informed that he speaks excellent Russian and Ukrainian, and his overt employers are a clique of Jews, mostly of Russian extraction. If you don't take him into custody tonight, now, here, you'll probably have no second chance to take him

easily or without a gun battle. You know how these Bolsheviks and Jew Anarchists are."

The lieutenant arose and looked about uncertainly, his
left hand hovering in the vicinity of his cased handcuffs,
the voice of authority, but ecclesiastical authority only,
ringing in his jug ears. The sergeant stood up too, but
made no other move, watching his superior.

Old Rosaleen had heard enough and more than
enough, however. "It's prayin' for your forgiveness I am,
fither, but you should be ashamed of yourself, and you a
holy priest of God and His Mither. That poor, weak
mortals like us all be easily tempted, you of all people
should be a-knowin', and if crawlin' mither-naked into a
man's bed of nights be not temptin', I'd like to know what
is. It's that—that scarlet woman you should be after the
punishin' of, not poor Mr. Moray.

"And although he's not of the True Faith, I'll warrant
he's no Jew, nor yet a godless Bolshevik or whatnot. He's
a good man, a decent man and godly in his own way . . .
far and away more godly than some who've sheltered
under this roof."

She stared pointedly at Irunn, who met that stare for a
brief instant, then hung her head and began to sob again.

Turning to the police lieutenant, she said flatly, her
hands extended before her at a little over waist level,
"Terence, if it's taking in Mr. Moray you're thinkin' of,
then you'll be takin' me, as well, so put the cold steel
chains on me old wrists. They cannot be more cold than
the Christian charity of this holy priest, I'm thinkin', I
am."

Milo thought that the lieutenant looked as if he would
rather be in hell with a broken back than here and now in
the warm, comfortable furnished parlor of Maggie and
Pat O'Shea. He could almost hear the wheels turning, the
gears grinding madly as the tall, lanky redhead tried to
think of a way out of his dilemma that would not offend
either the priest or his old friend's widow. And Milo felt a
stab of pity for the much harried man.

Then Gerald Guiscarde chimed in, "Lieutenant
Grady, Milo Moray is not, no matter what this priest
claims to have heard, a Bolshevik or an Anarchist. He's

not a Jew, either. I've physically examined him thoroughly, and believe me, I know.

"Yes, he speaks Russian, but he also speaks German, French, Spanish and a plethora of other languages, as well. His work for Dr. Osterreich's group is that of a translator, and I am told by Dr. Osterreich and others that he does his job in a good, thoroughgoing manner, that he's the best translator they've ever had in their employ.

"And if there are truly any radicals in this room just now, my vote would be for Father Rüstung. Were he as truthful as he demands others be, he'd register himself with Washington as an agent of a foreign power. That's what he really is, you know—he and his precious German-American Bund would sell out this country in a minute to Adolf Hitler and his gang of German thugs."

"Be very careful what you say of me, doctor," said the priest in icy tones. "A day of reckoning will come for you and your kind . . . and it may well come far sooner than you think."

Then, turning back to Terence Grady, the priest demanded, "Well, what are you waiting for, lieutenant? Are you going to arrest him and put him in jail where he belongs, or not?"

Ignoring on this rare instance the snap of command in the voice of the German-born priest—whose accent had become stronger and more noticeable in the last few minutes—Lieutenant Terence Grady drew himself up and said, "No, fither, I ain't. I'm a lieutenant of patrolmen, a harness bull, not a vice cop or even a detective, and taking Mr. Moray in would be a job for one of them guys, not for me. It wasn't like he was caught in the act or nothin', and not even a warrant for him, either."

"A warrant you want, lieutenant? Well, a warrant you will have, the first thing tomorrow morning, over the signature of Judge Heinz Richter. Do you recognize the name of my good, good and old friend, eh? Of course you do. And please to be warned that he will also hear quickly of your impertinence to me, your failure to follow my orders, to do the duty which I pointed out to you and arrest a malefactor who had publicly confessed his guilt to a terrible crime against God and man.

"Come, Irunn," he snapped and stalked toward the foyer.

With Irunn, the priests and their chauffeur gone, Rosaleen fetched in more food and a bowl of punch, to which last old Pat O'Shea promptly added a half-quart of Irish whiskey.

They all had eaten and imbibed in silence for some time when Fanny Duncan spoke, hesitantly.

"Mr. Moray, you said that she . . . that Irunn, that is . . . wasn't a . . . a virgin when . . . when you . . . when you and she . . . well, anyway, it all makes me think back to our training days. Irunn and me, we were roommates in training for a couple of years of it, and . . . and I've always wondered. The way she talked about her brother, Sven, and some things she said sometimes in her sleep and the way the two of them behaved when they thought nobody else could see them one time when she and I went up to the farm in Wisconsin for a week and . . ."

Maggie paled and hurriedly signed herself. "Fanny! Hold your tongue, as you love God. *Incest?* It's a nauseating thought. Only degenerates and idiots do such things."

"Oh, I wouldn't go so far as to say that, Mrs. O'Shea," remarked Gerald Guiscarde, adding, "Certain events in my own practice, plus confidential conversations I've had with other professionals, incline me toward the belief that incest is not anywhere near as rare a thing as most people, even medical people, seem to think or aver."

Maggie just shook her head in disbelief, but Milo could and did fully believe it all, for he recalled that on two separate occasions in a transport of passion Irunn had called him Sven and whispered endearments to him in Norwegian.

After finishing off the trays of foods and most of the strengthened punch, almost single-handedly, Lieutenant Terence Grady addressed Milo. "Mister, I don't want to take in no friend of Rosaleen O'Farrell's, and besides, you strike me as a good guy, but if that Kraut priest does get a warrant from that squarehead judge in the mornin', it ain't gonna be no like or not like to it, you see. I'm gonna have to bring you in or send some other cop to do it. It might be a good idea if you get out of this precinct—or, better yet, this city—before morning. I'll give you a ride as far's the train depot, but I can't do more'n that for you. I got my wife and kids to think about, see, and my pension, too."

"You're a very brave man, lieutenant, a good man, too, to offer help in the face of a vindictive and powerful man like Father Rüstung," said the doctor. "And I am certain that Mr. Moray recognizes and deeply appreciates your generous offer. But no, it would be just too much needless risk for you to undertake. Leave it to me. I have a motorcar, too, and I am not, thank God, in a position where that most unsaintly man can do me any harm.

"But I do agree with you that Milo must leave the city or even the state tonight. Technically, he is guilty of a so-called crime that could get him, if convicted, as much as fifteen years in prison. So, if you and the sergeant will leave now, the rest of us will make plans and save you the discomfort of having to arrest a friend of Mrs. O'Farrell's."

As prearranged, Milo descended from the train in South Bend, Indiana, and found an all-night diner near the depot, where he sat, drinking terrible coffee at a nickel the chipped mug and reading a day-old newspaper until the old wall clock said that it was nine a.m. He then made his way back to the depot, found a telephone and placed a reverse-charges call, person-to-person to Patrick O'Shea, giving him the name they had decided upon, Tom Muldoon.

"Tommy, lad? Yes, operator, this is Patrick O'Shea. Yes, I'll accept charges for the call. Tommy, I can't talk to you but a minute. The whole bloody house is full of cops. Some feller used to room here, they're after him, two carloads of them just come in and they're after searching this house from cellar to attic. Anyhow, that guy I told you about, he's been told you're coming and he'll be expectin' you and he'll take good care of you and if he don't you let me know lickety-split. . . . A'right, lootenant, a'right, it's just a old buddy from the War is all, and I ain't talked to him in a coon's age. What in hell you expect me to be able to tell you, the man's gone is all. I'm closes' thing to blind from gas, you know, I can't see the damn street from the front stoop, not any kind of

clear, so how can I tell you which way he went, huh? . . .
Bye-bye, Tommy, I gotta go."

By nine-thirty, Milo was aboard a train bound south
for Indianapolis. As the engine picked up speed and the
car began to sway, he settled down into the seat and
closed his eyes and thought back to his last few hours in
what had been for not quite a year the first home of
which he had any memory.

"First of all," said Gerald Guiscarde," we need to
figure out how you're going to live after you leave here,
your job and us, your friends. The last thing you want to
do is seek a job as a translator. That would be a sure give-
away of just who you are, and if that priest is as dead set
to clap you in jail as he gives every indication of being,
he'll probably have his Bund people all over the East as
well as the Midwest looking for you and ready to have
you picked up and extradited back here.

"Jobs of any kind are damned hard to find anywhere in
this country, and if you live anything like well with no
evident job you're going to stand out like a sore thumb
and attract the Bund. So where to tell you to go, what to
tell you to do, Milo? I must confess, I can't just now come
up with an answer."

"Well, I can, by cracky!" said Pat O'Shea.

"You always have the same thing on your mind,"
snapped Maggie peevishly. "Maybe Milo doesn't want to
join the Army."

"Well, it's the bestest place for him, the way things is,
Maggie. Look, doctor, I's a perfeshnal soldier back before
the war. I soldiered for twelve years, made staff sergeant,
too, afore my folks all died and I had to come back home
to try and run the brewery. And if it's one thing I knows,
it's the Army.

"If Milo enlists—and I can get him enlisted, I still got
frinds from the old days is recruiters, two of them—the
Army ain't gonna turn him over to no civil police for
nothin' he done as a civilian, not unless he'd murdered or
raped or kidnapped or robbed banks or somethin' really
bad. Them bugtit feather merchants do try to come after
him for fornicatin', for the love of mud, Army's gonna
perlitely tell them where to go and what to do to theyselfs

when they gets there, is all. Just as long's a man don't fu—ahhh, mess up as a soldier, the Army don't give a hill of beans what he done before.

"And as for them Kraut-lovers, that Bund and all, it's more'n enough old soldiers what fought in France in the War is still around to make short shrift of any them comes sniffin' around after Milo."

"You know, Mrs. O'Shea, your husband may be right. The Army may well be the answer we so desperately need to keep Milo out of that priest's clutches. I think the minimum enlistment in the armed services is three years, and by that time surely all of this sorry business will be ancient history. But the question now is, how are we going to get him down to the recruiting office and signed up before the police pick him up on that warrant and clap him behind bars?"

Pat chuckled. "I got the answer to that one, too, doctor. I knows thishere recruiter in Indianapolis, see. Milo can get on a train and get out of Illinois, tonight, see. I can call my old buddy firstest thing he opens up in the morning and tell him enough of what's going on to get him ready for Milo when he gets there, see. Milo'll just have to kill some time somewheres till the right time to go to the recruitin' office is all, but we can work that out in jig time."

At Pat's suggestion, Milo packed only his razor and a few toiletries, a few days' worth of underwear and socks, a couple of shirts and a few books. As an afterthought, the old soldier suggested adding the fine, strong padlock from off the moneybox chain, saying that such would be useful for the securing of issue lockers in the barracks. Milo threw in a wad of handkerchiefs, then closed and locked the thick briefcase which was the sole piece of luggage of any description he owned.

It was while he was packing that Rosaleen bore up the stairs to his room a picnic basket packed well-nigh to bursting with food "for your journey, love."

Reopening the briefcase, he managed to make room for but three of the thick sandwiches. But then Rosaleen took over, emptied the case and repacked it so competently that she was able to add two more sandwiches, a slab of cheese and a half-dozen hard-boiled eggs, a small jar of pickles and a brace of red apples.

"Do you have a pocket knife?" inquired Pat. When Milo shook his head, the old man dug deep into his pants pocket and brought out an old, worn, but razor-edged Barlow. "A soldier needs him a good knife, Milo; I don't, I can't even see good enough to whittle no more. Mrs. O'Shea, she'll be damn glad I give it to you, she's plumb sick and tired of fixin' up my cut fingers as it is.

"I'll pack up the resta your clothes and things, Milo, and put them in a old cedar chest is up in the attic with some mothballs, too. You can send for them whenever you wants them, see."

"No, Pat, thank you, but no," Milo told him. "Sell them for whatever you can, or give them away. One thing, though. Rosaleen, can you find me a legal-sized envelope and a sheet of blank paper?"

While the woman was gone, Milo opened his strongbox and emptied it onto the small writing table. He quickly divided the couple hundred dollars in smaller bills between his billfold and several of his pockets, then tucked a couple of fifties from the sale of the gold into each sock. The rest of the stack of bills he divided, and when the old cook returned with the stationery, he placed a thousand dollars into the envelope and dashed off a quick note.

"Sol, I am leaving town for good. Where I'm bound, I won't need all this cash, so I want you and your family to have it. With this for a nest egg, you might be able to finish law school, and I think you should. No, you can't give it back to me, for not even I know where I'll be when you get it. Milo Moray."

Adding the folded note to the contents of the envelope, he sealed it and put it in his coat pocket. Handing the rest of the cash, uncounted, to Pat, he said, "Now this, Pat, you can hold until I send for it, whenever. Okay?"

Then he looked up from the chair at old Rosaleen. "Mrs. O'Farrell, if I give you something, do you promise to take it without a lot of argument?"

"It's not one red copper I'll be taking from you, Mr.

Moray," she declared forcefully in a tone that brooked no nonsense or demur.

He shook his head. "No, it's not money, Mrs. O'Farrell. Will you promise to take it? Please, I haven't much time left."

"Well . . . if it's not money, love," she said uncertainly, "then, yes, I promise to take it."

"You heard her promise me, Pat?" Milo demanded.

"That I did," was the old soldier's quick answer. "She promised, indeed she did."

Picking up the ring box of dark-green velvet from the top of the writing desk, Milo pressed it into the old cook's hand. Opened it that she might see the carat of blue-white emerald-cut diamond in its setting of heavy, solid red gold.

"Oh, no, no, Mr. Moray, sir, I can't be taking sich a treasure! No, why it must be worth every last penny of . . . of fifty or sixty dollars."

Milo just smiled. "Actually, a bit more than that, Mrs. O'Farrell. But remember your promise—I hold you to it."

Old Rosaleen looked at him, then back at the stunning ring for a moment. Then she buried her wrinkled face in her work-worn hands and ran from the room, sobbing loudly.

Milo stood up and took from the tabletop the last two bills, a twenty and a five. "Pat, this is the twenty-five dollars that Irunn paid the jeweler, Plotkin, to hold the ring. If she or anyone else comes around demanding its return, you are to give them this. Your wife has the receipts. Understand me?"

Pat nodded briskly. "You damn tootin' I does, Milo. It's like I's said for a helluva long time—you some kind of a man, you is. You gonna make a damn good soldier, too, I can tell you that right now. You got the kinda style it ain't much seen of no more."

The leavetaking was an emotional one, to say the least, what with all of the women crying, save only old Rosaleen, who had done with her crying for the occasion and who now wore Milo's gift on a thumb, her other fingers being too small to give it secure lodgement.

As the old cook reached up to hug Milo's neck, she

stated, "It's gettin' this lovely, lovely present of yours sized to my finger, I'll be doin', Milo Moray, and then it's I'll be wearin' it until the day I die and buried with me it'll be. God and His Blessed Mither guard and keep you, now, and it's my prayers you'll be havin' of me that you fare well."

In the Mercedes-Benz, Milo took the sealed envelope from the pocket of his greatcoat and passed it to Dr. Guiscarde, saying, "The name of the young man this is intended for is on the envelope. Sam Osterreich can put you in touch with him. And make him take it, hear? He's way too bright a boy to waste his life peddling door-to-door."

"The old sarge, now, he was some kinda sojer, some kinda sojer, I tell you, mister!" stated Master Sergeant Norman Oates between and through mouthfuls of Rosaleen O'Farrell's hearty homebaked bread and butter and roast beef or country ham, sharp cheddar cheese and home-canned mustard pickles. "Won't no reason for him to get gassed like he did, you know. 'Cept of he put his own gas mask on that young lootenant who was layin' there wounded with his own mask shot fulla holes, is all. An' then the one what he took off a corpse won't workin' right, see.

"Naw, Sarge O'Shea, he was a real, old-time sojer, the kind like you don't hardly see no more in thishere new-fangled Army. You want some more coffee?"

Milo accepted, holding out his white china mug for a refill, for it was the best coffee he could recall ever having tasted, its flavor being the equal of its aroma.

Taking another hard-boiled egg in his thick fingers, the stout, balding, jowly soldier cracked it with the flick of a thumbnail, then expertly peeled off the shell, showered it with salt and pepper and bit off the top half before continuing.

"Yeah, I tell you, mister, it was plumb good to hear old Sergeant Pat's voice again, this mornin'. Way he tells it, you kinda on the run, like, right?" He chuckled, then added, along with the rest of the egg, "Didn' need to tell me that, even, none of it, 'cause I'd've knowed. If it won't important like for you to make tracks, he'd've got ole Castle in Chicago to 'list you up 'stead of me. So you tell me, what's the law want you for? Better level with me, Moray, 'cause I got me ways of findin' out and I don't cotton to being lied to."

When Milo had related an encapsulated version of the story, the sergeant pushed back from his desk, threw back his head and laughed and laughed and laughed, his huge beer belly jiggling and bouncing to his mirth. His already florid face became an alarming dark red, his eyes streamed tears, and he finally had to hold his sides and breathe in wheezes. At last, he was able to exert enough self-control to straighten up, pull himself back to the desk and wipe at his eyes and face with a wadded handkerchief, following which, he used the same cloth to loudly and thoroughly blow his nose, before jamming it back into a pocket.

Still grinning, he said, "Christ on a crutch, Moray, it's high time they took shit like that out'n the friggin' lawbooks. Goddam, man, fuckin's the most natcherl thing in the world. I don't go 'long with rape, see, but if the woman's willin', hell, the goddam cops shouldn't have no place in it a-tall. As for the damn preachers and priests and all, bugger the sour-faced lot of 'em, folks has got the right to some pleasure, no matter what they say or claim the Bible says. You ever read the Bible, Moray—I mean, really read it? Well, you should—it's chock-full of more begats than you ever saw in your life, and the onliest way to begat a kid is to fuck a woman.

"As for your trouble, don't you worry none about it no more, hear me? That shit back in Chicago, that is the damnedest bum rap I ever heard tell of."

Chapter V

Among the first things Milo had to do upon his enlistment in the Army of the United States of America in November 1938 was to quickly learn to understand and to speak—though not, ever, to write—a whole new dialect of English. No one of the many dictionaries, thesauruses and etymological works he had read through during his months of work in the confines of the public library had given him more than a hint of the slang, the depthless crudities, the euphemisms, the scatological references, the slurs, the obscenities and blasphemies that all went a long way toward making up the everyday language of the common soldier.

The standardized, non-obscene Army terms and abbreviations were very easy to assimilate, especially for those men who had no difficulty in reading basic English, not that every one of the recruits could do so. A few were just too stupid, more were simply ill-educated. With most of the rest, the problem was that English was not their native language, and it was in helping these latter that Milo soon proved his worth to the commissioned and noncommissioned cadre of his training company.

Not that his skill at languages spared him any of the training, details, fatigue duties, drilling, classes, weary route marches and endless round of bullying and general harassment suffered by the rest of his company and battalion. Early on, he was given an armband to wear, told that he was henceforth an "acting squadleader" and given responsibility for six European immigrants, a pair of Mexicans, a Turk, and a Lebanese who spoke Arabic,

Turkish and French fluently but had only a few words and so very few phrases of English that Milo privately wondered how he had gotten accepted for the Army at all.

His abilities to get through to the members of his squad earned him a measure of grudging respect from his superiors, but what really impressed them was his unerring marksmanship and other proven combat qualifications.

When once he had mastered the mechanical functions of the U.S. Rifle, Caliber .30, Model 1903, and the Pistol, Caliber .45, Model 1911A1, he consistently racked up range scores in the high-expert classification, and no one afterward believed his quite truthful answers to the questions that he could not recall ever having handled or fired either pistols or rifles before. But their under-standable disbelief was not confined to his statements only, for in the Army of that time, there was full many a man with a past to hide.

He also was given an expert's badge in the art of the bayonet. The grizzled but still-vital and powerful old sergeant who conducted the bayonet classes averred that Private Moray was one of the best that he ever had seen—fast, sure and strong in the attack, cunning and wary in the defense and so well coordinated as to be able to take instant advantage of an error made by an opponent. He added that he was convinced that the man was no stranger to the use of the bayoneted rifle, but he added that his personal style was unorthodox—not American, not French, not British, not classic Prussian, either. If Milo had told the training sergeant the unvarnished truth, that he too did not know just where and how he had learned bayonet work, that it only came to him as instinctively as breathing, the man would have been no more believing than had the range personnel confronted with the deadly marksmanship of this supposedly green recruit.

Sergeant Jethro "Judo" Stiles was the field first sergeant of Milo's training company, and he also doubled as the battalion instructor in hand-to-hand combat. Unlike most of the cadremen, he was neither loud nor arrogant nor a brutal, sadistic bully. When he was not demonstrating the best means of garroting an enemy sentry quickly and in silence, the most efficient ways of dislocating joints and shattering bones or how to take a pistol away from an enemy, breaking his trigger finger and wrist in one process, he was quiet almost to the point of introversion, kindly, gentle, polite, well spoken and well read. He neither chewed tobacco, used snuff nor smoked cigarettes, only a pipe, and then rarely; he drank little beer, but was a connoisseur of fine wines and a real authority on cognacs and armagnacs. He lived well in rented housing off post, owned an automobile and wore beautifully tailored uniforms. It was believed that he was a remittance man, paid by his family to stay in the Army as a way of avoiding a scandal of some sort.

After he had called a number of the biggest recruits before an open-air class beneath a towering stand of Georgia pines and demonstrated fully just how powerless was even the largest, strongest man against scientific methods of self-defense, he chanced to choose Milo as his opponent for the next lesson. Tossing him a Model 1920 bayonet which had been securely wired into its issue case, the sides and point of which then had been padded with cotton and wrapped with friction tape, the training sergeant beckoned.

"All right. Moray, is it? All right, Moray, try to stab me with that bayonet. Okay, if you want to do it under-hand, that's fine too. Come on."

Without conscious thought of what he was doing or why he was doing it just that way, Milo advanced in short but fast and sure steps which to the watchers looked almost akin to dance steps.

With all his training and practice, natural skills and experience, the sergeant had only seconds to wonder if he was going to be able to stop this recruit who moved as quickly and lightly as an Olympic fencer. "Oh, shit," he thought, "I chose a wrongo this time!"

From the crouch at which he had advanced, the bayonet held a little below his hip, pointing forward, his free hand held up and out and ready to either attack or defend, to stab fingers at eyes, ward off blows or grab a wrist, he suddenly sank even farther down upon deeply flexed knees, then used his legs to drive his body forward with the speed and force of a arrow shot from a bow. The point of that arrow was his hand and the weapon it held, his hand at about the waist level of his target, but the weapon itself angling upward.

All that Stiles saw was a blur of motion. Then there was suddenly an agonizing contact and he was doubled over, retching up his breakfast, fighting to draw breath and wondering just how the mule that had kicked him in the belly had gotten into his class area. Then he lost all consciousness.

The class was immediately called to attention, then marched into the adjacent field to unstack their rifles and fall into formation. They were marched back to camp and spent the rest of the morning at the wearily repetitive close-order drill with arms.

Sergeant Stiles was retained by the training company because of his unquestionable skills and his ability to impart those skills to trainees, but his solitary nature and off-duty habits, plus his erudition and cultivated tastes, alienated him from most of the noncoms and many of the officers of the company and battalion. He had few friends among his peers, but one of those few was the first sergeant of Milo's training company, James Lewis.

That afternoon, after recall, as he sat with the others in the barrack cleaning rifles under the critical eyes of their platoon sergeant, the company clerk came in with the message that Private Moray was to report to the first sergeant on the double.

Taking Milo aside and speaking fast in low, hushed tones, Platoon Sergeant Cassidy said, "You gotta unnerstan', Moray, with all the damn Bolsheviks and Wobblies and all we get's in, we jest cain't let reecroots git away with bestin' sergeants, is all. The first and some others is gonna have to take you out and beat the piss outen you—they *has* to, see. It'll hurt, sure, but you jest take it like a man and it won't las' long, 'cause they don't aim fer to do no real damage to you, jest give the resta the guys what saw whatall you did to Judo Stiles a coupla blacked eyes and a split lip and swoled-up jaw to look at fer a few days."

Milo headed for the office of the first sergeant, but was met by the noncom himself before he reached the orderly room. Ready for shouts, obscene abuse and manhandling from the senior sergeant, Milo was surprised and made very wary by being treated almost civilly, instead.

"Moray? Yes, you're Moray. Come on with me, Moray."

At the small parking area behind the orderly room, Sergeant Lewis stopped beside a three-quarter-ton reconnaisance truck. "Can you drive, Moray?"

"No, first sergeant."

"Okay, I'll drive. But you oughta learn to. Comes in damn handy to be able to drive a veehicle in the fuckin' Army. Get in."

In the post gym, after they had divested themselves of shirts and undershirts, after Lewis had laced Milo's hands into a pair of six-ounce boxing gloves, as they walked in sock feet from the locker room to the gym proper, the first sergeant said, "Moray, years ago, I was boxing champeen of the old Twenty-third for some years. I'm some older now, of course, but I ain't got soft and slow and fat, like a lot of the guys has let themselfs get.

"Now I heered what you done to Judo Stiles Today. It's all over the fuckin' battalion, and somebody's got to make a example of you for it, see."

"First sergeant," said Milo, "Sergeant Stiles ordered me to attack him, to try to stab him. All that I did was to follow those orders. I've tried to be a good soldier."

Lewis nodded, looking a little sad. "I knows, son, and if you sticks to it you gonna be a damn fine soljer, too. Hell, you'll have stripes, real stripes, in no time a-tall, 'specially whenever the nextest war fin'ly gets around to startin' up and the Army gets bigger. And that's part of why I'm sorry to have to beat up on you thisaway; but it's a whole fuckin' hell of a lot better for me to mess your face up then for three, four of the pl'toon sergeants to get you off in a latrine somewhere and work you over, son. I knows what I'm doin', see—I can give you just a few good ones in the right places for to make it look like you been dragged th'ough a fuckin' wringer by the cock."

At the raised boxing ring, Lewis held the ropes apart so Milo could step through them. Joining his victim, the gray-haired boxer went to a corner of the ring and waved Milo to the opposite corner. The few other men in the high, vaulted room of the sometime riding hall drifted over to watch, for Sergeant James Lewis was always worth watching.

"Move around on the balls of your feet, son," the noncom advised Milo. "And keep your knees bent some to help you take the force of a punch, see. I promise, after I's messed you up some, I'll stop. You ready?"

Milo sighed. "As ready as I guess I'll ever be." And then he advanced to the center of the ring.

Immediately he absorbed the first jarring jab to his face, Milo's body and limbs rearranged themselves without his conscious volition.

"Oh, ho, Moray," puffed Lewis. "Done had some time with a old-fashion bare-knuckle fighter, have you? Okay, I can fight that way, too, but I warn you, it'll prob'ly hurt you more in the end."

Lewis was good, skilled, experienced and had stayed in practice if not in unremitting training over the years, so he did land a few more blows here and there. But so, too, did Milo, once more letting his instincts guide his body and reflexes. His final blow put Lewis flat on his back on the canvas, and the watchers entered the ring to pound him on the back and heap flattering praise upon him before picking up First Sergeant Lewis and bearing his inert body back to the locker room.

When the noncom came around and pushed away the hand waving the ammonia ampoule under his blood-crusted nostrils, he just drew himself up on his elbows and stared at Milo for long minutes in silence. Then, slowly shaking his head, he swung his legs off the side of the massage table and sat up. He swayed then, and Milo quickly took a step to the older man's side and gripped a biceps, lest his recent opponent pitch onto the floor.

Lewis said precious little as they dressed and drove back to the company area. When he had parked nose-in and turned off the engine of the reconnaissance car, he said, "Moray, my boy, you punch like the kick of a fuckin' mule, I swear to God you do! You learn you modern boxin' and all, you'll be champeen of whatever division you winds up in, I don't doubt it one bit. I'm just thankin' God you had them fuckin' gloves on—you might of kilt me dead without them.

"When you gits back to your barracks, you tell Sergeant Cassidy I said to round up all the other platoon sergeants and bring them to my office, pronto. What you ain't to tell him or anybody elst is why I wants to see them.

"I didn' do hardly any damage can be seen easily on you, see, and I don't want none them takin' it inta their heads to try workin' you over, son, 'cause you just might kill one or two of them or they might kill you, and I don't want anyway to have to work out no L.O.D.s determinations on how a bunch of my cadre got themselfs beat half to fuckin' death; no man what hadn't fought you would believe it.

"A'right, Moray. You can go now. But you take care of yourself, hear? I'm gonna be keepin' my eye on you."

Milo never knew exactly how Lewis had phrased or explained his hands-off-Moray order to his cadremen, but from then on, Cassidy and the other noncoms treated him almost as an equal, and a few days prior to the completion of their basic training cycle, First Sergeant Lewis once more summoned him. This time, however, the senior noncom met him formally, in his office just off the orderly room.

When Milo had completed the required reporting ritual, he was told to close the door and stand at ease. "Moray, after you graduates Tuesday, you ain't gonna have far to travel. You're gonna go just down the road a ways to the advanced infantry basic battalion, and you do as good there as you done done here, your next stop is gonna be acrost the post to the NCO Academy. You're prime, Moray, and I ain't just flatterin' you when I says it, neither, and so lotsa the other units is gonna want to grab you up for to fill out their cadres, but you tell any as talks about it or tries it that they'll do 'er over the dead body of First Sergeant James Evans Lewis. You hear me, son?"

Lewis smiled the first smile that Milo had ever seen on his lined, scarred face. "I wants you back here, boy, to be one of my platoon sergeants, see. You got you more brains nor the resta the bunch I has now put together, 'ceptin' my field first. You play your cards right and you'll wind up as field first afore too fuckin' long, under

Stiles, as first. See, my thirty's gonna be up in only 'bout four years, come the thirteenth day of January, nineteen and forty-three, my hitch is up and I'm long gone. I means to leave thishere trainin' company in good hands, though, and you and Stiles is the plumb best I seen sincet the last war. It's damn fuckin' seldom the Army gets men like you two, see, and I ain't gonna let a prize like you get out of my hands. I ain't that big of a fuckin' fool, nosireebob, I ain't!"

The Sergeant Moray, Milo (n.m.i.), who stood before Lewis' desk after graduation with honors from both advanced infantry basic and the NCO Academy still could recall no single incident prior to his awakening in a Chicago hospital room, but he knew by then that Dr. Sam Osterreich and old Pat O'Shea had likely been accurate in their suppositions about him. The most of the business of soldiering just came far too easily to him for him not to have been one, somewhere, sometime, in some army, and probably for some little time, too.

Lewis had been obliged several times over to pull strings, call in IOUs for past favors, beg, wheedle, cajole and do everything except physically fight to retain his dibs on Moray. But he had done all of these gladly, partly for the joy of winning, of course, but also because the attempted shanghaiings of his peers reinforced his own statements and views as to the potential and value of the man.

He smiled up at the new-made buck sergeant. "Welcome home, son. Close the door and sit down." With the door shut, Lewis arose and stepped over to his filing cabinet, opened the bottom drawer and drew from its rearmost recesses two canteen cups and a quart of bourbon, still better than half full.

Immediately after work call the next morning, Lewis drove Milo down to the motor pool and introduced him to Master Sergeant O'Connor, the NCO-in-charge. "Teach him to drive, Harry. He missed learnin' how, see, and I can't spare him long enough to send him off to no fuckin' school. I'll be owin' you one, if you do."

A week under the motor sergeant's often impatient tutelage gave Milo the rudiments of properly handling the smaller wheeled transport vehicles. This was followed by a week on the deuce-and-a-half, the general-purpose two-and-a-half-ton truck. Then, of a day toward the end of that second week, O'Connor drove one of the brand-new general-purpose one-quarter-ton vehicles (which very soon were to be nicknamed "jeeps") up to Lewis' training company and closeted with the first sergeant in his office.

When they were seated and O'Connor had had a swallow or two of the bourbon, Lewis asked, "You ain't havin' no fuckin' trouble with my boy, Moray, are you, Harry?"

His hands seemingly absently occupied with a cigarette paper and his sack of Bull Durham tobacco, O'Connor replied, "Aw, naw, top, not him. He's a'ready a right fair driver, for all he's got him a kinda heavy foot now and then. I done got him famil'arized with alla the smaller stuff, four-wheel *and* two- and three-wheel, last week. This week I grounded him on the deuce-and-a-half, both the six-wheelers and the ten-wheelers, and he ain't half bad in them, neither. Man learns quick and remembers good."

The cigarette rolled to his careful satisfaction, the white-haired noncom cracked a wooden match alight with his thumbnail, lit up, took a puff and went on. "Thing is, top, I'd like to keep Moray down there at least another week, see. Right now, it's too fuckin' many drivers on thishere post don't know how to do nuthin' with a fuckin' vehicle *but* drive the cocksucker. I wants to make damn fuckin' sure this Moray knows at fuckin' least how to do basic maint'nence, see. Can you spare him that much longer, top?"

Lewis, just then sipping at his whiskey, nodded as he took the canteen cup down from his lips. "Sure, Harry, take a week or even two, if you can make him better for it . . . but I'm servin' a fuckin' warnin', too, Harry O'Connor. Don't you and Mr. Cobb get you the fuckin' idea you gonna make no OJT mechanic or suthin' out'n him, neither. I done fought and beat bigger fish nor you and Warrant Officer Cobb to keep Moray for this comp'ny and I'll fuckin' well beat your fuckin' asses, too, come to that."

Lewis could see that this jab had connected good and proper. O'Connor and Cobb *had* been up to something, but he also knew that now they would both back off rather than tangle with him and his web of connections in the battalion and regiment.

"So give Moray all the training you think he needs, Harry. It'll be three weeks afore the new bunch gets to us, and I'll be needin' him then. He's gonna be takin' over a trainin' platoon, then. More bourbon, Harry?"

While Lewis splashed more of the whiskey into his steel cup, O'Connor queried, "But, top, I'd heard you was full up, cadre-wise."

Lewis smiled. "The comp'ny is—we got all the Table'll let us have, now, but I done found a way 'round that, too. I'm shippin' Sergeant Carbone out, transferrin' him in grade."

"*Queer Guinea Guido*?" asked O'Connor in patent amazement. "Who the hell did you find was dumb enough to take on that dago gut-butcher, top?"

Lewis smiled lazily, obviously enjoying deep satisfaction at reciting his triumph for a properly appreciative listener. "Regimental Head and Head, that's who, Harry. If you go to old Martin, real quick-like, maybe he'll let you two room together."

Ignoring the last jibe, O'Connor looked pained, "Aw hell, top, ain't we got enough trouble in regiment a'ready? I was jus' talkin' to Mr. Cobb 'bout it the other day. Seems like we winds up with ever' fuckin' loony and loopleg, not to mention ever' damn asshole goldbrick and moron comes along. We a'ready got us all the friggin' cornholers and pegboys we can take in Head 'n Head, top. For the lova God, what'd you go and do that to old Homer Martin for? What'd he ever do to you?"

Lewis' smile evaporated. "Wished the wop carrot-grabber off on me'n this comp'ny to start off, that's what. But he agreed to thishere, once't I explained all to him, he did, Harry. I checked Carbone's 201 file real close, see, and I come to find he useta give classes in wire-layin' and stringin', see. So Martin, he ain't gonna keep the shit-stirrin' bastard around hardly long enough to cut a fuckin' fart. He's gonna cut orders, if he ain't done it a'ready, to ship Carbone over to Signal Comp'ny. Martin agrees with me that whatall happens when Sergeant Call, the first faggot of Signal Comp'ny, gets the fuckin' Prussian Eyetie in his claws after all this time and all, what happens over to Signal'll be a pure, fuckin' joy to watch, Harry, a pure, fuckin' joy to watch!"

Harry O'Connor set down his cup and just stared at Lewis, cigarette ashes dribbling unnoticed down the front of his blue denim fatigue uniform. "Top," he said finally, "that is the evilest, viciousest, rottenest scheme I ever heard tell of. Ever'body knows Guido's done stole away or leastways got into three, four, maybe five or six or more of Plugger Call's angelinas, and it ain't nothin' but bad blood between them two sods. Hey, 'member, Call damn near got hisself busted when he broke a bottle and went at Carbone with it at the regimental beer garden, two years ago.

"It's plumb beautiful, top. How much of all this does Queer Guido know about?"

"Not one damn thing, 'cept for that he's shippin' out to regimental Head and Head. And he better not hear nothin', neither, Harry. You don't tell nobody, hear? Not Mr. Cobb, not your bunkie, nobody!"

O'Connor nodded, then chuckled, "Naw, nobody, top, not me. I wouldn't want to miss this shit circus for the fuckin' world. Wouldn't surprise me none if them two plumb dehorned each other!" He chuckled again, grinning to show tobacco-stained teeth and rubbing the palms of his calloused, grease-stained hands together in an excess of anticipated glee.

"Milo, you done been taught how to run a trainin' platoon," said First Sergeant James Lewis, "so I ain't gonna give you a whole fuckin' shitpile of orders and all on it. The onliest thing's gonna be diffrunt from your platoon and the others in this comp'ny is I'm gonna shift all the furriners over to you, since you can talk with them and the resta us cain't. You gone have Corp'ral Perkins as long as you thinks you needs him with his first bunch, so you should oughta make out okay."

And Milo did, of course, being a natural leader and having been thoroughly schooled in the NCO Academy. The only desertion was that of a gypsy, but despite the black mark against platoon, company and battalion, Milo, Lewis and the rest of the cadremen felt more relieved than anything else, for the decamped man's appalling proclivity to petty theft from his mates and his utter aversion to even the basics of personal hygiene had earmarked him as a murder waiting to happen.

And all the regiment was gossiping already about the supposedly hushed-up affair in Signal Company, where First Sergeant Call had been attacked while asleep and horribly maimed, nearly killed, by none other than PFC Guido Carbone, who had been a platoon sergeant in a training company for some years. Following the crime, PFC Carbone had taken French leave and now, like the unmissed gypsy, was listed as a deserter.

Sergeant Jethro Stiles and Milo quickly became fast friends and buddies, a relationship strongly encouraged by First Sergeant Lewis, who occasionally joined them when his and their duties allowed for a weekend of ease and cards and talk and drink at Stiles' comfortable rented bungalow off-post. Surrounded by bed on bed of roses, peonies, chrysanthemums, asters, altheas, irises, lilies, tulips, hyacinths, daffodils and a dozen or more other varieties of flowering plants, all springing up out of ground-covering cushions of phlox and baby's breath and vinca minor, the bungalow had been Stiles' home for years and fitted him like an old glove.

There were few rooms—living room, dining room, bedroom, bath, kitchen, a small room furnished with only a desk and chair and floor-to-ceiling bookshelves packed with books; there was also a basement which housed a furnace and coalbin, a workbench and its tools and a varied, extensive wine cellar—but Jethro managed well, doing his own cooking, cleaning and gardening with obvious relish. The man was a superlative chef; Milo could not remember ever before having been treated to such culinary masterpieces, all of them served on a table agleam with crystal, sterling silver and fine china, the food invariably prepared with herbs from the garden.

After one such epicurean delight, he and Lewis both stuffed to repletion and beyond, all three of them sipping at hot coffee and a fine old cognac, Milo remarked,

"Jethro, you are always referring to yourself and to me, too, as a 'gentleman ranker.' May I ask why? What does that term mean?"

But Lewis answered first. "Means just what it means, Milo. You and Jethro is gentlemen, no two ways about it. You should rightly oughta be off'sers . . . prob'ly will be, too, afore long, when thishere shootin' war that's comin' sure as God made us all gets around to gettin' the U.S. of A. mixed up in it."

But their host demurred, saying, "Milo, yes, he'll make a splendid officer, but not me, James. If offered a commission, I'll have to refuse it. I prefer the basic anonymity of the other ranks; also, it is a part of my penance.

"I know you all wonder about me, who I really am, why I am here among you, but being true friends you never have been so rude, so crude as to ask, nor would I have told you had you done so. All that I will tell you is this: When I was far younger and foolish and full with the arrogance and selfishness of being born to wealth and position, I did a terrible, monstrously evil thing, and worse, I did it carelessly, without so much as a thought for whom my act might hurt and how much it would hurt them.

"I was protected, of course, from my due punishment by the power and influence and wealth of my family. Nonetheless, it was considered in the best interests of all and sundry that I leave the country for a bit. I left for Europe with a letter which allowed me to draw any amount I might need out of family accounts in certain Swiss banks. I never have returned to my home. My father and mother are long dead, as too are all of the other principals in the tragedy I brought about so long ago, yet still I am not free to resume the life I inherited, the position I degraded.

"I am a self-exiled man, and I shall continue to pay the price for my misdeed for as long as God gives me to live."

Then, in a soaring tenor voice, Stiles sang Kipling's "Gentleman Rankers" to them.

Milo was long in forgetting that evening.

The training cycles came and went, commenced and

ended, grinding out replacement personnel to meet the meager requirements of the small standing army which was all that the Land of the Free felt that it needed to remain that way, with the "war to end war" now more than two decades in the past.

Kept penurious by a depressed economy and an anti-military, tight-fisted Congress, they trained and drilled with the outdated, antique weapons and vehicles and equipment and tractics of the long-ago trenches of France. It was an army of orphans, threadbare and despised by the very people they were sworn to protect from enemies foreign or domestic. And the need to extend that sworn obligation would be upon them all too soon, and the soldiers all knew it, even if their employers chose to ignore the signs of the impending bloodbath.

They did what they could with what they had available, and they did well, as everyone learned before it was over, despite a general and appalling paucity of bare necessities.

While on extended training exercises the Army of the United States of America made do with "field expedients" to simulate the weapons and equipment they lacked— mockups of stovepipe and plyboard to give an unconvincing illusion of the missing heavy mortars and artillery pieces, rickety trucks standing in for the still-unsupplied half-tracks and tanks—the modern and fully equipped Wehrmacht was on the march ·in Europe and the Imperial Japanese Army moved deeper and deeper into China and strengthened the fortifications of Pacific islands with strange names.

But at long last, the sands of time trickled so low as to leave nothing in which the stubborn American ostrich could longer hide its head. Poland fell to German and Russian arms, then Russia attacked Finland. In the early spring of 1940 Germany conquered tiny Denmark and invaded Norway. Next to feel the might of the war machine of the Third Reich were Holland and Belgium, and even às French and British troops tried to hold the shaky line in Flanders, the panzers and the Wehrmacht infantry were racing through the supposedly impenetrable Ardennes to strike deep into France, rolling up her scattered bands of ill-trained, ill-equipped, ill-led troops.

And as the French and British armies, which had suffered many of the same injustices from their respective countrymen and governments as had the American army, were taken, utterly routed and thoroughly defeated, off the beach at Dunkirk by a makeshift fleet of civilian boats, leaving behind them the bulk of their weapons and equipment as well as any thought that this new war would be a static conflict as had been the last one, the sluggish American Congress began to face the fact that a large army, a modern army, a strong army might well be needed . . . *soon.*

The training regiment as well as the understrength combat-ready (which was a very unfunny joke) units scattered about the forty-eight states and its possessions overseas began to see a slow trickle of long-overdue equipment, weapons and supplies. New buildings began to be thrown up on existing open posts and on reopened ones as well as newly purchased or condemned-to-government-use land.

And then, on the 16th of September, 1940, the first peacetime Selective Service Act was signed into law, and long before anyone was ready for it, the onrushing floods of drafted men were virtually inundating every training facility.

Chapter VI

Almost overnight, the training regiment became a training division. With the overall size more than quadrupled while the available numbers of cadre remained almost static, new and exalted ranks fell like so much confetti. The captain of Milo's company became a light colonel and took James Lewis along with him to be his captain-adjutant in his new battalion command. The company exec should then have advanced to company commander save for the fact that he had already been bumped up to major and was serving on the staff of the division. Two of their three second lieutenants were also bumped up and shipped out, leaving only the newest officer, Second Lieutenant Muse, to become a first lieutenant and take over the company. As Lewis had long planned, this frantic shuffling left Jethro Stiles in the position of first sergeant and Milo, bumped to tech sergeant, as field first.

By the time they had managed to get the first class of draftees through their mill and off to advanced basic training, there were none of the original cadre contingent remaining at a rank lower than sergeant, and the resultant situation was so critical as to lead to the virtual shanghaiing of trainees showing even the bare minimum of needed talents or of prior military experience to fill empty cadre slots in the company Table of Organization and Equipment (TO&E). Nor were they alone in this practice; from division down it was the same story. The general preference was for enlistees, but they would take draftees, too, figuring—rightly, as it turned out—that all of the men would be around for however long the war lasted.

The world continued to turn, and the new training division and many another like it continued to painfully remold their quotas of soft civilian levies into reasonable facsimiles of soldiers. Class after class after class of them passed through the hands of Lieutenant Muse, First Sergeant Stiles and Sergeant Moray on the initial steps along a path that would lead, for some, to death or dismemberment.

Elsewhere on that same world, *Il Duce*, Benito Mussolini, launched the Italian army on an offensive against the small, weak army of Greece, moving out of already occupied Albania. The Greek forces of General Alexander Papagos not only stopped the numerically superior, vastly better-supplied and -armed Italian army, they launched two ferocious counterattacks that drove the invaders in full rout back over the Albanian border. Papagos then took the offensive, his troops pouring into occupied Albania in full pursuit of the demoralized Italians. Reinforcements of men and materiel poured in from Italy, of course, but even with these, the best that Italian General Visconti-Prasca could do was to hold a little over half of Albania, the rest being occupied by the Greeks. It is most probable that that unhappy man thought quite often of the hoary folk proverb involving the best treatment of sleeping dogs.

Completely lacking any air force, the Greeks had been aided in this regard by elements of the British forces engaged against the Italians in North Africa. Had the British not constructed airbases and supply points on the Greek mainland and on Crete, chances are good that Mussolini's Teutonic allies would have allowed Visconti-Prasca and his stymied, stalemated army to twist slowly in the wind of the Albanian mountains until hell froze over solidly. But the German high command, just then preparing to invade their sometime ally, Russia, and not at all savoring the thought of Greek-based British planes menacing a flank of their Russia-bound army, elected to drag the well-singed Italian chestnuts from out of the Greek fire.

When once the Nazi propagandists had thoroughly

cowed the leaders of Hungary, Rumania, Yugoslavia and Bulgaria, forced them in their terror to sign degrading treaties and sent in German troops to occupy and prepare for an invasion of Greece, Britain sent General Henry Wilson with upward of sixty thousand British troops from North Africa (where they, too, had recently inflicted a humiliating defeat on Italian arms in the deserts).

But Wilson's sixty thousand and the remainder of Papagos' hundred and fifty thousand proved just no match for the Waffen-SS, Wehrmacht and Luftwaffe units thrown against them in their hastily erected position. The German invasion had commenced on April 6, and by April 29 the shattered remnants of the Greek army had surrendered and the only British still remaining in Greece were either captives or corpses.

The conquest of Crete took only about ten days and was a purely Luftwaffe victory, even the ground troops being of the Luftwaffe Fallschirmjager or airborne troops. The lightning-fast victories of German arms made it abundantly clear to a closely watching world that only large, strong, well-trained and, above all else, well-supplied and well-armed forces could represent any sort of a match for the triumphant forces now scouring Europe and the Balkans with fire and steel.

The United States of America was not as yet formally a warring nation, but only fools could doubt that she soon must be such. This became more than abundantly clear when the U.S. Navy destroyer *Kearny*, while helping to protect a Canadian merchant convoy in the waters off Iceland, was torpedoed by a German U-boat on October 17, 1941. A brand-spanking-new vessel replete with all modern appurtenances, DD *Kearny* survived the torpedoing and limped back to port safely. But not so with the elderly four-stacker DD *Reuben James*, two weeks later. The *James* was torpedoed without warning, the deadly "fish" struck her main magazine and the explosion ripped her completely in two. The bow section sank immediately and the stern section stayed afloat only long enough to explode into millions of pieces; all of the ship's officers went down with her, and a bare forty-five of her men were saved.

"If you don't want to go to war," First Sergeant Jethro

Stiles remarked to Milo, "then isn't it a bit silly to allow your warships to escort the merchant shipping of a combatant? Roosevelt—or someone very close to him, at least—wants us in the war against Germany and Italy, you can bet your GI shoes on that, my friend. Of course, it may well be economics, pure and simple. Arming for a war and then fighting it is a surefire way of pulling a country out of a depression. He's tried damned near everything else, the crippled old socialist bastard, so maybe he figures this war business to be his last card. I tell you, Milo, the people of this country are going to live to heartily regret allowing that man and his near-Bolshevik cronies to play their socialistic New Deal games on the citizens and institutions and economy of this country. And now he and they are going about making damned certain that, like Wilson, they drag us into another war in which we have no real business."

Stiles sighed deeply, then shrugged. "Naturally, I could well be wrong on the whys. Roosevelt and his Red-loving friends may just be all a-boil to help Mother Russia, but that's as poor a reason to send Americans to be killed and butchered as any of the others. Josef Stalin is as much a murderous animal as is Adolf Hitler, if not more so; power corrupts, and absolute power corrupts absolutely, and Stalin has been in power for longer than Hitler, so we can be certain that he has become far and away more barbaric. And if proof of that last were needed, consider his recent purge of his own army's officer corps.

"If this is Roosevelt's reason for plunging our nation into another European war, it is akin to making alliance with a bear to fight a pack of wolves; even if we win, what is there to stop the bear from attacking and eating us? Maybe that's just what Roosevelt and his crew want to happen.

"Maybe it's what is ordained, too. Russell and Wells and not a few others seem to be of the opinion that socialism is the wave of the world's future. Sometimes I get the sinking feeling that we—the world's republics and monarchies—are at the best only fighting a grim, foredoomed, rearguard action against that which is to be."

Abruptly, he switched back to his everyday, workaday

voice and manner. "Oh, shit, Milo, if I keep on in this fucking vein, I'll be singing 'Einsamer Sonntag' and opening a few of the larger, more important of my own veins."

" 'Lonely Sunday'?" queried Milo. "I don't think I've heard of that song, Jethro."

"It's called 'Gloomy Sunday' in this country and other English-speaking countries. It was written some years ago by a Hungarian, I believe, and has become infamous because so very many people, worldwide, suicided while listening to it. Also, it is said, every artiste who recorded it has come to a bad end.

"Which, my friend, is precisely the end you and I are going to come to if we don't get cracking and have this report ready for our little captain to turn in to Colonel Oglethorpe on Monday."

One weekend in late 1941, one class having just finished and another not due until the middle of the coming week, Stiles and Milo had left the skeleton-manned company in the hands of a weekend charge of quarters and taken a few days of accrued leave together at Myrtle Beach, South Carolina. Free-spending Jethro had easily snagged a brace of attractive and complaisant "ladies" to share the beachside cottage he had earlier rented. When he and Milo were not fishing in the icy surf or enjoying their catch along with a plentitude of other foods and alcohol, they enjoyed the attentions of their bedwarmers.

On the Sunday afternoon, Milo and the two women sat close to the driftwood fire blazing on the hearth while Jethro basted for the last time a bluefish stuffed with herbs, spices, breadcrumbs, onions and finely chopped shellfish. The aroma of the baking fish, of the horse potatoes baking with it and of the other savories simmering in the battered saucepans atop the gas burners filled the small parlor with mouthwatering cheer every bit as much as did the opened magnum of champagne and the two unopened still-chilling ones nestled in a washtub full of cracked ice.

Pleasantly tiddly, Milo had but just arisen from his place to fetch a fresh magnum when he heard rapid footsteps ascending the shaky stairs, then an even more rapid pounding on the front door. He opened it to admit their landlord, Huell Midgett, a long-retired Coast Guard chief of about sixty years.

Politely ignoring the two female "guests," the old petty officer took a few breaths so deep as to set his beerbelly and multiple chins ajiggle, then said, "Boys, ain't none of my own bizness, of course, but you two is both of you Army off'sers. Ain't you?"

Jethro looked up from the fish and smiled. "Close enough, Chief Midgett, close enough. We're noncoms, but first-three-graders. Why?"

Midgett shook his head dubiously. "Funny, I ain't been wrong often, and I coulda swore you were both off'sers. But anyway, y'all better git on my telephone to your base, and real quick, too. 'Cause this mornin' the fuckin' Japs has bombed Oahu in the Hawaiian Islands. The fuckers caught the whole damn Pacific Fleet bottled up in Pearl Harbor, it sounds like on my shortwave radio. Feller I was talkin' to said all they could see from his place was black, oily smoke and fire way up inta the sky, them and the fuckin' Jap planes, was all.

"He said he was yet to see airy a one of our planes, so the Nip fuckers must've bombed the aerodromes afore any of ours could git up to fight the slant-eyed bastids. Afore he signed off, he allowed as how he 'spected to see Japs on the fuckin' beaches afore night. Don't thishere shit beat all, boys?"

The chaos to which Milo and Jethro returned was indescribable. At the hour of the Japanese sneak attack on the Hawaiian Islands, over half of the noncommissioned cadre and some two-thirds of the officer complement of the training division had been off post to lesser or greater distances. Although their post was thousands of miles from the Pacific Coast, although the only local Jap of whom anyone knew was the post commander's gardener, an unknowing witness to the pandemonium would never have guessed the truth.

During the two days it took Milo and Jethro to get back, the gates were become mazes of entrenchments, sandbagged strongpoints, machine-gun nests manned by edgy, sleepless, confused men with itchy trigger fingers. Sentries walked the perimeters, while details laid out barbed-wire entanglements just beyond those perimeters, unreeled and laid commo wire for field telephones, dug and roofed over revetments or excavated tank traps and laid land mines. Three-quarter-ton and the new quarter-ton scout cars mounting machine guns on pedestals moved here and there along the perimeters slowly, men with binoculars scanning both ground and skies lest they too be surprised by the treacherous yellow enemies.

Fortunately for all concerned, Milo still was wearing his identity plates strung around his neck under his mufti, but Jethro was not, and not until a Military Police staff sergeant who knew them both of old was summoned would the grim-faced, tommygun-armed guards allow them to drive onto the base.

In B Company's orderly room, the CQ, a buck sergeant named Schrader, all but wept openly at sight of the two of them. When he had rendered his report to Stiles, Milo demanded, "Where's your runner, Emil?"

"Some captain from up division come and took him and damn near ever other swingin' dick in the whole fuckin' area, Sarnt Moray. Said he needed bodies for to man the p'rimeter. That was Sunday afternoon, late, and ain't none of them fuckers come back, neither, not even to eat or sleep or shower or change clothes or nuthin'. I done been here since then all by my lonesome, checkin' fellers in and watchin' them all get dragged off for details and all, and I guess I'd've plumb starved to death if old Sarnt Trent hadn' sent me chow and all over here whenever he thought to."

"Okay, Emil, you did well, all things considered, you did very well," stated Jethro, clapping a hand on the haggard man's shoulder and smiling. "Now you shag ass back to your quarters and shower and get yourself some sack time, at least twenty-four hours of it, before you report back here to me. Now, go!"

When once the exhausted man with his dark-ringed, bloodshot eyes and his three days' growth of beard had staggered out in the direction of his barrack, the two noncoms began to go through the stack of messages.

"The captain called in Sunday, about the same time

we did," Jethro announced. "He should have been back from New Orleans by now, shouldn't he?"

"Maybe not." Milo shook his head. "Not if he was driving over the same kinds of roads we were, and his old Ford isn't a match for your car, either, Jethro. He might well have had a breakdown in some backwater without a telephone or a wire."

At that moment, the telephone jangled. Both grabbed for the receiver, but Stiles reached it first. "B Company, Sergeant Stiles speaking, sir." Then he smiled faintly and visibly relaxed.

"Hello, James . . . ahh, Captain Lewis, sir. What's our status? Odd that you should ask me that, sir. Sergeant Moray and I have just driven in from South Carolina to find that someone from up at division has taken it upon himself to strip this company of every man with the exception of cooks, first-three-graders and the company CQ. As of this moment, there are no officers, two master sergeants, one tech sergeant, one buck sergeant and three cooks in all of B Company."

He fell silent for only a moment, then exclaimed, "*Whaat?* My God, James, you can't be serious. That bad, is it? All right, all right, you can borrow Milo, but only if you help me get back some of my other men from whoever has them just now. War or no war, the last I heard there were inductees due in here on Wednesday, Thursday, latest, and my cadre are needed here, in the company area, one hell of a lot more than squatting in a trench somewhere out on the post perimeter. Besides, does any officer or man really think the Japanese are going to assault us here within the next day or so? Doesn't it stand to reason they'll hit California or Washington State first? And the last time I consulted a map, James, California was over two thousand miles from here."

He paused once more, and Milo could hear Captain James Lewis' familiar voice, though not his words. Then Stiles spoke again. "Yes, I understand, James. Milo will be over as soon as he can get into uniform and drive there. Yes, sir. Thank you, sir."

In the existing paucity of officers, Captain James Lewis ranked high enough to need very little bluster to free the impressed cadremen of his and Milo's training

battalion from the guard and labor details scattered here
and there about the periphery of the post. And those men
—tired, hungry, sleepless, filthy and shivering with cold
—were every one more than happy to clamber aboard
the trucks and be borne back to hot meals, showers, clean
clothes and their bunks.

By the time Milo had offloaded his company's men
before the mess hall and dispatched the trucks back to the
motor pool, then reported back to the orderly room,
Captain Muse and two of the other officers were back
and affairs were gradually returning to as close to the old
peacetime state of normalcy as any of them would again
see.

With the dastardly attack on Pearl Harbor and the
other military facilities on Oahu, the former flood of
trainees became a virtual *tsunami*, as patriotism, rage
and the declaration of war coincided to swell the ranks
with not only the hapless draftees, but enlistees by the
scores of thousands, the very cream of the citizenry
answering the call to the colors of their now-beset land.

Given better pickings from which to choose, the
training units began to flesh out, to replace stopgap
personnel with really effective cadremen and, conse-
quently, to turn out a far better grade of graduate from
the basic training courses. But the great and too-rapid
growth also necessitated the quick establishment of more
training camps and units. James Lewis was advanced to
major and sent to take command of a training battalion
somewhere in a new camp in Pennsylvania. Captain
Muse was given similar treatment, and all of the other
company officers were promoted and shipped out. For all
of his refusals, Jethro Stiles soon found himself commanding B Company with the silver bars of a first lieutenant
on his shoulders. Milo moved up to first sergeant, with
Emil Schrader, now a tech sergeant, as his field first.

Schrader hailed from Kansas and was a son of immigrants from Brandenburg. Though American-born and
-bred, he spoke better and more grammatical German
than English. Milo often chatted with him in that tongue
. . . and that was where the trouble started.

Jethro entered Milo's office and carefully closed and
latched the door one morning. "Milo," he began in a low,

guarded tone, almost a whisper, "something damned strange is going on concerning you. Have you made any application for OCS or for a transfer out of the unit without telling me about it?"

"Of course not, Jethro," was Milo's prompt reply. "Why?"

Lieutenant Stiles shook his head slowly. "Why? I don't know why, anything, Milo. But I just received an order to hold you ready here to be picked up and transported to an interview with an officer that I happen to know is connected with division CID . . . probably G-2, too, if not Army Counterintelligence. I can't imagine why a man like that would want to interview a noncom of a training company. Can you?"

Milo disliked Major Jay Jarvis from first laying eyes upon him. The man was short, skinny and pasty-white, save for his petulant, liver-colored lips, a multitude of facial pimples and muddy-brown eyes. He was of early middle years, balding and had chewed his nails to the quick, and his class-A uniform hung on his bony figure like a sack. His hands never stayed still for an instant, always playing with one of the profusion of stiletto-sharp pencils, a cold pipe which had strewn ashes from end to end of the GI desk, a stack of manuals and pamphlets, a higher stack of assorted papers and personnel files, the knot of his tie or the soggy handkerchief with which he dabbed at a dripping beak of a nose.

When Milo had been coldly ushered into the office by the armed second lieutenant and buck sergeant who had escorted him here from B Company, the door had been closed—and locked—behind him, leaving him to salute and report to this strange officer.

The major looked up at him, but would not look him in the eyes. "*Sprechen Sie Deutsch?*" he demanded in an atrocious accent.

"*Ja, Herr Major. Ich spreche Deutsch,*" he replied aloud, adding, to himself, "And one hell of a lot better than you do, you sourpussed bastard."

"You speak it well, too," said the officer grudgingly. "As well as a native, I'd say. Moray, you're being considered for a commission, but we need to know more about you, more than this"—he flicked a personnel file with the nailless fingers of one soft hand—"so-called 201 file of yours gives us. Where did you learn your German, Moray?"

Milo sighed silently. Here it starts again after all this time. "Sir, I don't know how or when or where I learned any of the languages I speak. I have been an amnesiac since the mid-thirties. My very earliest memory is of waking up in a hospital in Chicago, having been found clubbed down and robbed in an alley."

The major smiled coldly, showing uneven, scummy teeth. "Sergeant, am I really expected to believe that hooey? Please credit the Army of the United States of America with some small degree of intelligence. No, I am not one of your *Sturmbannführers*, Moray, or whatever your real name is, but I can sniff out a phony just as quickly as they can, mister! Can you offer me a single, solitary shred of proof that you are who and what you say you are? You'd better be able to, mister, because since we arrested Sergeant Emil Schrader, you're—"

"For the love of God, major, why did you arrest Emil?" Milo interrupted, and military protocol be damned.

Anger smoldered briefly in the officer's lackluster eyes and his mouth started to snap a reprimand at Milo's interruption. But then the anger died away without a wisp of smoke and he shrugged and replied, "Because he's a Nazi spy, Moray, that's why, as if you didn't know it all along. You've been heard time and again conferring with him in German. Those who heard you didn't understand what you two were saying, but they did recognize the langauge when they heard it, you see.

"You and Schrader identified the men we planted in B Company immediately, didn't you? I know that's why you began talking in code, right? Still in German, but in code."

"Major Jarvis," said Milo, "I find it difficult to credit any of this. You think, truly, that Schrader and I are Nazi spies? That you might entertain some questions about my background is perhaps understandable, all things considered. But Emil Schrader's background is completely documented from year one. He was born in Kansas; his family still lives and farms there. His parents came from Germany sometime back before the Great War, but all of their children are Americans, born."

Jarvis nodded. "And Emil Schrader, his parents and all of his brothers and sisters saw fit to become members of the German-American Bund, as coy a nest of traitors and spies as this country ever has produced. His father, Franz Schrader, is high on the Kansas councils of these home-grown Nazi-lovers."

In grim tones, Milo stated, "So you think that simply because Emil and his family joined and participated in an ethnic group, did so long before any American consid-ered the Germans to be our enemies, he is a spy. Major, don't you think that if the Nazis really wanted to use that poor dimwitted boy for a spy they'd at least put him someplace of more importance to the nation and the war effort than in a noncom slot in a basic training company? If you types are going after everyone who has some German in this division, you're going to have your hands full and you'll need to enlarge the post stockade to lock them all up.

"In addition to German and English, major, I speak Russian. Does that make me a Bolshevik? I speak Italian. Does that make me a Fascist? I speak Spanish. Does that make me a Falangist?"

Jarvis began to squirm in his chair. "Okay, Moray, okay. If you are what you say you are, I . . . we . . . are going to need some proof, some hard facts in corrobora-tion." He stood up. "You sit down at this desk and write me out a complete history of your life . . . well, of as much of it as you can remember. I want names, titles, dates, places, everything. Take all the time you need; you're relieved of all your other duties until this is done with, understand? But tell it all, Moray. If we catch you in a lie, that's it—you'll go to jail with Schrader. Better get to it, sergeant."

During the nearly forty days it took the authorities to run down and check out the persons whose names he had given in his handwritten account, Milo was allowed to carry on his work in B Company almost as normal. He was, of course, restricted in his movements; his pass had been lifted and he could not leave the post for any reason. Moreover, he was dead certain that he was under constant surveillance and that his quarters were being searched about once each week.

Not having been told not to do so, he had early on discussed the entire matter with Jethro, whose immediate reply had been, "Bullshit, Milo. You're no spy and neither is Schrader, for that matter. I'll see what I can do, and I'll get in touch with James, too. But you play along with the silly bastards, at this point. It would seem that the lunatics have taken over the asylum."

So Milo just sweated it out, doing his hard job as well as he could, breaking in a replacement field first and waiting for the other shoe to fall. He was in the field when the same armed duo sought him out, relieved him of his empty pistol and nudged him into their three-quarter-ton command car, then drove back to the division headquarters.

The file before Major Jarvis still was marked "Moray, Milo (n.m.i.)," but it was now much fatter and there were two other fat files of differing colors under it. When Milo had gone through the formalities, there was dead silence save for the tapping of a pencil point on the major's still-scummy teeth.

At length, the officer spoke. "Moray, I could almost believe that I was right about you to begin with, but if I believed that, I'd have to also believe that some damned big people are also involved with you, both military and civilian. So all I can say now is that, mister, you have some friends in some damned important jobs and places —two military medical officers, one of them a Navy captain, and a very well-connected JAG officer, to name but three of a lengthy list.

"Your story you wrote down for us checks out, all of it. But, Jesus God, mister, with the linguistic abilities you have, why in hell have you wasted so much time as a damned infantry sergeant? Christ Almighty, man, that's the hardest, most thankless drudgery in the Army, what you're doing. And we, my service, is desperate for people like you, and our need gets greater every day, too. I think I'm safe in promising you that if you make application for transfer to the Counterintelligence Corps, you'll be a commissioned officer inside a month and you'll probably outrank me before a year is up."

"Thank you, sir," said Milo. "But I'm happy where I am. I have no desire to be an officer. I'm needed in B Company, and my friends, my buddies are all there."

"Not good enough, mister, not good enough at all," snapped Jarvis. "Fuck what you want, mister, this is war! Go on back to your company, your friends, your buddies . . . for now. But I'm going to have orders cut transferring you and your abilities to where they'll do the most good for Uncle Sam and the U.S. Army.

"That's it, Moray. Dismiss. Lieutenant Carter will give you back your sidearm as you leave and Sergeant Lawford will see you're driven back to wherever you were when they found you."

Milo's hand was on the knob when Jarvis spoke once more. "You're no longer restricted, of course, Moray, and you'll notice a few faces missing from B Company in the next few days, too. I can no longer justify keeping them and you in place. But I still don't trust you, mister. I think, I feel that there's one hell of a lot more to you than meets the eye. My intuition tells me that there's something damned odd about you, and my intuition is never wrong, so I mean to take you and just what you are or are not on as a sort of personal crusade . . . when this war doesn't interfere, that is.

"Yes, you have scads of highly placed friends and supporters, but then so too do I, mister, and you'd better believe it, too. No matter how high you rise in rank, I'm going to keep digging at this secret of yours until I finally expose it and you.

"No, don't turn that knob, not yet, Moray. This . . . this thing that I sense about you is . . . well, if certain persons heard all of what I feel about you, they'd most likely see me tucked away in some back ward at Walter Reed in a straitjacket for the duration of the war.

"Moray, I feel about you the same as I would feel . . . well, almost the same as I would feel around some highly intelligent animal. It's as if you're not really a human being, just a . . . *something* masquerading as one of us. Had I the authority, I'd have you run through the most complete physical examination of which the post medical facility is capable, have them do or at least try to do everything until I was proved right about you. What do you think of that, mister?"

Milo just shook his head. "I think you've got what a very brilliant friend of mine, a man who had studied under Dr. Sigmund Freud, used to call a fixation . . . I think that that was the proper term. Yes, Major Jarvis, you probably would benefit from the attentions of a good psychiatrist and a well-equipped, modern psychiatric facility, for you are clearly disturbed. You are bound to be suffering delusions if you think I'm not human. What the hell else could I be, major? One of H. G. Wells' damned Martians, maybe?"

Chapter VII

Tech Sergeant Milo Moray found Fort Holabird tiny, as posts went, located almost within the actual city limits of Baltimore. Security measures were tight and stringently enforced by a profusion of well-armed guards. Badges and cards bearing photos and fingerprints were *de rigueur* everywhere on the minuscule post, and without the proper combinations of badges and cards, no individual could even come within close proximity to many of the buildings.

Not that all that much of seeming importance appeared to be happening within those buildings which Milo possessed the proper credentials to enter. After tests had established that he owned a decent command of Swedish, he was set to work that was very reminiscent of what he had done for Dr. Osterreich in Chicago five years before. Day after day, he was presented with Swedish periodicals, newspapers and trade or technical journals for translation. There was no need for a public library, however, at Holabird, for their dictionaries and references were extensive, and, as was often pointed out to him and the others in his section, they were not expected to understand, just to translate for specialists who did not read Swedish.

Milo would have liked being paid by the word as he had been in Chicago, for even with his quarters and food being all provided by the Army, along with uniforms and medical care (something of which he strangely had no need, since he never succumbed to anything worse than an occasional mild cold), his salary was nothing to boast about, especially not in the midst of a civilian economy new-swollen with the high incomes of hordes of war-industry workers. His pay as a tech sergeant was eighty-four dollars per month with an additional thirty dollars per month for his status as a first class specialist, which addition brought his monthly stipend to one hundred and fourteen dollars, within twelve dollars of that of a master sergeant. Even so, his money did not go far, and it was but rarely that he could afford the cost of a bus or railway ticket to meet and carouse with Jethro Stiles at some place between Baltimore and Georgia, nor did he feel that he could or should accept the generous man's frequent offers of money to allay these expenses.

Finally, one night, thinking of the thousand-odd he had left in the care of Pat O'Shea, he wrote to the old soldier. But the return letter came from Maggie.

"Dear Milo,

"I am so very happy to hear from you once again after all these years. Poor Pat, God keep the dear soul, has been with the angels for almost three years now, which was truly a divine blessing for him, as he had gone stone-blind and was coughing up blood from his gas-damaged lungs day and night. Old Rosaleen suffered a seizure and died in the kitchen during Pat's wake, and I have since retained a new cook, another policeman's widow, Peggy Murphey. But I now fear I may soon have to replace her, for her brother-in-law, a recent widower himself, is paying frequent and serious court to her and Police Lieutenant Robert Emmett Murphey strikes me as a man who gets his way, come —— or high water, as dear old Pat would have put it.

"We have heard nothing of my eldest son, Michael, since the Japs took the Philippine Islands and can only pray Our Lady that he be safe and well. Joseph was wounded at Pearl Harbor on the morning the Japs attacked the fleet there, but he has recovered and the Navy has him in a school now to make an officer out of him. Sally is nursing at the hospital now, and Kathleen was, too, but when the Nazis attacked Russia, she signed up to be a Navy nurse and she's now at a Navy hospital out in California, as too is Fanny Duncan.

"That terrible German priest, Father Rustung, was

arrested and taken away by the FBI when they arrested all the other Nazis, and good riddance to the lot of them, say I. They say the other priest, the sissified one, went into the Army Chaplain Corps.

"I hear that Irunn Thorsdottar went back to Wisconsin and was nursing at a hospital in or near Milwaukee, Wisconsin, and living there as man and wife with her own elder brother. Somehow, the two perverts were found out and prosecuted and sent to the penitentiary for criminal incest. More good riddance to bad rubbish.

"Dr. Guiscarde went into the Army only a week after the Japs attacked Pearl Harbor, and his last letter they say was from a camp in New Jersey. Dr. Osterreich is a captain in the Navy Medical Corps and is somewhere around Washington, D.C. Is that near you?

"Both of the maids I had when you were here married, and I have two new ones—a girl from Latvia and another little colored girl from Kentucky, who is lighter-complected than the old one and a lot easier to understand when she talks.

"I sure hope the Army is feeding you boys well. This new rationing they have now is just terrible, especially on meat and sugar and lard. If it wasn't for Cook's connections with some people at the stockyards, we would all be on very strict diets here. But if it will help win this war and get all of you boys home safe, then I say we will just have to put up with it until then.

"Milo, as you can see, I am not sending you much money, and the reason is that Pat took it into his head to invest most of the money you left with him in stocks. He bought you shares in the American Telephone and Telegraph Company and I am sending those certificates to you, instead. If I was you I would hang on to them, because they already are worth something more than what he paid for them back in 1938 and I don't doubt but what, with the war and all, they are going to be worth way more than they are now in years to come.

"I'd send you more money if I could, but it seems that poor Pat had borrowed against his insurance money and there was just about enough left to get him decently buried and pay for masses for the repose of his dear old soul, and I'm still saving money for a stone of the kind I know he wanted on his grave, too. What with property taxes and income taxes and the extra money I have to give Cook each week to pay for the meat and lard she gets without ration coupons, I am barely scraping by here, and I refuse to touch one penny of the money that comes from the government for the boys.

"Please remember, Milo, prayers to God and His Holy Mother never go unanswered. You might also pray to the Blessed Saint Sebastian, Patron of Soldiers, and I enclose a specially blessed medal of Saint Sebastian for you.

"Our prayers are always for you, Milo. May God bless and guard you always in this war."

There were four ten-dollar bills, a five and three ones in the package, and a silver medal on a flat-link neckchain of silver. There was also a stiff document folder secured with a cloth tie, and in it were the stock certificates, a bill of sale, transfer documents and a receipt for something over a thousand dollars.

But a second, smaller package had come in the same mail call. This one, too, was postmarked Chicago, but there was no return address and the handwriting was large, bold and most obviously masculine.

Fingering it, Milo wondered just who it could be who had written him. Guiscarde was in New Jersey, Osterreich was in Washington, Pat was dead, Rüstung was probably interned or in a federal prison or deported long since. So who was there left whom he had known back there, back then? Sol Brettmann? Or could it be one of the other men of Sam Osterreich's group? He tore the package open to find two envelopes. He opened the thinnest one first and read:

"Dear Sergt. Moray,

"You never met me, but I know you. I was the cop what found you when you got yourself clubbed down and robbed in Chicago. I done a awful thing to you that night, Sergt. Moray, and I ain't making excuses or nothing, but just then that night I had a awful sick wife at home and little children too and I couldn't barely take care of them on the money I could bring home honest-like. When I seen all of the money had been in the billfold the robbers had done took from you, I guess I went mad for a while is all. I've done confessed to God long since about all of this and more and I've done some heavy penances and all and still I know my poor soul will be in Purgatory for a good long while.

"My poor wife died a year or so back, God rest her soul. I've done rose up real high on the Force, too, in the last few years, and the onliest reason I ain't started paying back what I stole from you before this is just that I didn't know where you was and I was feared to ask them as I knew did know. But now I'm courting a fine widow-lady who does have a way of knowing your address and all and I've talked this here over with her and she thinks I should ought to start paying you back and so here in the big envelope is the first of your money.

"You had nine hundred and sixty-one dollars in bills in your billfold along of two gold eagles. I got ninety dollars for your gold watch and another fifty-four for the chain and fob. That all adds up to one thousand, one hundred and seventy-five dollars, Sergt. Moray. But my intended says that I rightly owe you more than that and I guess I rightly do, so she has calculated out that I should pay you three percent on all I stole off you until now for every year since I stole it and three percent on what I still owe to you after this every year until I gets it all paid off. So that means with this six hundred dollars I'm sending you here, I still owe you seven hundred and fifty-one dollars and twenty-five cents except that it will most probably be another year before I can send you more money so I actually owe you seven hundred and seventy-three dollars and seventy-nine cents.

"I ain't going to give you my name and I recken you can figure why I ain't, but I'll be keeping up with you from now on and praying for you and getting more money back to you just as fast as I can, but you got to realize I still got kids to see to and, God willing, I'll soon have me a wife again and it may take as much as two or three more years to get this all paid up. But I'll do it and you have my sacred word of honor on that, Sergt. Moray. You boys all give them Natzis and Japs hell. You got the whole dam USofA behind you.

"A man who wronged you long ago and has been truly sorry ever since."

In the other, thicker envelope was the six hundred

dollars. No old, wrinkled bills such as Maggie O'Shea had enclosed were these, but rather crisp, minty-new twenties, thirty of them, so stiff and fresh that Milo cut his thumb on the edge of one of them, winced and instinctively sucked at the hair-thin red line. But it had closed before he got it down from his lips. His rare razor cuts on cheeks or chin closed and healed very quickly too, and he had long since given up wondering about it and just gratefully accepted the fact that he was a quicker than average healer.

Until he could get an answer from Jethro, Milo found a lodgment for the stock certificates and most of the unexpected windfall of cash in the safe of his section commander.

The return letter from Stiles was short.

"Milo, old buddy,

"Congratulations on your luck in collecting your old debt—few are that fortunate, alas. As regards the stock, wait until I see you and it. If you can wangle a three-day pass next month, let me know the dates and perhaps we two can meet at someplace in the District of Columbia, where I'll be on training affairs. Come in mufti. I have someone I want you to meet at a place a bit south of the District, in Virginia.

"All my best,

"Jethro Stiles, Major, USA."

But, what with one delay and another on both ends, it was more than two months before Milo was able to rendezvous with his buddy in the spacious, sumptuously furnished lobby of a hotel in northwest Washington. Although the man he met was lean and hard and browned, the marks of worry and age were beginning to appear on the face and forehead and at the corners of the smiling eyes. The hair at Jethro's temples was stippled thickly now with hairs as silvery as the oak leaves on the shoulders of his carefully tailored blouse.

Without conscious thought or effort, Milo snapped to and crisply saluted his old friend.

Jethro casually returned the salute, his smile broadening, then extended his hand to grip Milo's warmly and strongly. "I am the guy who never was going to accept an offered commission, of course, Milo. Look at me now, huh? All that the bar will sell is beer or a very inferior selection of wines, I'm afraid. But don't worry, we won't go dry for long. I have some cognac in the boot of my car, and far more and better at our destination. Ready to go?"

Milo smiled in return, saying with only a bare touch of sarcasm, "The colonel's wish must be my command, sir."

"Can the shit, Milo, and let's get in the fucking car before I remember who and what I now am and bring you up on charges of gross insubordination." Jethro chuckled, leading the way out of the crowded lobby.

The Lincoln V-12 coupe was shiny and looked to be brand-new. Jethro was an accomplished driver, and he handled the long, heavy vehicle with ease. Nonetheless, before they had finally crossed the Potomac into the peaceful-looking Virginia countryside, Milo had concluded that his nation's capital was never going to be an easy or safe place to drive large numbers of motor vehicles with any degree of rapidity; the circles and spokelike avenues leading off them had no doubt been elegant in an age of horse-drawn carriages, but they were fast becoming deathtraps with their burdens of far faster, far more numerous, far less biddable automobiles, taxis, trucks and the like, many of them apparently operated by suicidal or homicidal maniacs.

"How in the name of God can you get enough gas to drive this thing, Jethro?" demanded Milo. "I'll bet that that engine drinks as much gas, mile for mile, as a deuce-and-a-half, at least. Or doesn't rationing apply to field-grade officers?"

Jethro laughed. "Oh, yes, rationing applies to me, too, at least for my private vehicle when I'm not using it for Army business. But, my dear Milo, there is in this land of the free and home of the brave a thriving sub rosa market for such things as foods and liquors. These markets sell for only cash, no coupons necessary, just so long as the buyer is willing to pay substantially more than said items are actually worth. One also can buy any quantities of ration coupons from these same sources, and this is how I can continue to drive this fine, but always horrendously thirsty, automobile."

"You, a high-ranking officer of the Army of the United States of America, are dealing on the black market?

Buying gas-rationing coupons that in all likelihood are counterfeits?" said Milo in mock horror. "Colonel Stiles, sir, I am frankly appalled!"

The heavy car ate away at the miles, and they drove into Loudon County, passing a sterling-silver flask of a fine cognac back and forth between them. At a turnoff from the main road onto a narrower, graveled one, Jethro pulled off onto a grassy shoulder beneath the spreading branches of a stand of stately, massive old oaks. Beside the car, skirting the road shoulder ahead, was a freshly painted white wooden fence some five feet high, and beyond the section of it immediately to his right, away in the distance across acres of grassy meadow, Milo could barely discern a scattering of animals that looked to be horses or cattle.

After taking a long pull from the quart flask, Jethro said, "Milo, my good old friend, you are about to be made privy to a secret known by no one else with the sole exception of Colonel James Lewis. I'll not ask for or expect any avowals that you'll not betray my trust in you, for did I not trust you implicitly, you'd not be here this day.

"Milo, forgive me, please, but I have not been completely candid with you in the years since I first met you. I am married, Milo, and you are about to meet my wife, Martine Stiles, as well as my two children, Per and Gabrielle.

"Before you ask the obvious, Milo, no, it has not been an easy life for her, but she understands me, my self-imposed exile and penance, she loves me deeply, and our children bind us one to the other despite my lengthy absences and necessarily brief returns. She is much younger than I am. I have known her for much of her life, you see, for she is the daughter of two old and very dear friends from my first days in Europe, years ago.

"I first bought this farm as a place for her to rear our children, before ever there were any to rear. It is fortunate that I happened to buy this particular farm, in this particular place, for now, with my necessary trips to Washington every so often, I am able to spend more time with her and them than ever before." He chuckled. "So much so, that now it would appear that Martine will be bringing forth a new little brother or sister for them in about six months' time."

Jethro's pretty young wife was not the only surprise awaiting him in the rambling, gracious brick house nestled among its bounteous gardens fringed by a profusion of outbuildings with rolling meadows stretching out on every hand.

While a servant drove the Lincoln away, the petite blond woman first greeted her husband with an embrace and unabashed kisses. Even after bearing two children, so slender and fine-boned was she that her three-month pregnancy was already obvious, but her face radiated her soul-deep happiness and her blue eyes glowed with love each time she looked at the graying officer.

She welcomed Milo in a cultured French tinged with both Parisian and the Swiss dialect, beckoned over another servant to take his bag, then herself ushered him into her home. There, in the comfortably furnished and lavishly decorated parlor to the left of the entrance foyer, four wing chairs faced a huge hearth on which a log fire was laid but not yet lit behind a pierced-brass screen. Two of these chairs were occupied.

Rank and increased responsibilities had not made an easily obvious change in one line or hair of James Lewis' appearance. His new pinks and blouse fitted him like a glove, as his uniform always had for as long as Milo had known the man; the silver eagles on his shoulders did not look at all out of place on the sometime first sergeant, and the row of campaign and award ribbons affixed over the breast pocket of that selfsame blouse told at a casual glance that here stood not just another new-made civilian-soldier. But even as he pumped Lewis' big, hard hand, Milo was reeling numbly in shock at sight of the other guest in Jethro's home.

Dr. Sam Osterreich's uniform was the dark blue of the Navy, the sleeves of his blouse encircled with the four wide, gold stripes indicating the rank of Navy captain, the full equivalent of James Lewis' rank.

Later, as the four men sipped wine and talked, the story came out. "You see, Milo," said Lewis, "back when I was twistin' tails to get that pissant shithead Jarvis from off of your ass, I come to find out you had been in a hospital in Chicago back in the late thirties and the doctor what had done first took care of you was just then a major at Dix, up in Jersey. When I got in touch with him, he said he'd do all he could for you because he knowed fuckin' well you wasn't no Nazi because of how you'd got in a lot of trouble when you got on the shitlist of some Nazi Bund priest in Chicago and that that was how you come to join the Army to start out with.

"But, besides that, he put me in touch with Sam here, who's still at Bethesda like he was then, and has some kinda pull—believe you me he has!—more'n you can shake a fuckin' stick at, too. It was him, almos' all him, what got your balls outen that crack, Milo, and give that dumb shitface Jarvis a comeuppance he had just been a-beggin' for for a fuckin' long time. Afore it was done, some first-class, fuckin' remain's had been done on him, too, a coupla fuckin' new assholes worth, I tell you. 'Cause of you and whatall he was tryin' to do to railroad you, Doc Sam, here, he not only was able to get you bailed outen the shit, but he got poor Schrader and two, three other guys from our division off the fuckin' hook, too. Like old maids sees burglars under ever' bed and in ever' closet, thishere fuckin' scabsucker Jarvis was seein' fuckin' Nazis ever' place he come to look; if a soldier could talk German good, to that fuckin' Jarvis, it meant he was a Nazi spy. The brass-balled fucker even had the gumption to ask *me*, flat out, if the real reason I was stickin' up for you wasn't because my mama's maiden name was Gertrude Bauer. And he damned fuckin' near got hisself busted down a whole helluva lot further than he did, too, when he asked Colonel Kessler if he'd been borned in this country and how long ago was the last time he was in Europe. Milo, that fuckin' li'l bastard's mouth's gonna dig him a fuckin' grave!"

Osterreich, looking chubbier than Milo remembered him, holding his crystal wineglass delicately by its stem, shook his head sadly. "The former Major, now Lieutenant, Jarfis is a sad case, misplaced to begin, then terribly overworked. He is not possessed of either emotional or of physical strength or endurance, unfortunately. He is seriously crippled by some rather sefere phobias and a most irrational belief he has in his intuitife powers.

"The unfortunate man is skirting perilously close to a nervous collapse at the best of times and I therefore made a recommendation that he be hospitalized or separated for the good of the Army. But he apparently possessed of some influential friends is and he only was reduced in rank, reprimanded and then sent on his way to continue, one supposes, to ferret out Nazi sympathizers and spies.

"And the saddest of all about him is that he most likely a real Nazi would not know. A real spy would easily hoodwink such a man as him, for he is far from truly intelligent and the most of his boasted intuition mainly is self-delusion.

"I know Nazis, gentlemen, I attended several meetings of the fledgling National Socialist German Workers' Party in the nineteen hundred and twenties, and in those early days of the party I was honored and welcomed and made much of as a former cavalry officer of the Imperial Austrian Army. All of this was, of course, before the fact of my Jewishness became all-important to them. I impart to you all no secret, here. It all is well known to any who wish to learn of it, for it was not only the National Socialists' meeting I attended now and then, but the Communists', the Monarchists', the Anarchists' and many another group, all of whom I found to be basically the same—a cadre of wild-eyed but cunning fanatics attempting to form hordes of troubled, desperate, demoralized German men and women into a political power base.

"The man Jarfis knows nothing about the Nazis, although had he been a German in Germany, he would no doubt have made them a good recruit, though he is too unstable to have been able to rise very far in their ranks. His ideas of Nazism are terribly skewed and twisted and distorted. I feel very sorry for him, for he truly is suffering, but there is nothing I can do for him. Under present circumstances, he is the responsibility and the very great problem of the Army, not the Navy."

Martine Stiles and Milo got along every bit as well from the start as had he and her husband. Throughout the courses of the sumptuous dinner served that Friday night, she chatted gaily with Milo and the others, slipping effortlessly from English to French, Danish, German, Italian and Spanish, though she carefully limited all general conversation to her British-accented English for the benefit of James Lewis, who was not a linguist.

The meal itself was a palate-pleasing blending of *haute cuisine* and Southern country cooking—terrapin soup, broiled fillets of shad, capon Provençal, a profusion of garden vegetables, a hot apple pudding topped with melted cheese and sprinkled with crushed walnuts, all accompanied by the best that the extensive wine cellar had to offer and capped at last with steaming coffee and an 1854 cognac, pale, smooth and very powerful.

Martine had grimaced in self-deprecation upon the serving of the capon, remarking, "This wretched war, gentlemen, please to accept my sincere apologies, but although almost all of the food is raised here, upon the farm, one still feels guilty to serve meat too often." Then, smiling, she added, "But never to fear, tomorrow night there will be a roast of veal."

Milo did not meet the Stiles children until the following morning. Almost four, Per was a grave, formal, quiet little boy, who sat and handled the reins of his Welsh pony with as much ease and authority as did his father and mother sit and control their thoroughbreds. Gabrielle was a tiny, chubby near-duplicate of her mother. Riding in a trap driven by the children's nurse, she bounced and chattered gaily, smiling and laughing throatily.

Earlier, in the stableyard, Osterreich, forking a frisky red-bay filly, had watched Milo mount and quickly take control of a mettlesome dark-mahogany-hued gelding. Kneeing his mount over, the doctor had spoken in a low voice in Russian—a tongue not thus far used in this multilingual household, but which he knew they both knew.

"Milo, old friend, now I know that I was right about you, years ago. I was right, and that old soldier Patrick O'Shea was right, also. Lieutenant Jarvis' vaunted intuition may well be accurate to the extent that even I am certain that you are not really an American. At least, if you truly are, you did not learn your horsemanship in America or in England, even.

"The way that you just mounted, the way that you sit your beast, the way that you hold the reins, these are all classic European military ways, Milo. I, too, was taught just so, in the Imperial Hussars, before the Great War, and I helped to teach them as a *Fahnrich* of cavalry."

The doctor smiled and patted Milo's bridle arm reassuringly. "This is no accusation, my old friend and comrade. I, of all people, know that you simply do not, cannot remember anything of more than five years ago . . . not on a conscious level. But your body and your unconscious, they remember, you see."

After that early morning, Milo was convinced that the doctor might well be right about him. He had ridden a few times in the recent past, for exercise—on rented horses in Chicago with Irunn Thorsdottar, now and again with Jethro on post and off—but those had always been on bridle trails. The morning at Jethro's farm was crosscountry on spirited, well-bred horses kept in the peak of condition by experienced handlers who had no other function and were never lacking for anything necessary to the well-being of their charges.

Jethro and Martine on their big Irish hunters led a fast, hell-for-leather pace across meadows, through little rills, over fences and hedges, ditches and the occasional mossy bole of a fallen tree. Through it all, for the length of that morning hell-ride, Milo's body reacted without his conscious urgings or instructions, making of him and his mount one single smoothly operating device for a safe, easy-looking transit of the rough, dangerous, but exhilarating course.

Nonetheless, the sudden, strenuous, rarely practiced spate of exercise left Milo disinclined to ride out that afternoon with Jethro, James Lewis and Sam Osterreich to look over the working parts of the farm. He found the library and, with a book and a bottle of sherry, whiled away the best part of the first two hours after luncheon. Then he was joined by Martine.

When she had selected and filled for herself a slender goblet of the straw-colored wine, she drew up a chair to face him and seated herself.

"Milo Moray," she said, using her British English on this occasion, "since first I set my eyes upon you yesterday, getting from out the automobile, I knew that we two have been . . . or, perhaps, will be . . . very close persons, soulmates, possibly even lovers. Do you, too, feel this . . . this unseen bond between us, Milo Moray?"

What Milo felt just then was a cold chill along the whole length of his spine, a prickling of his nape hairs and a rush of adrenaline similar to that he had felt when he had, once on bivouac, found a timber rattler coiled between his blankets.

Slowly closing the book, he said gravely, "Mrs. Stiles, your husband is my best friend, and I—"

Tilting her head back, she trilled a silvery peal of laughter, but then she looked him in the eye and stated, "Milo Moray, you misunderstood. Perhaps I said the improper words. English is not, after all, my native language.

"No, I very much love and respect my fine husband. I have loved him for the most of my remembered life and wanted to be nothing else than that which now I am—his wife and the mother of his children. Never would I even to consider betraying him or dishonoring my marriage vows with another man . . . not even with you.

"But still, I feel this strong feeling that we have been or we will someday be of a much and personal closeness. I cannot shake away this feeling, and I but wondered if you, too, had had this experience when you met me."

"No," said Milo simply. "No, I have had no such feelings, Mrs. Stiles. If this disappoints you, I am sorry. I but tell you the truth."

"No, no, I feel no disappointment, Milo Moray. Why should I feel such? If anything, I feel great joy that you have here proved to me just how good a friend to my husband you truly are. He chose well, I think, when he chose you as his—what is the word? buddy?—he chose well, indeed. You are a gentleman of the old mode, and you always will be most welcome in this house.

"But I want your solemn vow, Milo Moray. I want your firm promise that you will care for our Jethro, do all that the good God allows to keep him safe in the dangers that lie ahead. Will you so vow?" There could be, this time around, no mistaking her meaning or her deadly seriousness.

Milo was puzzled. "Mrs. Stiles, Jethro is in more real danger driving through the city of Washington than he could face down South, doing staff work in a training unit. Of course, I will do anything I can to protect him from whatever, but I'm based in Baltimore, over eight hundred miles away from his post. No two ways about it, I'd like to be back with him in the old unit, but the Army seems to feel I'm of more use to them up at Holabird."

"Our Jethro, gallant soul that he is, still abrim with a senseless guilt for something long ago that was not really his fault, has persuaded certain persons to give him a combat command, a battalion of infantry. He soon will leave for his new posting. Can you not find a way to join him again, there, Milo Moray?"

Chapter VIII

"Jesus H. Christ on a frigging GI crutch, Moray," stormed Major Barstow in clear consternation. "Have you lost your mind? Not only is a linguist like you of immense value here to Uncle Sam, but you're in the safest, cushiest billet you'll find this side of the damned Pentagon complex. Man, with your talents and your cooperation, I can keep you here for as long as the war lasts. What is it you're after? Rank? I can bump you up to master, within a week, no sweat. You want a commission, hell, man, I can get you that, too, a direct one. Just give me a little time and you'll have it all.

"But, please, for the love of God, don't hit me first thing on a Monday morning again with such a line of lunatic nonsense like you wanting an immediate transfer to an outfit that I know damned good and well will likely be in that meat grinder they're running in Italy inside six months!"

Barstow kept at Milo up until almost the very moment that he shouldered his barracks bag and entrained for South Carolina. His final words were, "You're a nut, Moray, but I guess that without your kind of nuts, no war would ever get won. I've put the very highest marks I can in your file; that's all I can do, now. Here it is; it's sealed, that's GI regs. If you unseal it, for God's sake, do it carefully so you can reseal it easily, huh? You do as good a job for the bastards where you're going as you did for us here, you'll be wearing three up and three down soon, don't fret about it. Good luck, Moray. Try not to get your head or any other essential parts shot off."

The entire unit, from division on down, was still in a state of flux, none of the components completely filled in. The grizzled master sergeant who checked Milo in still wore his Ninth Infantry Division patch. When once he had torn open the sealed records and seen that he was dealing with a Regular rather than another johnny-come-lately uniformed civilian, he unbent considerably and offered Milo a cigarette and a chair across the cluttered, battered desk from him.

"Thishere Colonel Stiles, he must know where some fuckin' bodies is buried to git that bunch in Holabird to let you go, Moray. You know him? What kinda fella is he? West Pointer?"

"Not hardly," Milo chuckled. "He's a gentleman, but he was a tech when the war started, first sergeant of a training company. I was his field first . . . and his buddy."

The master looked pleased at this news and nodded. "A Regular, huh, like us?"

"About thirteen, fourteen years service, sarge, all but the last two years of it in the ranks. He's hard, but he's fair, too, doesn't play favorites. You give him what he wants, what he thinks you can do, and he'll take good care of you. What else can you ask of an officer?"

The master shook his head. "Not a fuckin' thing more, Moray. Sounds like I fin'ly lucked into a good spot for a fuckin' change. And he's sure stickin' by you, too. All the fuckin' comp'ny commanders yellin' their friggin' heads off for trained noncoms, and he's got you down in a staff slot." He leafed through the personnel file for a moment, then grunted. "Shitfire, man! You talk Krauthead, Frog, Eyetie, Swede and all thesehere others, too? Hell, no fuckin' wonder they had you up to Holabird. The wonder —and it's a pure wonder!—is just how thishere Colonel Stiles managed to pry you away from 'em. He prob'ly has you lined up for S-2, but he better not let regiment or division hear too much about you or they'll jerk you right out of this fuckin' battalion afore you can say goose shit. But, say, how come *you* ain't a fuckin' of'ser, Moray?"

Milo shrugged. "Oh, I don't know, sarge, mostly probably because I never wanted to be one, I guess. Besides, I have no college degree, either."

The master made a rude sound. "Hell, Moray, that eddicayshun crap don't matter diddlysquat no more. Shit, piss and corruption, even I's a of'ser . . . for a while. Then me and a coupla good ole boys busted up a of'sers' club, bashed the fuckin' post snowdrops around purty good, too. We all got court-martialed, of course, and busted back . . . way back. The onlies' fuckin' way I could git my three and three back was to 'volunteer' for thishere fuckin' new division. But hell, it don't matter none, no way. I'm with you, Moray, I'm a lot happier as a master than I was as a damn, fuckin' of'ser anyhow!

"Okay, let's us get you settled in, Moray." He pulled a clipboard from beneath the mountain of papers on the desktop, precipitating a small avalanche, which he ignored. "I'm gonna put you in a squadroom with two other techs and a staff in, lessee, in Buildin' H-1907. Got that? The lockers and racks is a'ready in there, so you can lock up your stuff while you go over to Head and Head supply and draw your mattress and bedding and all. But you watch that fuckin' crooked-ass Crockett, hear me? Make damn sure he gives you blankets and all out of brand-fuckin'-new bales, les' you c'lects crotch pheasants for fun.

"Oh, by the way, Moray, I guess as how I'm the fuckin' battalion sergeant major, leastways till we gets in another master or a warrant or somebody better for the job. You done been a first—you wanta take over Head and Head Comp'ny till things get shook down some? I could give you a two-man room, then."

Milo shrugged. "Sure, sarge. Why not?"

The formation of the Sixtieth Infantry Division was best described as snafu—"situation normal, all fucked up"—all the way. Needed personnel and specialists slowly trickled in from every point of the compass, supplies and equipment came late or not at all or the wrong kind or in impossible quantities. For almost two weeks, the entire Head and Head—battalion headquarters and Headquarters Company—consisted of the cooks and mess steward, Sergeant Major/Master Sergeant John Saxon, Milo, four other first-three-graders—the battalion supply sergeant, Moffa, the battalion S-3 sergeant,

Evans, the signal section sergeant, White, and a staff
sergeant/specialist who was a clear case of misassignment,
since his specialty was medical records keeping—and an
agglomeration of eighteen drivers (with no vehicles to drive,
as yet), one corporal and one pfc (the both of them fresh out
of Graves Registration School), and two buck sergeants (one
a tracked vehicle mechanic and the other a dog handler
with his Alsation dog). But all of that began to change; the
state of hopeless-looking disorder began to fall into order at
about eleven on the morning of Milo's tenth day of service as
H&H first sergeant.

Even clear down in the battalion supply area where he
stood arguing with the slick and slimy Sergeant Moffa, all
could hear from the headquarters building the hoarse
bellow of *"Ten-HUT!"* and recognize the voice of Master
Sergeant Saxon.

Stepping out of the supply shack and looking up the
row of T-buildings, Milo could recognize even at the
distance and despite its thick covering of road dust the
long, sleek shape and maroon color of a Lincoln V-12
coupe. Lieutenant Colonel Jethro Stiles, Infantry, USA,
had arrived to take command of his battalion.

When once he had heard the reports of Saxon and
Milo, the commanding officer sighed deeply and shook
his head slowly. "John, Milo, it's the same, sad fucking
story from division on down, I'm here to attest to that
much. The Powers That Be really broke it off in this
division, and the general is so fucking mad that he's
chewing up twenty-penny nails and spitting out carpet
tacks. It seems that we got every fucking goldbrick and
fuck-off and miscreant and mother's mistake that any
other outfit wanted to unload somewhere.

"Howsomever"—he smiled lazily and tilted back his
head to gaze at the resinous rafters above him—"I just
may have helped the overall situation a bit. I made a few
telephone calls and sent a few wires from division, earlier
this morning, called in some markers and cadged a few
favors here and there. If it all jells, I think that I can
safely assure you that from now on, this battalion will be
at the very tiptop of the general's most-favored list."

"In that case, colonel," began Milo, only to be
stopped.

"Milo, John, when we're alone together, it's no 'colonel' and 'sergeant,' hear me? This rank of mine is only a wartime expediency, every Regular knows that, and I feel one hell of a lot more at home and properly placed among you and men like you than I do among most of the officers, anyway.

"Now, that matter aside, you have a problem, Milo?"

"*We* have a problem, Jethro, two of them, in Head and Head. Supply sergeants are always out for the main chance, everybody knows that, but this precious pair we've got here—Moffa of battalion supply and Crockett of Headquarters Company supply—take the fucking shit-cake. Somehow, between the two of them, they've managed to convert a shipment of two thousand brand-spanking-new GI blankets that arrived just last week into less than half that number of ragged, motheaten, thread-bare pieces of shit that it would be a fucking crime to issue to a fucking dog. And that's just their most recent sleight-of-hand with our supplies."

Without a word to Milo, Stiles picked up the receiver of the desk telephone and, after about fifteen minutes, was talking to his party. "James? Jethro, here. Can I have just one more? Gabe Potter, that's who. Well, isn't there any way you can get those charges dropped? I really need the fellow, James. Yes, yes, thank you, James, that's yet another one I owe you. Take care, you old bastard."

"Master Sergeant Gabe Potter?" Milo yelped, "Jesus, Jethro, he's the crookedest man at Fort Benning! He's the last thing we need up here. Moffa and Crockett are bad enough."

Stiles raised his eyebrows for a moment, then said, "That's right, Milo, you've been away for a while. Well, it's Captain Potter, now, and since he made captain he's kept the whole place humming with courts-martial hearings and reductions in rank, with sentences to Leavenworth and stockade time. He was a master crook himself, so he knows every fucking dodge there is, and he's ferreted out every racketeer in the whole damn training command. Of course, he's garnered a whole pisspot full of enemies at it, so he just might be glad to get up here into a new unit where he won't have every other fucker gunning for his ass . . . well, at least not for a while yet."

When they all finally straggled in and he got a look at them and their files, Colonel Stiles forced a captaincy back on Master Sergeant John Saxon, ignoring his loud and profanely voiced objections and opinions of officers in general. Then the old soldier was made the battalion adjutant.

Affairs in both battalions and the higher echelons were well on the way to normalcy when Milo was called to battalion headquarters one day. He found Stiles waiting for him outside the building, beside a jeep.

When he had returned the salute, he said, "Get in and drive, Milo. They raise pure fucking hell if I drive myself anymore, even in my own car. Drive somewhere out in the boondocks. We two need to talk, and I don't want half the fucking division hearing us."

When once they were off the built-up portions of the post and rolling along a dusty dirt road between brushy shoulders backed by stands of pine and scrub cedar, Stiles spoke again.

"Milo, there's something godawful fishy going on. I've twice tried to get you a commission, now, and each time the forms have been returned, rejected by higher authority, nor have I been able to wangle or worm out any explanation for any of this. I've run into a brick wall every time, and that's not my usual batting average in dealing with the Army. They won't even accept an application in your name for OCS, for God's sake, man. Have you got any ideas why?"

Milo was nonplussed and said so, whereupon Stiles continued his monologue. "Well, maybe we'll get to the bottom of it all in time. At last, we'll have a bit more of that commodity. Inside information I've acquired— and this is strictly not for repetition, Milo—has it that, what with all the fuckups we've had to put up with, we've been replaced by a more combat-ready division for the Italian business. They're going to give us more time to shake down and form up, see, save us for the big invasion, probably early next year. Somewhere in France, obviously, the Mediterranean coast, I'd guess, considering how well fortified the Krauts have made the Atlantic coasts and how assuredly costly an assault on those coasts would be certain to be.

"I own a villa in Nice, you know. Of course, I've not been there in almost twenty years, but until the war started I still received regular rents on it. It would be good to see it again, if we wind up anywhere near it.

"But that's all in the future and a bit speculative, at best. Look, Milo, I'm going up to Washington for a week or so next month on some business for the general. I'd intended to spend a bit of time out at the farm, and Martine wants me to bring you, too. Can you get away from the company that long, do you think?"

The slow, unhurried and quiet pace of life in the Virginia countryside was very restful, soothing, after the frenetic months of trying to whip nearly nine hundred strangers into a tight-knit unit, with every new disaster and shortfall landing squarely atop the last.

Jethro left early each morning for Washington and sometimes did not return until well after dark, usually too tired to do much other than eat lightly, have a few drinks, bathe and go to sleep in preparation for the next day. During his absences, Milo and Martine spent the days riding or walking the length and breadth of the thousand-plus acres of the farm, joining the children in playing with a litter of puppies, talking about anything and nothing in a half-dozen languages and otherwise lazing away the long days in trivialities.

Melusine Stiles had been just over six weeks old upon Milo's arrival with her father. Having no milk this time, and not caring to try the bottle method, Martine had sought out and hired a wet nurse for her newest child. However, she still spent time with the baby as well as with her two older children, and during these times, Milo, ever voracious for knowledge, always hoping against hope that some passage read somewhere would trigger his dormant memories of the past, made use of the well-selected array of books in the library of the house.

The week stretched into two weeks, then a third, but Jethro assured Milo that he was keeping in regular touch with the battalion as well as regiment and division and that their presence was not crucial to anyone's well-being. Milo never asked what Jethro was doing in Washington, and Jethro himself seldom volunteered much information, only advising that Milo make the most of his current period of relaxation as there would be no time or opportunity for such soon.

It had been Martine who had steered Milo, early on, to a set of treatises on varying aspects of military science—tactics, strategy, management of military units in the attack, in the defense, on the march, proper utilization of intelligence and a plethora of other subjects; most of these were written in French, but a couple were in German, as well.

"Milo Moray, I am terribly worried for our Jethro," she had confided to him. "At times, he seems foolishly overconfident in his abilities to command successfully so large numbers of the soldiers, lacking but the barest of training and educations in such matters. Milo Moray, my father is a graduate of Saint-Cyr, as too was his father and my late elder brother, and so I know—even if my husband will not admit to knowledge—just what is required to make a competent commander of a man. With the sole exceptions of the excessively rare military geniuses, years of education, training and experience are necessary.

"Now, my husband is well educated, but it was not a military education he enjoyed, nor is his a true military mind, for even I can consistently best him at chess. He means well, he is very conscientious, as we both know, but in a life-or-death situation that often is not enough, and I have a strong, terrible feeling that he may not come alive back to me from out of this war.

"But I have another deep feeling, too, Milo Moray. That is that you are very possibly one of these near-genius military minds still unsuspected and in hiding. The little Austrian naval officer has known you for long, yes? He has told me that he is of the firm opinion that before you lost your memory, you were at some time a military man, possibly a European cavalry officer, and if true this could account for my intuitions regarding you.

"So, please to read these books, Milo Moray. Even if they do not help you to recall your past, perhaps they will give to you knowledge with which you may help my husband to succeed in his chosen position and return safely to me and to his children."

* * *

Milo never was to know just what Jethro did or said during his three weeks in Washington, but whatever it was, it worked with a vengeance. Upon their return to South Carolina and the unit, things began to move. The slow, sporadic trickles of supplies and equipment became a steady stream and then a veritable flood. Empty slots were quickly filled as missing and badly needed specialists — commissioned, warranted and enlisted — were transferred in from other units, not a few of them from nearly the width of a continent away. Enough men soon were on hand to allow them the freedom to start weeding out the misfits and troublemakers with which they had initially been cursed.

An episode that was to haunt Milo for many years to come occurred on the day that the former battalion supply sergeant, Luigi Moffa, was brought up from the post stockade for sentencing on the multitude of charges of which he stood convicted.

With a clanking of his sets of manacles, the man in the faded, baggy, blue-denim fatigues (with a prominent bull's-eye painted in white on the back of the shirt) dropped down from the back of the weapons carrier and shuffled awkwardly up the steps into one of the buildings housing battalion headquarters. Milo's glimpse of the prisoner and his two beefy, well-armed grim-faced guards showed him a drastic change from the Moffa he first had met. It was not simply the lack of tailored uniforms and patent-leather field shoes, nor was it the loss of at least thirty pounds. It was not even the face that showed still-pinkish scars, fresh bruises and a barely closed cut above one eye. It was the eyes themselves and the general demeanor of the once-arrogant and abusive man—they contained no spark of life or any vitality. Moffa resembled nothing so much as an ambulatory corpse.

Milo sighed and went back to his work. He hated to think of any man being so thoroughly broken, but then reflected that if any man deserved it for his many misdeeds, it was certainly Moffa; that much had come to light during Captain Potter's very thorough investigations.

He had been back at work for a good quarter hour when the entire building reverberated to a booming pistol shot, followed rapidly by four more, then, after a pause, a man's scream ended by a fifth shot.

Suddenly, a wild-eyed major in a class-A uniform caked with dirty snow, his face and hands bleeding from a profusion of cuts and gashes, stumbled through the entry of the building.

"The prisoner!" he gasped to no one and everyone. "That Guinea bastard! He heard his sentence, then got a gun away from one of the guards and shot the other one. Then he started after us. I jumped through the window."

Just then, a soldier came pounding down the long central corridor and was narrowly missed by the pistol ball that tore its splintery way through the closed door of the room in which the board had sat for Moffa's sentencing.

"Goddam!" swore Milo, then turned to one of the clerks. "Turner, go outside to the other end of the building and tell those fuckers not to try to use the corridor until we can get this fuckin' mess sorted out." To another, he said, "Dubois, you and my driver get the major here up to the regimental surgeon on the double. Those cuts look bad, and he's bleeding like a stuck pig."

Before the adjutant, Captain John Saxon, and a bevy of men and officers had tramped through the snow around the safe side of the long building, Milo and a few of his men had conducted a cautious reconnaissance of the distinctly *un*safe side to find two officers safe, though gashed and shivering in the bitter cold, each crouched low under one of the two smashed-out windows. A third officer lay in the snow on his face, his head at such an impossible angle to the body that he could not possibly have been alive. A fourth officer hung backward out of one of the windows; he had a big blue-black mark on his forehead, and that head no longer possessed a back to it.

Working along the sides of the building, as much as possible out of the murderous prisoner's sight and line of fire, Milo got up to first one, then the other of the two living officers and dragged them back to where other men could take charge of them. He saw no point in risking anyone's life to retrieve the two dead men, officers or no.

Back in the environs of his office, he rendered John Saxon a report through still-chattering teeth. The old soldier nodded brusquely, then gripped his shoulder. "You done good, Milo, but then, you a Reg'lar."

"Sargint majer!" he then roared. "Take you some bodies and git ovuh to the arms room and tell Jacoby I said to issue you three Thompsons, a hunnert rounds of ball for each one, a half a dozen smoke grenades and a coupla Mark Two pineapples. Git!"

Milo grasped Saxon's arm, hard. "John, you can't just pitch hand grenades into that room. Moffa may not have killed all of them—some could be lying wounded in there still."

"You got a better ideer, Milo?" demanded the grizzled officer. "Besides just leavin' the fucker in there till he grows him a long gray beard?"

Milo cudgeled his brain frantically. "John . . . how about tear gas? That ought to get him out."

"Where we gonna get any quick, Milo, huh? It ain't none in the arms room, I can tell you that."

"Then how about letting me try to talk him out, John?" Milo was shocked to hear himself say the words.

"Moray, you off your fuckin' gourd, man. That fuckin' Moffa he's sure to be plumb mad-dog crazy to've done all he's done. You think he won't kill you too, you just as loony as he is," Saxon snapped.

Moffa used his jaw teeth—he no longer had any front ones adequate to the job—to draw the cork of the bottle of bourbon, all the while keeping his eyes and the muzzle of the automatic pistol locked unwaveringly upon Milo. After a long, gulping swallow of the alcohol, he lowered the bottle and spoke sadly.

"You shouldn' of come in here, top. You know I'm gonna have to kill you, too, now. You know that, don' you? And you dint never do nuthin' to me, but I gotta kill you enyhow."

He took another pull at the bottle then, impatiently waggling the pistol when Milo started to speak.

"See, top, them fuckers over there"—he jerked his head at the overturned table and the bodies that lay behind it—"they was gonna send me to break rocks in Leavenworth for the nex' thirty years. Top, ain' no fucker gonna send me to Leavenworth, and not back to that fuckin' stockade, neither, you hear me. The fuckin' bastids in that stockade, they done beat me and starved me and made me crawl for the lastes' time. Naw, I'm gon' make some fucker kill me, top, that's what I'm gon' do. I druther be dead and burnin' in hell than in Leavenworth or back in that fuckin' shithole stockade, top. So, like I done said a'ready, I'm sorry."

There was a half-heard roar, a dimly seen flash of fire-streak from the muzzle of the heavy pistol, and, with unbearable pain, some irresistible force flung Milo backward to bounce off a wall and land, face down, in a heap beside the gory body of one of the dead military policemen.

He knew that he was dead. He knew that it would only be a matter of a very short amount of time before all sensation, all pain ceased. But he wished that before his mind stopped functioning forever, he could remember just who and what he had been before his awakening in Chicago, years ago.

But the pain did not stop. It got worse, if anything. He heard shouts from outside the room, heard them clearly. He even heard the wet gurglings as Moffa worked at the bottle of whiskey. Those wet gurglings it was that awakened in him a sudden, raging thirst for whiskey, water, anything wet; his entire body was insistently clamoring for fluids.

Slowly, more than a little surprised that his arms and legs still would function, Milo gained first to hands and knees, then to his feet, swaying like a tree in a gale, groaning and biting his lips and tongue against the fire-ball of superheated pain lodged in his chest and back.

He did not see Moffa, who just stared at the blood-soaked apparition, wide-eyed, the pistol dangling from one hand and the near-emptied whiskey bottle from the other.

"Goddam you, top," he finally gasped, "lay down! You *dead*, you fucker you! I put that slug clean th'ough your fuckin' heart!"

Milo heard the words, though he did not see the

speaker, not clearly. Later he was to remember those words. Nor did he see the fragmentation grenade that sailed through one of the shattered windows and bounced twice before it came to lie spinning in the middle of the floor.

But Moffa saw it. Dropping both pistol and bottle, he dived upon it, clasping it, his instrument of salvation, close against his chest and sobbing his relief, even while he used one foot to kick the nearest of Milo's wobbly legs from under him.

Immediately in the wake of the searing explosion, the door came crashing inward and a burst of submachine-gun fire stuttered through the opening until a voice shouted and brought silence in place of the deadly noises.

In his second fall to the blood-slimed floor of the room, Milo had thumped his head hard enough to briefly take away his consciousness.

Captain John Saxon moved warily into the room, the still-smoking muzzle of his M1 Thompson at waist level, his horny forefinger on the trigger. One of the two men behind him took but a single look at what was left of Moffa, dropped his own Thompson with a clattering thud and was noisily sick.

"Somebody come in here and get Danforth," said Saxon, in a quiet, gentle tone. "The poor li'l fucker and all the rest of you's gonna see more and worse nor thishere when you gets in the trenches, over there.

"Somebody go ring up the medics and get some litters over here, on the double, seven . . . no, eight of 'em. Sargint majer, have your men git all the weapons together and get 'em back to the arms room, then git back here, and don't you swaller none of Jacoby's shit 'bout 'em havin' to be cleaned afore you can turn 'em in; allus remember, you outranks him."

As he put the safety on his submachine gun and passed it to the waiting hands, he caught a flicker of movement out of the corner of his eye and spun about to see Milo, his uniform soaked in blood, his hands smeared and streaked with it, twitching feebly, his lips moving soundlessly.

"Sweet fuckin' Christ," Saxon whispered, then turned and roared out the doorway, "Git that big medical kit down here, *fast*, and tell the medical comp'ny to get a fuckin' surgeon over here on the fuckin' double. I think Moray's still alive!"

By the time the medical officer arrived in the charnel house of a room, John Saxon was squatting beside the semiconscious Milo, an opened but unused medical kit behind him.

"The onlies' thing I can figger happened, lootinant, is that the fuckin' slug tore th'ough his shirt, in the front and out of the back—the holes is both there for to show for it. In dodgin', someways he musta tripped over the MP's body and cracked his fuckin' haid when he fell, and he fell right in a big puddle of the fuckin' MP's blood and Moffa just figgered he was dead meat. It ain't no wounds on him, 'cepting that goose egg on his fuckin' knob. Don't nobody but fools and Paddies mostly have that kind of luck."

All of the injuries and deaths save only Moffa's were determined to be L.O.D.—line-of-duty—and Milo found himself being accorded vast respect by officers and men alike for all that his personal choice of the real hero of that terrible day was old, combat-wise Captain Saxon.

"Now, goddam you, Milo," Stiles had railed at him in private, "you're not immortal, you know—you can bleed and die, too. You're not paid to take that kind of stupid chance. That's what we have eight hundred odd GIs in this battalion for. You're too valuable to the unit. You're too valuable to me, too, you fucker. I happen to know you've promised Martine to try to keep me alive through the rest of this war. How the bloody hell are you going to do that if you go and get yourself shot and killed for nothing?"

Then he had grinned. "By the way, even if our last trip up north had accomplished nothing for the division, at least it accomplished something positive for the future. Martine is pregnant again."

Jethro Stiles had attested his belief in Milo's mortality. But Milo himself was beginning to wonder about that subject, to entertain certain doubts. Much as he tried to rationalize these insanities away, still did they come back to haunt him.

Everyone else might believe Saxon's assumption that

the shot fired at him by Moffa had missed, but Milo knew them all to be wrong. What he had to face was that he had been shot in—or close enough not to matter—the heart with one of the most powerful and deadly combat pistols in existence and at a point-blank range of less than a dozen feet. He clearly recalled the force of being hit and flung against the wall, and he could still remember the agony of the heavy ball tearing through his body, though that particular bit of recall was slowly fading, he noted thankfully.

Moffa had known that his shot had been true to its mark—drunk or sober, his emotional state notwithstanding, the well-trained old soldier could hardly have missed at a range of four yards or less. Milo could still hear ringing in his ears the dead man's admonition to "lay down! You *dead!*" And dead he should have been, well dead. So why was he not dead?

Careful examination of the back and the front of his torso, when once he got back to his quarters, had shown Milo only a slight indentation of about a half-inch diameter in the skin above his heart, this surrounded by discoloration that resembled a fast-fading bruise. On his back, a bit below the shoulder blade, was a larger, deeper dent—about an inch and a half—and a wider discoloration. However, when he showered the next morning, he had been hardly able to locate a trace of either of them, front or back. That he told no one of these oddities was partly because he hardly believed them himself and partly because his job just kept him far too busy for another visit to the surgeon.

Chapter IX

Like some vast herd of huge beasts grazing the restless waves of the North Atlantic Ocean, the convoy of troop transports, supply ships and naval vessels sailed a course that was deliberately erratic, lest that course be guessed out by the wolflike packs of German submarines, the bane of wartime shipping. On front and rear and along the flanks of this convoy of men, materiel and armaments, speedy, hardworking destroyers flitted back and forth, with every crewman's eye, every technological device aboard on the alert for the slightest trace of one of the feared submersible raiders of the seas. Should such a trace be suspected, it was the mission of these flankers to interpose their own lightly armored cockleshells between the attackers and the lumbering quarry, while others of their kind steamed to the supposed location of the foe and let off salvos of depth charges—steel drums filled with powerful explosive charges designed to create sufficient concussion to rupture the hulls of the submarines, thus drowning the crews or forcing the craft to rise to the surface, where shells from deck guns could sink them easily.

Because of the dangers presented by the U-boats, because of the fact that despite all precautions, submarine-launched torpedos still found their marks, sinking or heavily damaging ships, killing or injuring men and sending to the bottom billions of tons of valuable equipment and supplies, each cargo ship was packed to utter capacity, and so too were the troop carriers, to such a point that the only men aboard who made the passage in any degree of comfort were the sailors and the higher-ranking officers. The troops were packed like so many canned sardines in a 'tween-decks hot and thick with the reek of humanity, with no room for organized calisthenics and few possibilities for the make-work details traditionally used to keep units and individual soldiers out of trouble, their principal activities consisting mainly of endless gambling and even more endless bull sessions, interspersed with the occasional fight—a welcomed relief from boredom—and noncoms were hard pressed to prevent their troops from becoming just so many slothful, dirty, vicious beasts. They were able to maintain order, discipline and at least a degree of cleanliness only by dint of near-brutality.

So many men were crammed into the ship that only by shifts could they be allowed up into the fresh air topside, there to gather in clumps or to walk the narrow ways around and between the vehicles lashed to the decks; and even these few brief forays into natural light and clean, crisp air were only allowed in daylight on clear, calm days without deckwashing seas, lest any of these land-lubbers be lost overboard.

On such a day, a rare day for the season and the location—the sky of a silvery blue and utterly cloudless—the troopship plowed through a sea almost as calm-looking as a pond. Far away on either hand could be discerned other ships of the convoy, but to the naked eye these were merely large dots; only with magnification could details of them be seen. Headquarters and Headquarters Company of Milo's battalion were taking their brief sojourn upon deck. Leaving his subordinates to maintain order and discipline among the troops, Milo had sought out a secluded spot—actually, in the cab of a truck—to converse and confer with his commander and old friend, Lieutenant Colonel Jethro Stiles.

"Milo, certain of the staff feel that we—I—ought to make regular inspection circuits down below decks. John Saxon demurs, but then he seldom agrees with much of anything the staff decides. What do you say?"

"I say John's right . . . as usual, Jethro. Remember, he went to France on a troopship back in the Great War, so he knows just what kind of hell it is. No, best to let us noncoms handle it alone," was Milo's solemn reply.

Stiles regarded him narrowly. "That rough down there, is it?"

Clumps of muscles worked at the hinges of Milo's clenched jaws. "Jethro, whoever designed that slice of purgatory down there was not only utterly sadistic but a certifiable lunatic, as well. How in hell are you supposed to keep up the morale and the self-respect of men who have to wallow, day in and day out, in their own filth? The so-called showers are an insult to the intelligence— the hot water lasts just seconds, you have to soap up fast as blazes before it turns into live steam, then you have to rinse yourself in cold, salt seawater, which leaves you feeling sticky, tacky all over; you may *be* clean, technically, but you sure as hell don't *feel* clean.

"The latrines have round-the-clock lines of men waiting to use them, and what with the cases of seasickness and diarrhea and whatnot, a lot of the men in those lines are unable to wait as long as necessary, so there are mop details at work damn near any fucking time or place you look.

"The men are without exception bored, damnably uncomfortable, irascible and getting stiffer by the hour from a lack of decent exercise. Classes are an unfunny joke. They nod and sleep through them."

"Why don't they sleep at night, Milo?" demanded Stiles.

"My God, Jethro," Milo expostulated in heat, "you saw those racks down there before the troops moved in, didn't you? There's only a foot or less of space between each one even when they're empty. At night, a man has to slide in either on his back or on his belly, because after he's in, there'll be no room for him to turn over all night long. The only thing they wear at night is dog tags and jockstraps, and still they stream sweat. A man would have to be utterly exhausted to sleep under those conditions, Jethro, and they have nothing to do to exhaust them and no room to do it in.

"So under every light there's an all-night poker game or crap shoot, and the noise they generate just adds to the echoing snores of the lucky few who have been able to sleep. We feel it would be most unwise to try to break the games up, for at least when the men are gambling the nights away, they're not contemplating the wretched conditions under which they're forced to live, the swill they're expected to eat, their complete helplessness inside the fucking steel torpedo target, their sexual frustrations, the nonavailability of booze and beer or even fucking Cokes, the suffering to be ended, maybe, by their deaths where we're sailing to.

"One of the few good things I can report is that there's been damned little theft reported down there, but that's most likely just because there's simply no place to hide anything and a thief would be found out very quickly . . . and probably killed or seriously injured on the spot, despite us NCOs. As it is, for the best we can do or try to do, the fights down there are frequent and vicious. We've locked up issue weapons, bayonets and every other item that looked like it could be used to kill or badly incapacitate a man, of course, but as you and I both have reason to realize, fists and feet and fingers and knees and elbows can do more than enough damage if a man knows precisely how to utilize them in fighting . . . and that's exactly what instructors have been drilling into most of those men since their basic training."

Stiles frowned through most of the monologue. "Well, Milo, I can do nothing about the shower facilities. Ours are no better up here, you know; the ship simply does not —could not—ship aboard sufficient fresh water to give fresh-water showers every day to so many men. For your information, I did lodge a strenuous objection to all these fucking trucks and jeeps being jammed onto the deck of this ship, but my objections were overridden by higher authorities. If these vehicles were not here, taking up space, we could have organized physical training classes up here in the air and the light . . . but then if a bullfrog had wings, he'd not have a sore ass most of the time, either.

"You and the other NCOs and the men will just have to put up with the latrines and the sleeping accommodations until we get where we're going. There's nothing anyone aboard can now do to change or ameliorate those conditons, unfortunately. But what's this about the food?"

"These cooks of ours," said Milo, "are virtually without effective supervision. The head cook, Sergeant Tedley, has been ill since the day we set sail, so much so that off and on, the medics have thought he might die of dehydration. His second-in-command is so inefficient, so weak in leadership, that most of the cooks do absolutely nothing to speak of except stay drunk on lemon extract and the like and keep well out of the reach of the men."

"Well, Jesus Christ, Milo," snapped Stiles, "why hasn't Lieutenant Jaquot either set this matter straight or reported it to me or John Saxon?"

Milo shrugged grimly. "Probably because he's unaware of it, Jethro. I don't know of anybody who's seen the mess officer below decks since we left New York Harbor. Although the scuttlebutt is that he's won himself a fucking pisspotful of money in some high-stakes poker game up in officer country."

Stiles nodded, a hint of anger smoldering in his eyes. "So he has, Milo, so he has, some of it from me, too. He's won so consistently, the Belgian bastard, that some of us are beginning to wonder just what he did for a living before the war. Of course, the fucking money doesn't matter to me, I don't have to try to live on what the Army pays me, after all, but, by God, I'll have that fucker's hide for neglecting his duties to have more time for his precious fucking cards.

"I'll also talk to the ship's captain and see if there's some way we can get more ventilation down into those spaces you inhabit, particularly at night. As regards all of the rest of your many tribulations, old pal, all you and any of us can do is to just keep on keeping on until we get landed, wherever. Then if we're lucky we'll have the time and space and the opportunity to whip the company back into shape before we have to fight."

The battalion landed in England one cold, wet, blustery day, and that weather remained with them for months, so that many a man and officer was soon looking back to warm and often bone-dry South Carolina with fondness and real longing. So easily did the heavy soil on which their camp was set retain water that most of those who knew anything about such matters were dead certain that the area had been a swamp in the not-too-distant past; moreover, though not within sight of the sea, the land lay sufficiently close to the coast to be buffeted by every storm or gale that chanced to come boiling in from off the North Atlantic Ocean as well as to be pervaded by each and every one of the incredibly damp and icy-cold sea fogs of that season. Nor, in the flat and almost treeless countryside, was there any natural break against the frigid winds and storms that winter brought lashing down from the Highlands of Scotland, Iceland and the arctic wastes of Ultima Thule, far to the north. But in the rare good weather or in the usual foul, the hard training had to continue, day in, day out, night in, night out, week after week, month succeeding month. Big and bloody operations were now afoot, aimed at Fortress Europe, and everyone, from generals down to lowliest privates, knew it for fact.

"I jest don't unnerstand it none, Milo," attested Captain John Saxon, as they sat in the adjutant's office of a wintery day, drinking from canteen cups of hot coffee laced with whiskey and waiting for the office space heater to build up sufficient warmth to at least partially disperse the enervating, bone-chilling, damp cold. "Thesehere folks should oughta be in our debt, after all we've done and is doin' right now for to pull their sad asses outen the fuckin' fire for 'em. More'n that, they's s'posed to be our kinfolks, for all that they all talks damn funny, like damnyankees, kind of. But shitfire, man, you'd think the fuckin' shoe was on the other fuckin' foot, the way thesehere fuckers act. I allus was sorry I dint get to England back in the Great War—jest to France and then back—but I guess I plumb lucked out after all. I wouldn' of put up with being treated like a fuckin' mangy stray dog, the way thesehere fuckin' limejuice bugtits treats our boys.

"Take thishere Hulbert bizness, fer instance. Did you talk to the man after they brung him back? Yeah, well, so did I. He's allus been a good 'un, draftee or not, and I'm damn sure that that Limey cooze is tryin' to get the poor horny fucker railroaded, is what I think. She let him buy her drinks, the first night, see, leadin' him on, sweet-talkin' him inta gettin' a cook to give him butter and powdered eggs and Spam for her, plus three fuckin' cartons of cigarettes. She kept up smoochin' the fella and a-squeezin' his cock in dark places and promisin' him ever'thing. Then when he had give her a whole passel of stuff and tried to get her to put out like she'd been promising him, the cowcunted candlebasher broke a fuckin' bottle over his head and yelled '*Rape!*' Did you see what them damn fuckin' Limey cops done to the poor bastard's face?

"But even so, he just may've been lucky, luckier thin some I could name what did get into a few Limey cunts and was too drunk or too fuckin' lazy or too damn dumb to use the fuckin' pro-kits like they been told to. Don't you look for that fuckin' Jacquot back anytime soon—the fuckin' cardshark has done got hisself clapped up twenny fuckin' ways from Sunday from all the Limey codfish he bought and slammed his wang into right after we got here. And he's just one, too. You wouldn't believe how many men *and* fuckin' of'sers, too, in the division has done gone and got theyselfs done up brown with syph, shank, clap, crabs and ever-fuckin'-thing elst the damn fuckin' Limeys is got for sale.

"I tell you, Milo, till we gets to France or wherever, I'm stickin' my prick into nuthin' but Madam Friggley" —he held up one big hand and waggled the fingers— "and you'll be smart to, too."

Milo himself had been lucky, he decided. None of the women, either in England or in the States, whom he had swived had apparently been diseased, or if they had been, at least, he had failed to contract any of their afflictions. It was just as well, too, for with the accelerated training and the normal day-to-day minutiae of running the oversized company, he would not have had time to undergo treatments for venereal disease or anything else, and he could only again thank his lucky stars that he obviously was immune to such other annoying discomforts as flu and bronchial infections, scabies, boils, sore throats, intestinal problems and even hangovers. For all that in the perpetually wet and cold climate some of the men around him always were sniffling, sneezing, and hacking, he seldom caught a cold, and then only a mild, short-lived one. The outbreak of crab lice soon after the battalion came ashore which had necessitated the shaving of everyone's head and body hair had pointed out the amazing fact that the tiny creatures apparently found his body fluids distasteful, as not a one was ever found upon him.

In the near future years, Milo was often to remember the crab lice episode and wonder about himself, about his decidedly unusual physiology. He was to wonder especially when those about him were suffering from the attentions of body lice, fleas, ticks, bedbugs, the various parasitic worms and leeches, while his flesh and blood and organs remained whole and inviolate. It was to be long, long into that then-unguessed future that he was to add together a myriad of assorted facts—his patent immunity to all of mankind's diseases, his ability to survive clearly fatal wounds by way of unbelievably rapid regeneration of tissues, his complete freedom from parasites, and many another notable curiosity—and begin first to question and then to believe himself to be, as mad Major Jarvis' intuition had told him, either super-human or not truly human at all.

The training went on and on, becoming more and more realistic and dangerous for the trainees, which now included almost every one of the nine hundred and seventeen officers and men in the battalion. Simply for the hard exercise, Milo joined them whenever he could find or make the time to do so. He soon found that it heartened the men to find an officer or a senior noncom wriggling among them in the cold, sticky mud under the fanged wire, while the .30 caliber machine guns fired ball ammunition bare inches overhead, so he not only made more time to join the training exercises himself, but encouraged others to do so in the interests of heightened morale.

Early in February 1944, Jethro and the officers of his staff were summoned to a series of meetings at regimental headquarters. A week later, the division engineers arrived with trucks and tools and boards and plywood with which they quickly built on the frozen ground full-size mockups of landing craft, each one complete with a hinged front ramp of corrugated steel. The experienced, hardworking men had the mockups completed before the day was out, then moved on to the next battalion on their list.

On the following morning—fortunately, one of the rare, bright, sunny days—this newest phase of their training was commenced. And the training continued despite the very worst of weather conditions—weary officers and men burdened down with full packs, personal weapons, heavy weapons, steel boxes and wooden cases of munitions and explosives, cartons of field rations, spools of commo wire and field telephones and all of the other impedimenta of modern, mid-twentieth-century warfare. They trooped into the wooden boxes and arranged themselves as ordered, sitting or squatting or kneeling on the slick, wet, muddy boards in the damp fog or cold drizzle until the command came to arise and exit down the dirty, slippery ramp, then trudge back into the roofless structure to do it all over again. Milo participated in this training, too, and was soon to be very glad that he had done so.

In early May, Jethro suddenly appeared. Framed in the doorway of Milo's private cubicle of the Quonset hut that housed Headquarters Company, Battalion, he beckoned, saying, "Get your jacket and come with me. We need to talk . . . privately."

When Milo had driven the jeep out to a spot sufficiently far from the other humans for Jethro's satisfaction, he switched off the engine and turned in the seat to face his old friend. "So? Talk."

Colonel Stiles sighed. "Milo, I still can't get you commissioned. I can't understand any of the fucking mess and neither can regiment or division or even corps, for chrissakes. They all figure there's a fuckup somewhere in the War Department records, and for want of anything more certain or concrete, I guess I just have to agree with them. I'm sorry. I did try."

"So, what the fuck does it matter, Jethro? Am I demanding a fucking bar? Hell, I'm happy right where I am, in my present grade, doing the job I'm doing." Milo was puzzled, and his voice reflected that.

Stiles just sighed again and shook his head sadly. "It

matters, Milo, because of this: I'm leaving the battalion soon—division staff calls, and I've put them off for about as long as I can. The man who's coming in to replace me will be bringing along his own adjutant, sergeant major and H&H first, which is, of course, his right and privilege and much better for all concerned, since he and they will no doubt work more smoothly together than he would with strangers."

Milo frowned. "So what happens to John Saxon, Bill Hammond and me?"

"I was told I could bring up to three officers of company grade with me to my new posting and job, Milo. Bill's commission is in the mills, and I'd hoped yours would be too, by now, but . . . Hell, Milo, are you sure, are you fucking positive you don't know of any reason why somebody somewhere for some fucking reason would be disapproving all the damned commission requests I've sent in on you over the last few years? So I can't take you along in your present grade. If you want to take a bust down to corporal, I might—might, mind you—be able to justify you as a driver, but it's a mighty long chance and too fucking much risk, I think, for you to sacrifice your stripes for."

"So, you've found a slot for me, Jethro. Right?" Milo asked tiredly.

Stiles nodded once. "I have. Did you hear about the cases of spinal meningitis in Charlie Company? Yeah, well, that left them minus two of their sergeants. You've met Captain Burke, of course."

Milo nodded. "Yes, good officer. West Pointer, isn't he?"

"Virginia Military Institute, Milo, pretty close to the same thing, and a whole fucking hell of a sight better than the frigging NGs and ROTCs and CMTCs we're all so burdened with.

"Anyway, I've talked to Burke, and he would flatly love to have a noncom of your experience in Charlie Company. As you well know, you have the respect and admiration of every officer and man in this battalion. But his problem is this: his first sergeant has done and is doing as good a job as anyone could, and replacing him for no reason would make for a lot of fucking bad blood, and, of course, that's the last fucking thing Burke wants with combat looming so close up ahead."

"He wants me to take field first, then, Jethro? Okay, it's a job I know, too," agreed Milo readily.

"No, Milo." Stiles spoke in a low and hesitant tone. "He's got a good field first, too. He wants you to take over as platoon sergeant of his second platoon." Then the officer added hastily and a bit more cheerfully, "But he swears, and you know it's bound to be true, that if any fucking thing happens to the first or the field first, you're the man for the slot."

Milo shrugged. "Just so long as I go over in grade, don't have to take a bust, Jethro, it's okay with me—the diamond will come off very easily. It'll be good to get back to doing some real field soldiering for a change, too. The way things were, it looked like I'd have sat out the whole fucking war behind a fucking desk."

Although he sat slumped, Stiles looked and sounded much relieved. "Thank God you took it all so well, buddy. Look, I did all they'd let me do to sweeten the pill a little. You can take off your tech stripes completely and sew on a set of masters and you'll go over to Charlie Company in that grade, too—I've already cleared it with Burke. And, Milo, believe me, I'm still going to keep pushing on a commission for you. If any of us old Regulars deserves one, it's you, my friend."

Leo Burke, Captain, Infantry, USA, was a young man in his twenties. An even six feet in height, with dark-blond hair and snapping blue eyes, he was every bit as hard and fit as any man under his command. He spoke a cultivated English in the soft accents of his native Virginia; his handclasp was firm and his boyish smile infectious. He greeted the reporting Milo warmly, clearly desirous of real friendship with his new platoon sergeant.

"At ease, Sahgeant Moray. Sahgeant Coopuh, why don't you have a man fetch us fo' cups of cawfee back here. Oh, and see if you can run down Lootenant Huni-cutter, too. Tell him ah'd like to see him on the double."

When the first sergeant had departed, closing the door that led out to the busy orderly room, the young officer gestured to one of the side chairs, saying, "Please sit

down, Sahgeant Moray." When both were seated, with
cigarettes offered and lit, the company commander said,
"Sahgeant Moray, you just can't know how happy and
truly honuhed ah am to be able to add you to my
company. You are what every offisuh and man in this
whole battalion thinks about when they hear of professional sojuhs, Old Line Reguluhs. It's sho good to
know I'll have a man like you to lean on in days ahead if
the going gets as rough as it may get. Welcome to mah
comp'ny, sahgeant.

"Lootenant Terence Hunicutter is the platoon leaduh
of second platoon, and if evuh a second lootenant needed
a sahgeant like you, it's Terry. He means well, sahgeant,
he's conscientious, hardworking, and he truly does feel
fo' the men in second platoon. But he's one of the Civilian
Military Training Corps offisuhs and he just doesn't know
a whole lot of things he should know and needs to know if
he's going to keep them and him alive and well when we
get into combat. Ah'd considuh it a personal favuh if
you'd take Hunicutter unduh your wing, sahgeant, and
do all you can to help him become the kind of offisuh ah
think and know he can be.

"In strict confidence, Moray, if ah had my druthuhs,
ah'd have you as platoon leaduh and Terry as the
sahgeant, but ah don't, and ah guess we just will have to
play this hand we were dealt. And, also, like I told
Colonel Stiles, if anything should happen to Sahgeant
Coopuh, ah mean to have you out in that orderly room as
mah first so fast it'll make your head spin. You're wasted
as a mere platoon sahgeant and ah know it, but ah still
am glad to have you even as that.

"Oh, and by the way, sahgeant, Colonel Stiles told me
you are a very accomplished riduh. Well, I have some
distunt relatives who live near a town called Somerton,
inland a ways from here. They keep a remahkable stable.
If we can find time, ah'd like to take you up to meet them
and we could then get in a little riding, maybe. It would
be a pure favuh to them and to the po' horses, too. One of
their sons is a pris'nuh of the Nazis, taken in Greece, and
the othuh has not been heard of or from since the fall of
Singapore to the Japs. Their mothuh is terribly arthritic

and their fathuh can't ride too often because of the wounds he suffuhed in France in 1940."

But the outing with Captain Burke was never to be, for the pace of the training increased to frenetic. Equipment and clothing and weapons were inspected and reinspected time after time, and all defective or badly worn or seriously damaged items were replaced with new ones. And as the days of May trickled into June, no officer or man had to be told that the time of sudden death would very soon be upon them all.

Milo found Lieutenant Terence McS. Hunicutter to be much like a puppy, painfully eager to please anyone and everyone without really knowing how. He lacked any real shred of leadership ability, and the four squad leaders had been covertly running the platoon for want of any better arrangement, all knowing that true command was simply beyond the young officer's capabilities. The four men gladly, relievedly turned the platoon over to Milo, asking only that he "take it easy" with Hunicutter, for they all liked the boy.

By the time that young Terence Hunicutter was cut almost in two by a burst of fire from a *Maschinengewehr* hidden behind a Normandy hedgerow, old John Saxon, now a major, had been sent back to replace the dead battalion commander, and he was quick to approve Captain Leo Burke's recommendation of a battlefield commission for Master Sergeant Milo Moray.

There were no significant changes to Milo's life in the wake of the promotion, for he had been doing the identical job since they had waded ashore on the 6th of June, anyway. He just cut off his stripes and pinned the pair of gold bars gifted him by Leo Burke onto his epaulets. Then he buckled on his pistol belt, shouldered a packload of ammo and grenades for his platoon, clapped his battered steel pot on his dirty head, picked up his Thompson and departed the Company CP.

Taking a long and circuitous but relatively safe route, Milo got back to the somewhat reduced platoon tired but elated that at least they now had their expended ammo replaced and a musette bag full of chocolate D-bars and cigarettes to help keep body and soul together until someone got combat rations up to them again.

His inherited command now included the remnants of three rifle squads—one of eleven, one of nine and one of eight men. The last remaining light machine gun section had been pulled away from him two days earlier to be added to the CP guard lines; indeed, he had seen and traded friendly obscenities with two of those men while in the CP area.

Calling over Sergeants Chamberlin and Ryan and Corporal Bernie Cohen, who now led the third squad, Milo laid the two golden bars out on the palm of his filthy hand, saying, "Take a good, long look at them, gentlemen, because this is the last time you're going to see the fuckers until we get somewhere where nobody's shooting at officers and noncoms, in particular. The pack has ammo and grenades—divvy them up equally. I couldn't get more than four new BAR magazines, so give the extra one to Pettus—he's better with the weapon than the other two are.

"Tell your boys they better all start saving their Garand clips. There's been another fucking snafu in supply, I'd say, because I got the last clipped .30-06 that company had. All the new ammo that came in on the last truckload is linked for machine guns, and I brought along a couple boxes of that, too, for the BAR men. No rifle grenades came, only pineapples and no adapters for those, so no point in lugging along the grenade launchers on tomorrow morning's patrol, Greg."

The hulking Greg Chamberlin nodded. "First squad is it again, huh, Milo . . . uhh, lootenant?"

Milo grinned briefly, his teeth gleaming against his dirty stubbled face. "Yep. Always a bride, never a bridesmaid, right, Greg? That's what happens when you're the best—or claim you are—though. And Greg, Gus, Bernie, so long as I'm the highest-ranking man around, it's still Milo to you.

"Okay, let's get the ammo distributed, then you can hand out some D-bars and smokes I brought. Then, Greg, come back here and I'll go over the map with you; I'll be going along on this one."

"Don't you allus?" remarked Chamberlin, chuckling.

The patrol set out at dawn and had moved well out into the unknown countryside by the time it was light enough to see clearly for any great distance. It was then that Pettus slammed his body sideways into the high, grassy bank on his right, his slung BAR under his lanky body, a hole in his head just under the rim of his helmet, blood beginning to dribble from it as tobacco juice was dribbling from the corners of his slackening mouth. He was already down and dead before any of the rest of them even heard the sound of the shot that had killed him.

Before any man could react in any way, a 7.9mm bullet took Milo in the pit of the arm he had just raised to dash the sweat away from his eyes. The bullet bored completely through his chest before exiting in the left-frontal quadrant and going through the biceps, as well, prior to speeding on. Milo later figured that it had skewered both lungs as well as his heart. The lancing agony had been exquisite, unbearable, and Milo screamed. He drew in a deep, agonizing breath to scream once again, and that second scream choked away as he coughed up a boiling rush of blood. He almost strangled on the blood.

All of the patrol had gone to ground. Chamberlin wriggled over to first Pettus, then Milo. After the most cursory of examinations and a brief, futile attempt to wrestle the BAR from under Pettus' dead weight, the big sergeant got the men off the exposed section of roadway without any more losses. Having fortunately spotted the flash of the shot that had struck Milo, Chamberlin and Corporal Gardner divided the riflemen between them, then Chamberlin set out in a wide swing with his section, going to the left fast, while Gardner's section moved more slowly, almost directly at the objective, now and then having one of his men gingerly expose himself to keep the attention of the sniper on this nearer unit.

Milo, back at the ambush point, just lay still, hoping that by so doing he could hold the pain at bay until he had lost enough blood to pass into a coma and so die in peace and relative comfort. But he did not, he could not find and sink into that warm, soft, all-enveloping darkness, and the pain went on and on, unabated, movement or no movement. In instinctive response to his body's demands, he of course continued to breathe, but he did so

as shallowly as possible, lest he bring on another bout of
coughing and choking on his own blood.

The pain grew worse as he lay there; so bad was it that
he gritted his teeth, grinding them and groaning. But
then, strangely, the pain began to slowly ebb away, to
lessen imperceptibly. Although he felt weak and terribly
thirsty, he felt no more drowsiness than he had before he
had been shot. He opened his eyes then, to find that he
could see, and see very clearly, which last surprised him.
What he saw was the two sections of Chamberlin's squad
parting and wriggling, then proceeding at a crouching
run in two directions clearly intended to converge upon
what must be the sniper's nest—the jumbled stones and
still-standing chimney of a burned-out farmhouse.

Something deep within him told him to take a better
look, a closer look at the distant objective against which
his last full rifle squad was now advancing. He cautiously
raised himself just enough to drag from beneath him his
cased binoculars, gritting his teeth against the renewed
waves of pain that never materialized. What he saw
through the optics was three figures clad in Wehrmacht
Feldgrau, busily setting up a light machine gun, an
MG-42, by the look of it, and fitted out with one of the
Doppeltrommel drum magazines. The thing was on one
of the rare tripods, which would serve to make its fire
more accurate and devastating than the usual unsteady
bipodal mount.

With no base of fire to cover them and their advance,
he knew that those men of his would be slaughtered.
They would not know of that deadly machine gun—
for, after all, they thought themselves to be stalking only
a sniper and an assistant or two and could not see from
their positions just what a hideous surprise the Krauts
were setting up for them—until the high rate of fire of
the MG-42 was engaged in ripping the very life from out
of them.

He immediately dismissed his Thompson. The submachine gun was a superlative, if very heavy, weapon at
normal combat ranges, but in this instance, he knew it
just could not reach the needed distance. Forgetting his
wounds and his pain in his worry for his men in such a
state of deadly danger out there, he allowed his body to

slide down the bank, then wormed his way back to where Pettus lay.

All of his strength was required to shift the big man's weight enough to get both the BAR and the six-pocket magazine belt off it without standing up and giving that sniper a new target. Then, laden with his own weapons and equipment, as well as the twenty-odd pounds of automatic rifle and its seven weighty twenty-round magazines, he crawled up the bank to its brushy top and took up a position that allowed him a splendid field of fire.

A pair of mossy boulders situated close together provided both a bracing for the bipod of the BAR and a measure of cover from return fire, almost like the embrasure of a fortification.

He took the time to once more scan his target area with the pair of binoculars and shrewdly estimated the range at about eight hundred yards, give or take some dozen or so yards. With the bipod resting securely on the gray boulders at either side, he slid backward and calibrated the rear sights for the range he had guessed. Then he set the steel-shod butt firmly into the hollow of his shoulder, nestled his cheek against the stock, took the grip in his hand and crooked his forefinger around the trigger.

Chapter X

Expertly feathering the trigger so as to loose off only three rounds per firing until he knew himself to be dead on target, Milo cruelly shocked the understrength squad of Wehrmacht as they were preparing their deadly surprise for the two small units of attacking Americans.

As the bursts of .30 caliber bullets struck the fire-blackened stones and ricocheted around and about the area of the ruined house, the *Gefreite* reared up high enough from where he lay to use his missing *Zugsführer's* fine binoculars to sweep the area from which the fire seemed to be coming. It did not take the twenty-year-old veteran long to spot the flashes of the BAR, and as the present danger to his squad superseded in his experienced mind the planned ambush, he pointed out the location of the automatic weapon that now had them under its well-aimed fire to the *Maschinengewehrmann* and ordered return fire.

When he had caught the glint of sun on glass, Milo had anticipated counterbattery fire and had scooted his body off to one side, behind the larger and longer of the two boulders, pressing himself tightly against it and the hard, pebbly ground, so he only had to wait until the German machine gun ceased firing, brush off stone shards and bits of moss, then get back into firing position. As he dropped the partially emptied magazine into a waiting hand, then slipped and hooked in a fresh one, he smiled coldly. Now he knew he had the range.

As Chamberlin later stated it, "Well, when I heard that damn fuckin' tearing-linoleum sound, I knew fuckin'

well it was more up there ahead than just some friggin'
Jerry sniper in that place, so I just stayed down myself,
and I hoped old Gardner would have the fuckin' good
sense to do the same thing, and of course he did.

"Then, when the BAR cut in on full—for some reason,
I hadn't heard the fucker before then—and I realized it
must be shooting at the Jerries from the fuckin' road, all I
could figger then was that old Pettus, he hadn't been
killed after all and was giving us covering fire, keeping
the fuckin' Jerries down so's we could get up to hand-
grenade range of them. So I waved my boys on, slung my
MI and got a pineapple out and ready."

Milo was working on the seventh magazine when he
saw the flash, then after a pause heard the *cruummpp* of
the first grenade explosion within the perimeter of the
German position. At that point, he ceased firing lest he
find himself shooting at his own men. When he had
collected the emptied magazines, he reslung the BAR and
Thompson, slid down the bank and was there to greet the
two sections as they straggled back to their starting point.

When Sergeant Chamberlin saw Milo standing there,
his eyes widened, boggled out, and he almost dropped
the cased pair of fine Zeiss binoculars he had stripped
from off the now incomplete corpse of the Wehrmacht
Gefreite, and he still was just standing and staring, trying
to comprehend the incomprehensible, as the others came
up behind him.

"Fuck a fuckin' duck!" Corporal Gardner exclaimed,
letting the holstered broomstick Mauser that had been
the machine gunner's sidearm dangle in the dust beside
his worn field shoes. "Sarge . . . I means, lootinunt, we
thought you's daid, fer shure. I know damn well that
fuckin' bullet hit you, Gawd dammit! I seen the dust fly
up outen your fuckin' shirt, I did. So why the fuck ain't
you a'layin' dead, like old Pettus there, huh?"

And Milo had no real answer for the understandable
questions of the squad members—Chamberlin, Gardner
and the rest—or for his own, not then, not for years yet to
come. So recalling old John Saxon's explanation of the
last unexplainable incident of similar nature back in the
States, he spun a tale of the bullet passing through his
loose-fitting field shirt without fleshing anywhere,

opined that he must have struck hard enough when he
dove to the rocky ground at the sound of the first shot, the
one that had killed Pettus, to briefly stun him. The blood
still wet in his clothing he blamed on wrestling with the
BAR man's gory corpse to free the automatic rifle and its
belt of magazines.

Although he still caught the odd stare from Chamberlin and Gardner, now and again, for weeks, they and the
squad members all ended up believing him, for disbelief
would have meant a descent into madness, after all. But
Milo himself did not, could not put any stock in his glib
fabrications. He knew damned good and well that the
sniper's shot had been accurate and should by all rights
have been his death wound. In a logical world, he should
be back there rotting in a shallow grave beside Pettus,
with a steel pot and an identity tag for a marker, waiting
for the attention of a graves registration unit. But he was
not, and that inescapable fact cost him more than one
sleepless night of wondering and speculation as to just
what made him so different from the millions of other
men now fighting and dying on the continent of Europe
and elsewhere around the world.

In August of that momentous year of 1944, a second
Allied invasion of Fortress Europe took place, this one in
southern France, and eventually elements of this force
hooked up with General George Patton's hell-bent-for-
leather Third Army. But these events were of little
interest to the men of a certain battalion of General
Courtney Hodges' First Army. They had all they could do
just trying to stay alive and still do the tasks assigned their
much-reduced, worn-out, fought-out units. When, in
early September, the entire forward movement ground to
a halt through lack of gasoline, lubricants and most of the
other sinews of modern mechanized warfare, the respite
was none too soon for the common soldiers and the
company-grade officers.

In their encampment by the side of a meandering
tributary stream to the nearby Meuse River, the twenty-
two men of Lieutenant Milo Moray's platoon moved like
automatons and as little as possible, their exhaustion and
malnutrition writ large upon their dirty, stubbly faces

and staring from the deep-sunk, dark-circled bloodshot eyes. With a seven-man strength, Chamberlin's still was the largest "squad" of the "platoon"; Bernie Cohen had five men left in his third squad, but Ryan had been seriously wounded and the second squad now was being led by Corporal Gardner.

But high as had been the losses of enlisted personnel in Charlie Company during their hotly resisted advance across France, the proportionate loss of commissioned officers had been even higher; Milo was now not the only platoon leader commissioned from the ranks since D-Day. None of the original second lieutenants was left with a platoon, in fact. Captain Leo Burke had lost part of a leg when his jeep had triggered off a land mine. He had been replaced by his exec, First Lieutenant Tom Beverley, like Burke a Virginian and a graduate of the Virginia Military Institute, though a year or so after Burke. His new exec was an OCS second lieutenant sent down to Charlie Company by division, a replacement officer who had still been Stateside on D-Day, Lieutenant John Brettmann.

Even after a full, uninterrupted—thanks mostly to Sergeants Cohen and Chamberlin—twenty-four hours of sleep and a luxurious bath in the riverlet with *soap*, even with his too long empty belly now gleefully working on a can of beans with pork, one of grease patties, one of hard crackers and two D-bars washed down with a pint of coffee that really was hot and sweet, even after being able to shave with hot water and throw away his tattered, incredibly filthy clothing for a new issue that had included no less than four pairs of thick socks and a pair of new field shoes that had broad, thick pieces of leather secured by brass buckles sewn to the top to go around and protect the lower leg and ankle, even after he had pared his fingernails down to the very quick and scrubbed away the last of the ground-in, fecal-stinking black filth that had for so long found lodgment under his nails, he still was not quite the old Milo Moray when he responded to a field-telephoned summons and came into the Charlie Company CP area.

Because the other two platoon leaders had not as yet made their appearances, Milo seized upon the oppor-

tunity to pick through the small hillocks of recently
delivered supplies, principally in search of new ponchos
for him, Chamberlin and Cohen, but not intending to
turn down any odd but necessary goodies he should
chance across. He already had been able to stuff several
items into his ready duffel bag—soap and shaving soap,
some GI spoons, a brand-new carbine bayonet and case,
four ponchos, a number of new magazines for pistol,
Thompson and BARs, two, new canteens with cups and
covers, a compact carton containing a gross of book
matches, another of chewing gum, a dozen toothbrushes
and cans of toothpowder, foot powder and some dozens
of razor blades. He had just dragged his bag over to
another pile and squatted before it to delve when he
heard a vaguely familiar nasal whine of a voice behind
him.

"You need a haircut, soldier. Who gave you permission
to paw through those supplies, anyway? They belong to
the unit as a whole, not to you personally, you know. You
could be charged with theft, for misappropriation of
government materiel, and I think I should do just that,
here and now, and . . . *eeek!*"

Upon hearing a strange voice behind him, Milo's
combat-honed senses had reacted, and the drawing and
aiming of the pistol, the spinning about on his deeply
flexed legs, had been as instinctive as breathing. Not until
then did his still-tired mind register that the figure
standing there was clad in a too-clean GI uniform and
polished boots, and was staring—wide-eyed and pale-
faced, trembling with very obvious fear—at the gaping
.45 caliber muzzle pointing up at him. As it all registered,
including the gold bars pinned to each epaulette of the
pressed, flat-pocketed field shirt, Milo grinned and
lowered the pistol, rapidly disarmed it and returned it to
its worn holster.

"Sorry, lieutenant. Are you a replacement? You must
be, else you'd know better than to come up behind a man
and startle him like that. I could've blown your silly head
off, you know? The next time around, you might not be
so lucky." Then, recalling just how the new officer had
looked, Milo chuckled and added, "You scare easy, don't
you, sonny?"

The officer turned and screamed at a noncom just coming out of a squad tent. "Sergeant, *sergeant* . . . yes, you, over here, on the double! I want this man placed under arrest, *now!* And seal that bag of his, too. I'll prefer charges against him. Well, are you going to obey my orders to arrest him?"

First Sergeant Dixon looked quizzical. "You want *me* to put Lootenant Moray under arrest, Lootenant Brettmann? What in hell for? Why don't you go in and talk to the captain about it?"

The new officer was stunned. "You . . . you mean . . . are you trying to tell me that this . . . this larcenous, insubordinate, murderous ragamuffin is a commissioned officer of the Army of the United States of America?"

Catching Milo's eye, Dixon raised his eyebrows and shook his head, but spoke to the new officer slowly and distinctly, as if to an idiot child. "Thass right, Lootenant Brettmann, sir. Thishere's Lootenant Milo Moray of the secon' pl'toon, sir."

At the sergeant's mention of the surname, it all finally came back to Milo—the vaguely familiar voice and the pointy, ratlike features. Smiling coldly, he said in Dutch, "Well, Comrade Jaan Brettman, how are things in Moscow?"

Later, seated on a wooden case of small-arms ammo across a folding field table from Tom Beverley, with a white-faced, trembling Brettmann standing stiffly off to one side of the small tent, Milo said tiredly, "He's full of shit, too, Tom, he always has been. If I'd really tried to kill him, *ever*, the little fucker would be pushing up daisies by now, and you know me well enough to know it, too. Don't you?"

Beverlyy just nodded; he did know Milo that well. He fumbled briefly in a bag at his feet to come up with a bottle and a pair of battered tin cups. After pulling the cork with his teeth, he filled both cups and shoved one across to Milo. He did not even glance at Brettmann.

"Okay, Milo, division wished the Jewboy here off on us, and ah don't know him from Adam's housecat. He says you tried to kill him years back and again just now, so you must've known him before this, unless he's completely round the bend . . . and that's possible, too. If you did know him sometime and someplace else, tell me about it. Ah need to know all ah can about mah men and officers."

Milo sipped appreciatively at the smooth single-malt whisky and sighed with pleasure. "There's not all that much to tell, Tom. I knew him only very briefly. We met on only one occasion, in fact. He was from a family of Dutch Jewish immigrants; all except him were good, decent, hardworking people. Out of the proceeds of a tiny one-man tailor ship, his father was sending both him and his elder brother, Sol, to college . . . and all this was in '37, too, mind you.

"Sol Brettmann was in law school, but Jaan here apparently was a major in revolutionary Bolshevism, while on the side he was teaching impressionable, sheltered young girls the finer points of burglary and sneak-thievery. When I caught him trying to break into my strongbox in my room of the house I was then calling home, he tried to knife me, and I broke his arm for him. Because he had involved a daughter of my landlady in his criminal activities, the police were never called into it, and after he was deemed fit to travel, he was sent back East somewhere to live with relatives. Until today, when he surprised me and I drew my pistol on him, I'd never seen or heard of him again, and I'm here to tell you that even this meeting, seven years since the last, was way too soon."

Beverley drained his cup, refilled it, then leaned across to pour more into Moray's half-empty one. He nodded. "That's all we need, Milo, all we need. We don't have enough troubles with the comp'ny more than forty percent understren'th and another fucking push coming fast as sure as God makes road apples? So ah told John Saxon ah had to have an exec, hoping ah'd get a mustang like you or him that knew shit from Shinola, and what did those division shitheads send down here? A lying, thieving kike bastard of a pinko who's so damn dumb in important things that ah don't think he knows which end to wipe the shit off of! And ah cannot imagine how he ended up in Charlie Comp'ny, to begin with, Milo. His frigging 201 file says he's a fucking quartermaster officer, for Christ's sake!"

Momentarily forgetting his circumstances in his righteous wrath, Second Lieutenant John Brettmann abruptly burst out, "It was all a conspiracy, I tell you, a hideous capitalistic conspiracy, to send me over here to die. I was at Camp Lee, Virginia, showing the enlisted men how they could form a union and teaching those who wanted to learn about progressive ideas the philosophy of Marx and Engels and the teachings of Lenin. Then, all at once, I was ordered to report to a port of embarkation and found myself being sent to Europe as a replacement infanty officer. I don't want to be here any more than you foul-mouthed, anti-Semitic alcoholics want me here. I'd never have gone into the Army, anyway, if the Party hadn't said to."

Captain Tom Beverley just looked at Milo and Milo looked back at him. No words were necessary between them, not on this matter. For the sake of bare survival of the men who depended upon them, this officer could not ever be allowed in a combat-command position, and for just such a position he was currently in direct line.

Leaving the tent, the three officers paced across the CP area, passed the perimeter and walked on several scores of yards beyond it before Tom Beverley halted.

Pointing to the blackened, rusting hulk of a Mark III panzer squatting some fifty yards away just beyond a flat field with knee-high grass growing around shell craters, the captain said, "Brettmann, your ticket back Stateside is in the turret of that tank. Go over there and climb up on it and open the hatch and fetch me back the musette bag that's hanging in it, heah? And be damned careful with it, too, boy. You break airy one of those bottles and ah'll have your guts for garters."

Brettmann paced rapidly across the field, clambered clumsily onto the hull of the gutted tank, then jerked at the flaking handle of the central hatch until it came open with a shrill protest from rust-eaten hinges. After a moment, he shouted back, "Captain, there's nothing in here that even looks like a musette bag."

Beverley cupped his hands around his mouth and bellowed, "A'raht, then, just come on back here, on the double!"

Second Lieutenant John Brettmann had trotted about

halfway back in their direction when, with a flash and an ear-shattering explosion, his body was flung a good ten feet into the air to flop down sprawling, unmoving and incomplete.

"Do you think he's dead, Tom?" asked Milo coolly.

The captain shrugged. "Looks to be from here, and ah'm not about to send any of mah men into a minefield to find out one way or the othuh. Whenevuh regiment or division gets around to clearing that field, they can take his tag and bury him. Let's us get back—the othuhs ought to be there by now, and ah need to hash out some things with the bunch of you."

Reinforced with replacements to only about twelve percent under their D-Day strength, the battalion took part in the attack on and capture of the German city of Aachen, just behind the broken Siegfried Line. But it did not prove a bloodless victory. Quite a few of the ill-trained new men were lost in it, along with irreplaceable men like Sergeants Gardner and Cooper and Captain Tom Beverley. Major John Saxon was wounded, but before he would let them take him back to the division hospital, he ordered the necessary promotions and transfers to keep his battalion running as smoothly as possible under the circumstances.

At battalion headquarters, where he had been ordered to report, Milo dropped off a handful of dog tags with the clerk assigned to handle KIAs, then sought out the harried adjutant, Captain Davies.

Looking up but fleetingly to see who stood before his cluttered field desk, the cadaverous-looking man muttered, "Moray, you're bumped up two notches by order of Major Saxon and some single-star at division. Take over Charlie Company and get ready for another push . . . soon. You'll be needing a first sergeant, since yours was killed along with Captain Beverley, but, no, I cannot supply you a noncom, or any other warm bodies, for that matter. Maybe soon, but not now. If you can beg, borrow or steal a truck and dragoon a driver for it, I can authorize you to pick up ammo and rations, and that's it. Questions?"

But despite Captain Davies' assurances of new actions,

there was no fresh push, not for either battalion or regiment. All had just been too badly chewed up for anything until once more up to at least near strength. They were moved back to their original areas south of the Meuse River.

Slowly, in dribbles and drabs, the decimated units were resupplied and reinforced with replacements, mostly green, partially trained men fresh out of basic training Stateside, with a sprinkling of veterans just released from various medical facilities and dumped into the replacement depots or "repple-depples." When one of these somehow wound up in the unit that had been his before his wounding, the scenes could be heartwarming. This was exactly how Sergeant Bernie Cohen came back to Charlie Company, to be immediately grabbed by Milo and made first sergeant. Chamberlin had declined that job and had also declined an offered commission; he still was running the second platoon, but as a master sergeant.

In November, the other two battalions, the mortar company, the tank company and most of the medical company were sent off to join in the push through the Hurtgenwald, their objective Cologne. But the drive quickly bogged down in the face of the stiff resistance offered by the troops of General Walther Model.

On the banks of the Meuse, the battalion camped, licking its wounds, integrating the trickles of replacements for the men and equipment and weapons lost and serving as perimeter guards for the regimental headquarters complex. They ate class-A rations and loved it, not often having had access to fresh, hot food since leaving England months before, though they still bitched and groused about it as soldiers always have and always will. They were issued winter clothing and, as the weather worsened, devised ways to supplement their bedding and windproof their shelters. Old John Saxon, now a lieutenant colonel, came back with some facial scarring and a slight limp to take over his command, and still the battalion just sat in place. But it was, for them, the calm before the storm of death that awaited too many of them.

In early December, First Sergeant Bernie Cohen and a

detail had gone into the regimental complex and there scrounged or "liberated" enough material to construct of wood and corrugated metal a smallish, airtight building centered by a wide firepit filled with coarse gravel and small boulders which would retain heat well. The resulting steam baths had become very popular, and that was where Milo and Bernie were when the CQ runner found them to say that battalion was on the wire for Milo.

John Saxon was clearly agitated when he spoke with the officers gathered in his heavily guarded headquarters tent. "Gentlemen, the fuckin' Krauts have done broke through in the Ardennes. Division is damn near as short-handed as we are, what with all them men tied down up to Hurtgenwald, and the word is to send them ever' swingin' dick can be scraped up here, and that means us, thishere battalion. So git back to yore comp'nies and saddle up, fast. And I mean ever' fucker you got on the mornin' report, too—clerks, cooks and all, ever'body that can shoot a rifle. Full packs, all the clothes they can wear and still fight, three days' worth of C-rations and weapons. Two hunnert rounds for each MI, and ammo in proportion for all the other weapons. Send your tents and records and all up here on the trucks you send to pick up ammo and rations and gas and all. Okay? Git!"

The drive down into the Ardennes was pure hell, as Milo recalled it. A snowstorm of near-blizzard proportions started up soon after the convoy took to the so-called road. Visibility quickly became bare feet, and this meant that each vehicle had to drive close enough to see the vehicle ahead with the narrow, dim "cat's-eye" head beams that were all that regiment would for some reason allow. The inability to see meant that the lead vehicles were plotting direction with map and compass, and this kept the advance painfully slow while the men huddled together for warmth in the backs of the trucks, forbidden to smoke and thoroughly miserable.

When at long last the trucks ground to a skidding halt, the men were all instructed to leave on the trucks everything save their weapons, ammo, rations, entrenching tools and ponchos. Thus stripped for immediate action, they were marched, single-file, past a long line of GI cans fitted with immersion heaters. Each man had his canteen cup filled with hot coffee and was allowed to hurriedly fish a can of C-ration out of the boiling water.

Milo thought that the greasy corned beef hash had never before tasted so good. The coffee could have served equally well as battery acid, but it was hot, and that was just then the important thing to him. But he had had only a single drag on his postprandial cigarette when the order came down to form up and move out into the numbing cold. The snow seemed to be slacking off, but what was still falling was being whipped on by an icy-toothed wind. As he tucked away his canteen cup, he reflected silently that this was damned poor weather in which to be expected to fight, but then any weather was.

Two days later, Milo crouched in the snow among the nineteen men that were what now remained of Charlie's headquarters platoon and first platoon. It could well be all that remained of the entire company for all he knew, since there had been no contact with Chamberlin of the second or Hogan of the third for . . . ? He was just too tired to remember how long.

There gradually approached unseen an ominous grinding-clanking-roaring, and lumbering over a low saddle came a German tank, a big one. A black-capped man stood with his black-leather-clad torso sticking out of the turret hatch, and a dozen or so rifle-armed soldiers rode clinging to the hull behind him. As the tank began to descend the slope into the little vale that lay between his hill and Milo's, the front of the half-track appeared in the saddle behind the lumbering steel behemoth.

"Are there any rockets left for the bazooka, Bernie?" said Milo quietly.

"Yeah, Milo, two," whispered First Sergeant Bernie Cohen. "But they won't do no good—that's a fuckin' Tiger tank. They'll just bounce off the fucker."

Milo nodded. "Well, tell the bazooka man to take out that half-track back there, while the BARs and the rest of us try to kill those infantrymen. They're what we really need to worry about—this slope is too steep for that tank or any other to make it up here."

"He won't need to," said Cohen sadly. "The fuckin' hill ain't too steep for fuckin' eighty-eight shells to climb. He can just sit down there and blow the whole fuckin' top off this fuckin' hill, and us with the fucker."

The flash and *whooosh* of the launched antitank rocket coincided with the tremendous explosion capped by a huge, black-smoky fireball rising from the saddle and announcing that the vehicle had been carrying gasoline, not troops. These sounds also coincided with the spraying of a deadly hail of small-arms fire on the Tiger below. The black hat spun from off the head of the man in the turret, even as that turret began to turn toward the hilltop, its long-barreled 88mm cannon beginning to rise. The unprotected *Panzergrenadieren* fared poorly, with no cover or even concealment to shelter them from the rain of death.

"Okay, okay!" Milo shouted. "Cease firing, cease firing, and let's get the hell off this hill before the Krauts blow us all to hell!"

The men needed no further urging, rolling out of their firing positions and running, sliding, rolling down the more gentle reverse slope as fast as was humanly possible. Not until yet another snow-covered hill lay between them and the Tiger did they halt, panting, listening to the main armament of the Tiger bombarding their late position relentlessly.

Milo clapped Sergeant Cohen on the shoulder. "Well, it worked, didn't it, Bernie? Why're you still so glum?"

"Yeah, it worked, a'right, Milo, that last time, but it ain't gonna work again, not for us. We down to *one* rocket for the bazooka now, and damn little fuckin' ammo for any fuckin' thing else. One of the BARs ain't workin' no more, and Bailey's ankle is either busted or sprained real bad. We gotta find either battalion or regiment, Milo."

But they did not; what they found instead and very soon thereafter was a full company of Waffen-SS, who were as much surprised at the encounter as were Milo and his fragments of Charlie Company. The battle was short, of course, and very bloody, and the outcome was certain when it began there amid the whirling snow. Most of it was hand-to-hand, the firearms fired at such short ranges that they often set afire the clothing of those at whom they were aimed.

Milo fired off the magazine in his Thompson, but had no time to put in a fresh one. He used the submachine gun as a club until his icy-slick gloves lost their grip on it. He managed to draw and arm his pistol then, but had fired off only two shots when something struck the back of his neck and darkness descended on him.

When things had been sorted out and the *Hauptscharführer* had made his report, *Obersturmführer* Karl Greisser waited until the *Sanitätsmann* had finished dabbing ointment on his powder-burned face before remarking, "There weren't many of them, God be thanked, for just look at the mess those few made of this company. Did any get away?"

Untersturmführer Egon Lenge shrugged. "One would doubt it, but in this snow and wind, who can say? There are a few wounded Amis. What do we do with them?"

Greisser raised his eyebrows. "On the advance, Egon? You know what to do."

Lenge nodded and tried vainly to click his bootheels. *Zu Behfel, mein Herr Obersturmführer."*

Pacing over to a knot of soldiers, he bespoke a *Rottenfuhrer.* "Get two men and fix your bayonets."

Milo came slowly out of his stupor and groggily raised his body up on his elbows. That was when the *Rottenführer.* "Get two men and fix your bayonets."

Milo came slowly out of his stupor and groggily raised his body up on his elbows. That was when the *Rottenführer* jammed the full length of his bayonet into Milo's chest, then again and yet a third time. With a groan, Milo sank back into the trampled, bloody snow.

Satisfied, the *Rottenführer* moved on to perform another mercy killing. He thought well of the company commander for ordering this. Only a very humane man would take time out from an advance to see to it that wounded enemies were not simply left to die of pain and shock and freezing.

Although in severe pain from the penetrating stabs of the bayonet, Milo stayed completely still until the last sounds of men and vehicles had faded into the distance. Although someone had taken his wristwatch, he discovered that the American weapons and clothing and equipment had been left where they lay by the Germans.

"The bastards must be running on a tight time schedule," he muttered to himself. "They didn't even search us for cigarettes . . . not that they'd have found any on this bunch."

His own searching showed him fourteen bodies, fifteen, including his. So as many as five could have gotten away clean. Of course, there could be some he had not found in the deep snow, too, and some of those not here could have crawled away wounded to die nearby.

He found his Thompson, checked the action, cleaned and dried it as best he could, then jammed his last full magazine into it. His pistol still hung by his side on a lanyard he affected, and he cleared and holstered it. A careful search of the bodies of his men gave him a handful of dog tags, a few more rounds of .45 ammo for his weapons and nothing else; they had all been down to the bare essentials days ago.

Search as he might, however, he could not find his map case, and as he thought of it, he could not recall seeing it within the last twenty-four hours or so. He reflected that it and its contents would not do him much good anyway, because he did not know where he was except in the very broadest sense, and he could spot no prominent terrain features or landmarks amid the wind-blown clouds of snow and the very low overcast. He did still have his compass, however, hanging unbroken in its case on his pistol belt; thank God for small favors. If he took a course a few degrees west of due north, he should eventually come out of the Ardennes somewhere in friendly territory, unless the German counteroffensive had rolled the invading Allies clear back to Antwerp by then.

Colonel John Saxon was in an exceedingly foul mood when he hustled into the commo tent, not liking at all being bothered for any reason at his daily bowel movement.

Taking the microphone into his hairy paw and appropriating the radio operator's seat, he growled, "Saxon here. What is so fuckin' all-fired important, Mr. Whoever-you-are? And I'm warnin' you, it better be fuckin' good! Like capturin' old Schickelgroober, that kinda good."

A cool, precise, obviously unflustered voice replied, "Colonel Saxon, your regimental headquarters says that you have or at least had an officer named Milo Moray, a captain and company commander, in your battalion. Is this true?"

"Yeah, it's so," attested Saxon, the still-recent hurt of loss taking a good bit of the fire of anger out of him. "The fuckin' Krauts wounded him and then bay'neted him and a whole bunch of other wounded fellas to death. Two, three boys come to get away and make it back and tell us 'bout it. Why? Have you found his body?"

"In a manner of speaking, colonel, in a manner of speaking. This is S-2, Second Armored Division. I'm Major George Smith. A man was captured by one of our advance units a few kilometers southwest of here yesterday. He was wandering around alone in bloodstained clothing, and that in itself made him suspicious, since there were no wounds to be found on him. After the regimental S-2 questioned him, found that his German was as fluent as his English and that, although he claimed to be a captain, there were no indications of rank on his uniform or in his effects and his identity tags carry an enlisted man's service number, he was sent back here under guard.

"Whoever he is, colonel, he is a linguist. He speaks not only English and German, but French, Dutch, Flemish, Yiddish, Scottish, Spanish and Romanian, and those are only the ones we've been able to check out. He has the order of battle of your battalion and regiment down pat and about as much of that of your division and First Army as one could expect the captain of a line company to know. I like the man and I'd like to believe his story . . . and it's a hair-raising one, too. But I've got to have more proof of his identity than he can give me, or has given me up to now, anyway. With all these phony GIs wandering around the countryside and speaking German when they think they aren't overheard, we have no choice but to be damned sure just who or what we've got."

"I unnerstand, major," said Saxon. "You cain't be too fuckin' careful, out in hostile country. I tell you what— you got this man there with you?"

"In the next room, colonel," replied Smith.

"Then ask him or have somebody else ask him these-here questions I'm gonna tell you and then tell me what he answers."

When the major resumed transmission, he said, "Colonel, the man states that his high-ranking buddy is Brigadier General Jethro Stiles, that the clapped-up cardshark of your battalion was a Belgian named Jaquot, that the name and rank of the man who tried to kill him back in the States was Sergeant Luigi Moffa, and that—"

"Never mind, major, never mind," crowed Saxon, grinning from ear to ear. "You got the genyewine article there, not no Kraut. Send Milo home."

When he finally got through to Brigadier General Stiles, Saxon said, "I hope you sittin' down, gen'rul. Okay? Milo ain't dead. Naw, he turned up and was picked up by some Secon' Armored fellas, two, three days back, and their fuckin' S-2s has had him sincet then, tryin' to figger if he was who he said or a fuckin' Kraut in GI clothes. I give the dumbass fuckers some questions could'n anybody but Milo answer right, and when I got the right answers, I told the bastards to send him back to battalion. I thought you'd wanta know, gen'rul."

During his long, solitary sojourn through the winter wastes of the Ardennes, dodging German panzers and infantry units and finding himself forced by these and by natural obstacles to bear farther and farther east of north, Milo had had much time to think. He now was pretty certain that there was something extremely odd, to say the very least, about the way he was put together. He had been knifed in Chicago by the late Jaan Brettmann, shot by Moffa back at Jackson, shot again by that German sniper and now bayoneted two or three times over by that SS man, yet he still was here to think about it all, and any one of the wounds he had suffered could have, *should* have, killed him outright. Not only was he still alive, he didn't even have any scars from these terrible wounds.

All around him since D-Day, men—good men, strong men, healthy and well-trained and intelligent men—had been dying, many of them of injuries far less outwardly serious than those he had sustained and survived. So, why? He was human in every other way saving that he never sickened and that he could come unscathed out of patently deadly situations and incidents. He breathed, ate, digested, defecated and urinated. He functioned perfectly well sexually (at least no woman had voiced any complaints about his performances). He slept when he could. He was capable of pity, disgust, hate, respect, anger, possibly love too (but he had never found himself "in love," not in the classic sense, so how could he be sure?), the whole gamut of human emotions. So what made him so different?

He did not formulate any answer before he stumbled across a tank crew engaged in replacing a damaged track link on their Sherman, screaming profane and obscene invective at the tank and each other and offering prime targets, had he been a German.

First Sergeant Bernie Cohen had been in a state approaching traumatic shock since battalion had called down to announce that their long-lost company commander, Captain Milo Moray, had somehow gotten out of the Ardennes alive and well and would be along whenever Second Armored could get him in. He still could not believe it even when Milo alit from a jeep and came into the Quonset hut orderly room of the reforming company.

Not until Milo had racked his Thompson, dumped his pistol belt on the table he called a desk, laid his helmet atop the belt and started to remove his jacket could Cohen manage to speak.

His thin lips trembling, the noncom said, "But . . . but Milo, I *seen* it! A Kraut jammed a K98 bayonet in your chest at least twice. I *know* I seen it. I was in the trees not fifteen yards away. That's why I told everybody you was dead."

Milo just smiled and gripped the stunned man's shoulder, saying, "I know, Bernie, I know you saw some poor bastard bayoneted, more than one, too, for they did that to fourteen men there. But they did miss me. I'd been cold-cocked during the fight, and I guess they thought I was already done for. When I did come to, the Krauts were long gone and the bodies of our guys were already stiff. I'm sure you did think I was dead, so forget it."

Chapter XI

The German counteroffensive of December 1944 was stopped, of course, crushed under the tank treads of General George Patton's Third Army, bombed and strafed incessantly by Allied air power and driven back with over 200,000 casualties. The so-called Battle of the Bulge quickly became history.

While Charlie Company was dug in on the eastern bank of the Rhine River, at Remagen, helping to hold that precious span from recapture by the Wehrmacht, Milo received orders to report back to battalion headquarters. He found there a jeep and driver waiting to transport him farther back, to division headquarters. Ushered into a warm, dry building and given a chair, he promptly fell asleep.

When at last he sat across the polished desk from Jethro, savoring his glass (real glass, cut and faceted) of cognac, he became unpleasantly aware of the fetid odor —compounded of wet, dirty woolens, gun oil, foul breath and flesh long unwashed—of himself.

As if reading his mind, Jethro said, "Finish your drink, Milo, and Sergeant Webber in there will drive you over to my quarters. You can have a bath and a shave, Webber will trim your hair—and he does it well, too— then he'll take your clothes out and burn them. There's a full kit waiting for you in one of the lockers there, boots too. Then you can rest or sleep for what's left of today. If you want anything else, just tell Webber. We'll have dinner tonight, and I have to talk to you about some things. I need a promise from you."

When he was as clean as hot water, GI soap, a GI

handbrush, a GI toothbrush and GI tooth powder could render him, Milo used one of Jethro's matched set of razors and shaving cream to take off the stubble that had been well on the way to becoming a real beard. Before dressing, he had the most solicitous Sergeant Webber take off most of his just-washed but still-shaggy hair, leaving a half-inch or less overall.

The clothing left for his use looked like GI issue, but a mere handling established that it was not, it was of far better quality—the mesh of the jockstrap felt like and looked like silk, the shorts and undershirt were of an incredibly soft cotton, and, although certainly of wool, the long johns and the padded boot socks were almost as soft and unscratchy as the cotton.

Before he could even start to dress, however, Sergeant Webber, armed with a can of DDT powder and other assorted paraphernalia, said, "Uh, sir, don't you think you should oughta let me go over your body for lice? It won't none on your head, but that don't prove nothing, of course."

"You're more than welcome to try, Webber," agreed Milo, "but it's a waste of your time. The critters don't seem to like me, for some reason, never have. Nor do fleas, either."

The noncom wrinkled up his brows. He did not want to call the officer a liar to his face, but that he did not believe him was abundantly clear. "Uhh, captain, sir, you better let me check anyhow, huh? Typhus ain't nuthin' to fuck around with. The Krauts is dyin' of it right and left, and so was the fuckin' Belgians and Dutch and Frogs, too."

The well-meaning sergeant still was shaking his head and muttering to himself in utter consternation at finding no lice or any other kind of parasites on Milo's body as he stuffed the worn, filthy, discarded clothing into what looked like an old gunny sack. But as he reached the door, he turned back to Milo.

"Sir, if you're hungry, the gen'rul said I should go over to the mess and bring you back anything you wants, so what'll it be, sir? Roast beef? Po'k chops? Sumthin' else?"

His mind fixed on the neat, tightly made GI bunk in the next room, Milo replied, "Thank you, sergeant, but no, what I need is sleep, and that's exactly what I'll be doing before you get that jeep out there started. If you want to stop by and drop off a can of Spam and some C-ration crackers, that will be fine; I might even wake up long enough to eat them."

A look of sympathy and solicitude entered the sergeant's gray eyes. "It must be pure hell up there where you come from, sir. Here, sir." He fumbled out an almost-full pack of Camels. "The gen'rul, he don't smoke nuthin' but a pipe, now, and I noticed you ain't got but one or two left in that pack of Chesterfields."

"Thank you, Webber," said Milo, then asked, "You're not a Regular, are you?"

The noncom grinned and shook his head. "Nosir, not me. I was in the CCC for near on three years when the fuckin' Japs come to bomb Pearl Harbor; that's when I 'listed up and went to drivin' school at Fort Eustis. But I likes the Army—I gets three squares mosta the time, a place to sleep, good clothes and shoes to wear and sixty dollars a month besides. I don't think I could do that good as a civilian, sir, so I means to stay in after the war's over, and the gen'rul says he thinks as how I oughta, too. Does the captain think I oughta? I knows you and the gen'rul was sergeants together in the Reg'lars, back before the war, so you oughta know."

Milo nodded. "Yes, Sergeant Webber, I agree with the general. I think you'll make a fine professional soldier."

Milo came fully awake suddenly, with the knowledge that there was another person in the room with him, moving quietly, sounding too light to be Jethro or Webber. The light steps seemed to be approaching the bunk on which he lay. Looking out into the near-darkness through slitted eyelids, Milo sent his fingers questing to find the hilt of the knife strapped to his right thigh. With as little motion as possible, he drew out the honed length of steel blade, took a good grip on the tape-wrapped hilt and then waited, tensely, for whatever was to happen next.

A presence hovered above him for a few heartbeats of time, then receded, and he half wondered if this was only a waking-dream sequence, for all that he knew it to be very real. The bright white glare of light that burst through the briefly opened door to the outer room made it impossible for him to see anything much of the short person who exited and then drew shut the portal. But by straining his ears, he could hear the low-voiced conversation in the other room, and he could even identify one of the speakers, all of whom were conversing in Parisian French.

"He sleeps, M'sieu General. I was about to waken him, but thought that I first should ask you."

Jethro's voice replied, "You were wiser than you realized, *m'petite*. Had you laid hand to him he might very well have killed or at least crippled you."

"This Captaine Milo Moray, he is so much a brute, then?" inquired a second, less husky female voice. "The general should have mentioned this thing earlier."

"No, no, Angélique, he is a good man, a very good man, a true gentleman. It is only that he has been almost without any hiatus in combat since last year. And, *ma cherie*, one never should be so unwise as to awaken a man fresh from active warfare suddenly and unexpectedly in a darkened room."

The woman called Angélique still sounded unconvinced. "It might be wise if we were to not waken him, *mon general*, for our Nicole is too precious, too vulnerable, to become the toy of some brutal and uncaring man. She is a gentle girl, convent-reared, and despite all that was wrought upon her by the Boches, all that I have taught her since, she still is far from hardness. No, *mon genéral*, I will give you back your gold and you will please to send Nicole and me back to Paris."

"You are of a wrongness, Angélique," sighed Jethro, "and I am surprised that you will not believe me on this matter, for I have never lied to you about anything. Have I? But I will make you a proposition: I will awaken Captain Moray and then introduce Nicole to him. We will leave them alone, and should he offer her any violence at all, I will double the gold I gave you and immediately have you both taken back to Paris. Is that agreeable, Angélique?"

There was more conversation after that, but Milo had once more sunk into sleep. When next he opened his eyes,

the room was flooded with the white light of a gasoline
lantern and Jethro was shaking the bunk and saying,
"Milo? Milo! Come on, old buddy, come out of it. It's
me, Jethro. Wake up and have some champagne."

Fifteen minutes later, Milo sat cross-legged on the head
of the bunk, twirling his empty champagne glass between
his fingers, watching the slim young woman who sat
stiffly on the foot of the bunk, sipping at her own glass
and puffing nervously at a Camel, carefully avoiding his
gaze or at least refusing to meet it. From the other room
could be heard an unclear mutter of conversation and
squeakings from the bunk that had apparently been
moved in while Milo slept. In the light of the lantern, he
could see that she was pale, her dark eyes were enormous,
her breathing was fast and her hands very tremulous.

He leaned a bit toward her and extended a hand. She
flinched from his touch, then returned her body to its
former position, clearly steeling herself for whatever. But
Milo sat back and spoke to her softly in French.

"Nicole, you need have no fear of me. I have been
many long months without a woman, but it has not killed
me, nor will I be injured by further abstinence. Had
Jethro not brought you in to me, I still would be sleeping,
and I can easily go back to sleep still, for I am very
weary. I do not even need the bed; you may have it for
the rest of this night. The floor is carpeted—just let me
take one blanket and I will be fine. I am not really
accustomed to such luxury as this anymore."

He was as good as his word. Taking a last long drag, he
stumped out his cigarette, then rolled off the bunk, taking a GI blanket with him. When he had turned down
the lantern as low as he could without extinguishing it al-
together, he removed the seat cushion from the chair,
found a section of carpet that looked good, lay down and
wrapped himself in the blanket and presently was softly
snoring.

Not until she was certain that the strange officer was
truly asleep did Nicole Gallion even begin to relax. She
now knew that all of this had been a grave mistake, that
she never should have let the worldly-wise Angelique talk
her into essaying such a thing, no matter how much the
general had offered to pay. Angélique had reassured her

over and over on the way from Paris how easy it would be to earn her share of the gold sovereigns. She said that she had acquaintances who had known and done business with the general twenty years ago, before the war, who said that he was a very rich man and generous.

But now she knew that she could not go through with it, any of it. Not even for the vast number of francs that the gold and cigarettes would bring could she force herself to do this thing. She would just have to try to find some other way to provide for Papa—poor Papa, once so big and strong and vital, now all twisted and bent, crippled and blinded by the savageries of the Gestapo, yet still too proud to accept the charities of his fellow countrymen.

She did not want to disrobe, but reflected that as she had but the one presentable dress it were best not to sleep in it. In search of a hanger for her garment, she eased open the door of a narrow wardrobe and found a man's silken robe, far too big and long for her, of course, but it would serve as a fine sleeping garment.

The girl quickly removed her slip of American parachute silk, hung it beside the dress and, now covered in gooseflesh, slipped into the smooth, soft robe and padded over to the disarrayed bunk with its promise of thick blankets, not even thinking of extinguishing the lantern. As she slid under the sheet and blankets, she encountered a long, hard object. In wonderment, she drew the length of razor-sharp, needle-tipped, blue steel from out its rigid case, tested edge and point, then returned it to its case with the hint of a smile. Snuggling against herself, the knife close to her small hand, she settled for sleep.

The moans and whimperings brought Milo out of his sleep. His first thought was, "Oh, God, who's been wounded now?" Then, "Why the hell didn't they turn the poor bastard over to the fuckin' pill-pushers instead of bringing him down here into the CP bunker?"

The moans and whimperings continued unabated. He rolled over and sat up, looking in the direction from which the pitiful sounds were emanating. He wondered for a moment where he was and who the young girl on the bunk was, her pale face twisted, with tears squeezing out from beneath her closed eyelids, shaking all over,

shaking hard, like a foundered horse. Just as he remembered, the girl began to speak, both in French and in
halting, schoolbook German.

"Oh, no, no, no, please, I beg of you, do not hurt him
anymore. Oh, please, *mein Herr Hauptsturmführer*, for
the love of God, he knows nothing of the things you are
asking, neither of us do, we are not the people you seem
to think we are.

"Oh, no, *no*, please, *NO!*" The last word was
screamed, shrilly. The girl sat straight up in bed, her
teary eyes wide open, the look in them compounded of
infinite horror, her small hands clenched so tightly at her
sides that red blood was welling up over the nails.

Before Milo could move, the door burst open and a
nude woman stormed in, her red hair wildly disheveled,
her step firm as her jouncing breasts, and blood in her
eye. "You pig," she snarled, "what are you doing to her?
What . . ."

Her voice trailed off as she noticed the widely
separated sleeping arrangements.

"I didn't touch her, Angélique," said Milo, concern
patent in his voice. "I haven't laid one hand on her all
night. I was asleep long before she was, over here. I told
her she could have the bunk."

"Then what . . . ?" Angélique began.

Milo shook his head. "A nightmare, I'd presume. She
woke me up moaning and whimpering and pleading with
someone in French and in German. She was begging
some man not to hurt some other man was all that I could
understand."

Jethro, just as unabashedly nude as Angélique, came in
then, saying, "I think you might have chosen better than
you did at the sum I'm paying you, my dear. Why did
you choose to bring this strange creature?"

The red-haired woman sighed and sank into the now-
cushionless chair. "I brought her because she needs the
money, needs it desperately. Except for the . . . the *things*
that were done upon her by the Boches, in prison, where
I first met her, she is an utter innocent. She was born to a
class in which no trades ever are taught, so how else but
this way could she support her father, who is now all the
family she has left and is blind and crippled from being

severely tortured by the Gestapo who suspected him of activities connected with the Resistance?

"They did the worst things to him in front of her, forced her to watch . . . and to listen, the beasts. That was most probably her nightmare, living once again that night of hell, the poor child."

While they had been speaking, Nicole had slowly sunk back down onto the bunk and was once more breathing rhythmically, clearly sound asleep.

In the outer room, all three of them wrapped in OD field shirts until the hard coal that Jethro had dumped into the space heater had time to get started, Milo, Jethro and Angélique sipped at a mixture of cognac and champagne and nibbled at cold Spam and C-ration crackers.

When he had gotten his pipe going, Jethro said, "Milo, I'm sorry about all of this. I only was trying to help you get your ashes hauled tonight, since I doubted you'd been laid since you left England last June; and going without that long at a stretch can lead to recurrent bouts of stiffness in the neck . . . among other places."

Milo shook his head. "In a way, I'm just as glad it all worked out this way, Jethro, because I'd have felt like some kind of animal if I'd found out about all this *after* I'd screwed that kid in there."

Switching effortlessly to French in order to be certain that she understood, he said, "Angélique, the general will pay you two the full amount. As I told Nicole earlier, I reelay need sleep far worse than I need sex, just now. I'll just go back to that spot of nice, soft carpet and get back to it; if you're worried about my sincerity, leave the door open and the light lit so you can see the bunk and her."

Turning back to Stiles, he said, "And that girl has more than enough problems, it sounds like, without having to try to whore to take care of her father. Do you recall those stocks that my late friend in Chicago bought with the money I left him? I told you of them and you had me place them in your safe at the farm."

At Stiles' nod, he went on, "Well, what would you say they're worth now? That is, how much would you be willing or able to pay me for them, if you knew the money was to go to Nicole and her father?"

"I am not at all conversant with the current market, Milo," said Stiles dryly. "But when last I had the time and the opportunity, I think they were worth in the neighborhood of two thousand or two thousand five. Yes, I'll buy them from you, if that's what you wish."

To Angélique, Stiles said, "Do you understand, *m'petite*? The captain has just sold to me certain personal possessions and has ordered that the monies be paid to Nicole, that she no more will lack of the means to care properly for her father. It will come to some sixty ounces of gold, or the equivalent in francs, pounds sterling or American dollars. Do you still think the captain to be a callous, unfeeling brute, Angélique?"

Despite Milo's protests that he would be comfortable with just his carpet bed, Stiles opened a storage room, brought out one of several rolled-up mattresses and another blanket and a pillow, then helped to spread them in the place chosen by his friend.

"I always keep spares on hand, Milo. Sometimes my guests get so drunk they'd fall out of their jeeps on the way back to their own quarters, were I to let them leave here. And we simply can't have our field- and general-grade officers lying drunk around the cantonment area, you know." He chuckled.

Milo was almost asleep again when a slight noise from the direction of the door brought his eyes open. As he watched, Angélique eased the door shut and moved soundlessly over the carpet past the bunk to where he lay. Shedding the field shirt, she knelt, lifted his blankets and slid in beside him.

"What in . . . !" he began, only to have her clamp a hand over his mouth, whispering into his ear on a rush of warm, cognac-scented breath.

"Hush, *mon capitaine*, do not to waken Nicole. You are a good, a truly good, man, m'sieu. You are, in fact, too good to be a man—which species I know all too well. I think that the saints must have been like you in their goodness. You give everything and ask for nothing in return, and . . . and I cannot allow it, you must not go back across the Rhine with no reward for your generosity. *Le général* agrees with this."

Even while she had been speaking, her cool hand had

gone seeking along his body, had found that which it sought and had grasped it, gently but firmly. When she had said that which she felt that she must say, she slid about fully beneath the blankets so that her tongue and lips might caress that which her hand held.

Milo's body instinctively responded. He felt as if he were being bathed in liquid fire, and after so long a period of celibacy, he discovered that his power of restraint had gone. His first ejaculation was long-drawn-out agony, and he groaned in ecstasy. But the talented fellatrice was not done; she lingered, first draining him utterly, then, with tongue and lips and kneading, maddening fingers, rearousing him once more to full tumescence. Much, much later, Angélique left him to return to the outer room and Jethro, but Milo did not hear her go or even know that she had gone.

When next he awakened, bright sunlight was creeping around the blackout curtains, the lanterns were extinguished, and the bunks were empty of occupants. When he entered the bathroom, it was to find a handwritten note tucked into a corner of the mirror above the washstand.

"Milo,

"All play and no work makes generals into colonels or majors. Whenever you wake up and get yourself together, our good Sergeant Webber will be waiting outside for your orders or whatever. There will be no ladies tonight; they will be on their way back to Paris by then. We will have dinner and a talk and a bottle or three. Tomorrow morning, I have to leave on a trip for division and you'll have to go back to the front. Enjoy today, old buddy.

"Jethro."

The dinner brought in by Sergeant Webber and two privates was a masterpiece by any standards. Milo could not imagine where or how in a war zone Jethro had managed to get such foods and have them prepared so exquisitely—green turtle soup with sherry and herbs, poached sole in aspic, squabs roasted whole and stuffed with butter-soaked breadcrumbs, tiny mushroom caps and truffles, a dish of carrots and parsnips in a sauce flavored with ginger and nutmeg, tiny new potatoes boiled then sauteed with pearl onions in herbed butter, fresh and crusty long loaves of white bread, a selection of nutmeats roasted with garlic, an assortment of cheeses and cherry pastries soaked in rum and brandy. Jethro apologized for the lack of variety in wines, having only champagne to accompany the meal and his fine cognac or Scotch whisky to accompany the coffee.

As the two old friends sat over their coffee, stuffed to repletion and beyond, Jethro said, "I had wanted a suckling pig for this occasion, Milo, but the Germans simply wanted more than I thought I should pay for one."

"The *Germans*?" blurted Milo, taken aback. "Where the hell would the Germans get a pig of any description? They're all starving hereabouts, lining up at every camp to get our mess garbage."

"Oh, not from Germans around here, Milo. Most of this meal came from Marburg and points beyond, though the bread and the pastries were brought up from Paris by Angélique, along with the nuts and most of the cheeses. I have a contact for the purchase of various items I might want, and, Milo, you would be truly astounded at just how much can now be bought in Nazi Germany for American dollars, pounds sterling or gold—especially for gold. All of the Nazi rats know that the ship of state is sinking fast, you see, and they're making urgent plans for their futures elsewhere, which futures will require hard monies are they to be."

"Trading with the enemy, huh?" said Milo. "Jethro, if it ever gets out, they won't just bust you, they'll shoot you or hang you. Division might just slap your wrist a few times, but corps and army. . . ."

Stiles laughed aloud, saying, "Oh, Milo, you are a true *naif*. Old friend, I am not so stupid as to be in this alone. Some of the highest-ranking officers in this army are with me in these ventures . . . not in person, of course, but in spirit and in investment. There is over twenty-five troy pounds of gold coin concealed in this *pied à terre* of mine, along with some hundreds of thousands of dollars in various Allied currencies. Do you honestly think that I could receive or store that much without the willing con- nivance of my military superiors? Here, try the

Antiquary now, it's one of the best of the single-malts."

After a longish pause while Stiles fiddled with stuffing and lighting his pipe, he said, "Milo, what are your plans for after the war? The Army will be reduced drastically, you know. It's that way in America after every war, and that means you won't stay an officer. They'll likely only keep you in—a Regular or not—if you return to the grade you held before this all started.

"Milo, I keep having presentiments and disturbing dreams. I don't think I'm going to come through this war alive. No, now, just hold it, don't say anything, let me finish. My father, my mother, my first wife and the child I had by her all are dead, and my only living relatives are certain distant cousins most of whom I've not seen in years and never cared much for, anyway. If I do die over here, there will be no one to care for Martine, for she now has no family left, either.

"Milo, old friend, I want your solemn promise that should something happen to me, you will take my place, will give Martine the care and the companionship she deserves and will try to bring our children up properly. Will you give me such a promise, buddy?"

As men and the sinews of war poured across the Rhine over the Ludendorff railway bridge and the pontoon bridge that replaced the damaged span when finally it collapsed into the swift, swirling waters, the invading U.S. Army surged forward. Marburg fell to elements of General Hodges' First Army, then on April 1, 1945, his army and General Simpson's Ninth Army met near Paderborn and the encirclement of General Model and his half-million-man army was complete.

No one expected the skillful, determined and well-supplied German army to surrender simply because they were surrounded, and they did not, but fought on, fought stubbornly and well, against overwhelming odds, to defend the vital Ruhr. But it was an effort foredoomed to failure, for there no longer was a Luftwaffe and the defenders suffered day and night bombing in addition to the fire of guns, howitzers, rockets and heavy mortars, and, by April 14, Model's army had been split in half. On April 18, the valiant General Model, refusing to be

responsible for the loss of the lives of more German
soldiers, ordered his remaining units to surrender to the
Americans, then put his pistol to his head and suicided.

Milo had established the Charlie Company CP in a
house that still had its roof, on the outskirts of the town of
Delitzsch, just northeast of Leipzig. Since the drive from
the Rhine had begun, the company had lost two officers
and more than fifty enlisted men, but now replacements
were catching up to them and the other battered, understrength units of battalion, regiment and division, along
with much-needed supplies.

After a morning spent at battalion headquarters in the
middle of the nearby town, Milo returned to resume his
paperwork. First Sergeant Cohen entered and said without preamble, "Captain, when are we due to cross the
Mulde and head for Berlin? Do you know?"

Milo looked up and smiled. "Scuttlebutt up at
battalion is that we aren't. It seems that Ike means to let
the Russkis take Berlin, and we'll probably end up
hunting out diehard SS and Nazis in Bavaria. At least
that's what the adjutant thinks, and he's been right more
times than wrong, Bernie."

"Well, shit, captain," the sergeant burst out heatedly,
"we're no farther from Berlin, right now, than the
Russkis are, so why the hell just give it to them on a
fuckin' silver platter? Our armies fought just as fuckin'
hard as theirs did to get this close. We're less than a
hundred miles away, and all these Krauts are flat beat,
no fight left in any of the damned fuckin' Master Race
anymore."

"True enough, Bernie, but only around here. The
adjutant says that the Russkis are having to fight like hell
against troops every bit as stubborn as those we faced in
the Ruhr. D'you want to go through another helping of
that kind of shitstorm? I don't! I'd much rather think of
dead and wounded and missing Red Army troops than
American GIs, if you don't mind, Bernie. We'll no doubt
take casualites in those mountains down there"—he
gestured at a map of Germany tacked to a hardwood-
paneled, bullet-pocked wall—"but I guarantee we'd take
more if we moved on toward Berlin."

"Captain, by the way, it was a radio message came in while you was up to battalion. Your friend what use to be battalion CO, Gen'rul Stiles, is going to be passing through this afternoon and is going to stop by here to see you about something."

True to his word, Jethro roared up in a big, long, powerful Mercedes touring car, its brand-new GI paint job streaked and splashed with mud, its tires and under-carriage thick with huge gobs of the gooey stuff.

"Where the hell did you get the car?" asked Milo. "And how the hell do you, a lowly BG, get away with driving around in it?"

Stiles smiled and shrugged languidly. "Spoils of war, Milo. I acquired it from the widow of a . . . shall we say, a former busineess associate in Marburg." To Milo's raised eyebrows, he added, "Yes, that particular one. It seems some of his SS buddies killed him and took away all of his hard funds and all of his other small, valuable items, as well. So I got the automobile at a very good price, dirt cheap, actually.

"What I detoured by here for was this." Delving into the thick briefcase he had brought in, he withdrew two bulky sealed and taped manila envelopes and placed them on Milo's desk. "Scoff if you wish, old buddy, but I feel that my demise is very, very near, and—"

"Your demise from what, pray tell?" said Milo. "Jethro, this war is as good as over for us. The Krauts around here are all beat down flat and begging for peace; this whole fucking town is aflutter with white sheets hung out the damned windows. My company and the rest of the battalion and the regiment might well run into some stickiness if we are sent hunting holdout Nazis and SS, but you can bet your arse that division HQ isn't going to be anywhere near that fracas. So, unless Webber piles up that fancy new auto of yours, or you decide to take a stroll through an uncleared minefield, I can't think of any possible danger you might be in."

"Nonetheless, Milo," Stiles went on mildly, "put these in a safe place for me, please. Open them if you hear of my death. Otherwise, I'll pick them up within a few weeks or send for you to bring them to me."

He threw down the last of the schnapps and stood up. "Now I must be going, Milo. Remember your promise, my dear old friend. God bless you."

Out at the big automobile, Sergeant Webber opened the rear door and stood beside it at attention. After tossing the now lighter and less bulky briefcase in, General Stiles turned back and took Milo's hand in both of his own and opened his mouth to speak, and that was precisely when the first shot was fired.

Chapter XII

Stiles gasped, grimaced, then his legs flexed, and he would have fallen save for Milo's grip on his hand. The second shot was fired, and Milo felt something tear through the left shoulder of his Ike jacket. Almost at the same time, there was a third shot that struck the muddy boot-cover of the automobile and caromed off, whining.

Webber had stood for a bare moment in shock, then he had sunk to his knees beside the door. As he slid forward on his face, Milo saw the red-welling hole drilled into the back of his neck, just at the base of the skull.

Forcibly pulling his hand free from the powerful grasp of his friend, Milo reached for his pistol, slapped his hip and cursed; his pistol belt still hung on a hook beside his desk.

"Bernie!" he roared, "Get me a fucking weapon of some kind out here, and some grenades, too. Snipers. Snipers in the big front upstairs window of that house two doors up on the other side of the street. At least two of the Kraut fuckers. And get Nicely to see to the general —he's been hit."

Stiles lay quietly, his face whiter than pale and his breathing ragged. Milo could see no wound on the front, so he gently eased the man partially over. Then he could see it, and it looked far from good—a rapidly growing blotch of blood at just about the center of the left shoulder blade. With a retching, tearing sound, Stiles coughed up a thick spray of red blood, then, with the blood still dribbling from his mouth and nose and down his chin, he spoke, hoarsely.

"Milo . . . for the love of God, prop me up . . . can't breathe!"

Milo saw the long barrel of a Mauser K98 poke out of the window opening once again, and he ducked down, shielding Jethro as much as he could with his own body. But the shot was obviously aimed elsewhere, at another target. Milo heard it hit something more solid than flesh and bone, though it did elicit a vile curse from someone who sounded like Master Sergeant Chamberlin.

Sure enough, as he looked up at a nearby scuffling sound, it was to see the hulking Chamberlin belly-crawling toward him, a Thompson cradled in his thick arms.

When the noncom had come close enough, Milo grabbed the submachine gun from him. "Give me the magazine pouch, too. I'll keep the fuckers down. You hightail it back and get some more men, good ones, too, not any of these fucking johnny-come-latelies. See if you can run down an M7 launcher or at least some hand grenades."

The rifle barrel had withdrawn into the darkened room behind the window, but still Milo took no chances. Using the boot of the Mercedes for both cover and a shooting rest, he sprayed half a magazine of big .45 caliber slugs across the window, parallel to the sill. From the first-floor window came a flash and the booming sound of a pistol and the simultaneous smack of the bullet into the far side of the tire beside which Milo crouched. With a drawn-out hissing the tire began to flatten. But he didn't flinch, he just lowered the muzzle of the smoking Thompson and put the other half of the magazine across the width of the lower window; his reward was a high-pitched scream.

As Milo leaned back against the shot-out tire, ejecting the spent magazine and replacing it with a fresh one from Chamberlin's pouch, Jethro, now sitting propped against the side of the auto, extended a hand to grip his arm . . . very weakly.

He opened his mouth, then closed it long enough to feebly spit out a mouthful of blood. In a voice so faint that at times Milo could not hear it at all, he said, " . . . long, long road, for me. Martine and you . . . the last few years of it much happier . . . more real happiness than I ever deserved.

" . . . see things now, Milo. You, you . . . like us but not really us . . . ageless, timeless, immortal. You and . . . people like you . . . rule an empire . . . different world, then. You will keep . . . promise, see you keep . . . ing it. Then fight a . . . nother war . . . many other wars. Savior of a race . . . little children. New world . . . talk to . . . cats, horses, other animals.

"Be good . . . Martine, Milo, buddy . . . know you will. . . ."

Then the rifle was firing again and Chamberlin shouted, "Keep that Kraut bastard down, Milo, he just got Jackson in the leg. *Medic!*"

Again taking his position behind the boot of the Mercedes, Milo feathered the trigger, firing bursts of three or four shots each at the window. By the time the magazine was empty, Master Sergeant Chamberlin and four other men were crouching behind the bulk of the automobile—three with Garands, one with a BAR, the sergeant bearing another Thompson and a bag of grenades.

"Foun' two M7s, Milo, but not one fuckin' grenade cart'ridge in the whole fuckin' pl'toon. Would you b'lieve it? Shit!"

Before Milo could speak, First Sergeant Bernie Cohen came crawling out from the company CP, a carbine slung across his back and a bazooka in his arms, with a rocket for it in each hand.

Milo set aside the Thompson and grabbed the rocket launcher, but Chamberlin protested, "Jesus Christ Almighty, Milo, you'll blow that whole rickety place down, even if you don't burn it down. A fuckin' bazooka?"

Ignoring the admonition, Milo said, "Bernie, the minute the first one's clear, load the second one. There's snipers both up and down, looks like. Even if we do blow the whole house in, they've got it coming for hanging out white sheets, then firing on us the way they are. Okay, I'm set. *Load!*"

Three bodies were dug out of the tumbled wreck that once had been a house. Milo felt sick at first when he saw them, saw the faces; the eldest could not have been any more than thirteen or fourteen. But one of them—the one with a big-bore bullet hole between his neck and shoulder with the scapula brown away on that side—was still gripping in his dead hand a Mauser HCs pistol with three shots gone from its magazine. Seeing this helped him to recover quickly. In addition to the smaller pistol, they found a P38 9mm pistol, a K98 rifle and an Erma MP38/40 with a burst cartridge case in the chamber. There were in addition to the firearms two SS daggers, about two dozen more rounds for the rifle, another magazine for each of the pistols and one for the *Maschinenpistole.*

"Just a bunch of fuckin' little kids." Chamberlin shook his head in clear consternation. "Hell, the way they were shootin', I thought we was up against SS or Wehrmacht, anyhow. Where did three little boys get aholt of stuff like that, you reckon?"

"Fuckin'-A right they was good shots," exclaimed First Sergeant Bernie Cohen. "I'll lay you dollars to doughnuts these three here was Hitler Youths and been learning to shoot and fight since they was five, six years old. As for the guns and all, you can bet on it that them fuckers was hid by a coupla blackshirts what all of a fuckin' sudden come to think they didn't want to be in no POW camp and that they's ackshu'ly been innocent civilians at heart all along. And you can bet its a whole lotta fuckin' Krauts just like them in thishere town and from one end of Germany to the other end, right now."

As he stood looking down at the body of his old friend, Milo said to no one who could hear him, "What a waste, old buddy. You got through almost all of it without a fucking scratch, only to be shot down by a fanatic little kid who wasn't even old enough to shave, right at the tail-fucking-end of the fucking war.

"I was wrong, you were right about knowing you were going to die soon. But, hell, if you hadn't come up here to give me those fucking stupid envelopes, that little Krautling would never have had a fucking chance to get you in the sights of that fucking rifle, either. But who's to say, Jethro, who really knows? You could have run over a stray antitank mine on your way to or from wherever you were going after you decided not to come here today, too, or Sergeant Webber could've plowed that car into a half-track loaded with explosives and you'd both be just as dead. Goodbye, Jethro, goodbye, buddy. Yes, I'll do my best for Martine and your kids . . . but, then, you knew I would, didn't you?"

Old Colonel John Saxon looked his near-fifty years, every bit of that and far more, but for all his aged appearance, he still was the same tough, profane old soldier that Milo first had met back in '42. By May 5, 1945, with Hitler dead and the Russians fully involved in their savage, barbaric rape of the stricken, shattered capital and its surrounding areas, a staff NCO rang up Charlie Company and Milo dutifully reported to the onetime town hall, now the battalion CP.

"Milo," said Saxon, after they two had each partaken of the powerful schnapps that the American troops called liquid barbed wire, "you ever heard tell of a Colonel Eustace Barstow, a fuckin' counterintelligence type?"

Milo nodded. "Yes, John, he was a major back then, but he was my section chief at Fort Holabird, before I transferred down to the battalion at Jackson. Why?"

Saxon snorted. "Well, the fucker's a full bird now. He's runnin' some operation down Munich way and he wants you some kinda fuckin' bad. Was you his angelina or suthin, huh?" He grinned evilly, mock-insultingly.

The Colonel Barstow who warmly welcomed Milo was not very much different from the Major Barstow who had grudgingly approved his requested transfer to a combat-bound unit. He was become a little chubbier, perhaps, but still was very active and fit-looking in his well-tailored uniform, which latter was the old-fashioned one of long blouse, pinks and low-quarter shoes.

"Had God intended me to wear an Ike jacket and combat boots, He'd have had me born in them," he chuckled merrily. "But sweet Jesus Christ, old man, did you try to win the fucking war single-handedly or something? The only thing you're lacking from that collection on your chest is a Purple Heart and the Croix de Guerre. Don't worry about the Purple Heart—you want one, I can see that you get one. They hand them out now for bleeding piles and ingrown toenails, you know. Another thing—you give me a few good months of work, in my chaotic little hashup here, and you'll have a pair of gold oak leaves to replace those tracks, that's a promise, old buddy."

"Exactly what are you doing down here, colonel?" asked Milo warily. "Or is that restricted information?"

Barstow's eyes twinkled as he laughed. "Of course it is, Milo. It's restricted as hell, it's so fucking restricted that every swinging dick—American, British, French, German, Russian, Pole, Czech and, for all I know, Tonkinese, too—knows exactly what me and my boys are up to here . . . or so they think. But there are wheels within wheels within other wheels. I'm a fucking devious son of a bitch, Milo.

"Milo, we've got an unbelievably fucked-up mess in Germany just now. The Krauts brought in hundreds of thousands of so-called voluntary workers—slave laborers, actually, a page they took from the Russians— from all over the European continent. Every nationality and every race native to Europe and Russia is represented, many of them speaking *outré* languages we can only guess at.

"Then, there are the hordes of political prisoners freed from the various camps and prisons, the Jews and gypsies who were lucky enough to survive the death camps, the POWs of various nationalities from out of the scattered *Stalagen*—and it seems like five out of every six of those is a Russian whose native language is not Russian, who does not even speak Russian very well and who hates and despises Russians as much as or more than he hates and despises Germans.

"Then we've got the Germans—civilian Nazis, all the varieties of SS and Gestapo, Wehrmacht, Luftwaffe, Kriegsmarine, Hitler Jugend, former police of various kinds, a real hodgepodge. And, to really complicate matters, there's too a sprinkling of the Axis countries— Eyeties, Vichy French, Hungarians, Rumanians, Albanians, Poles, Vlasoff's Cossacks, Danes, Swedes, some few of Quisling's Norwegians, Spanish Falangists, Finns, Ukrainian nationalists, Serbs, Croatians, Dalmatians, Montenegrans, Latvians, Esthonians, Lithuanians, Dutch, Flemings, Walloons, a few Swiss nationals, Bessarabians, Turks, even one or two Syrians have turned up. Up north, the British chanced onto some Japs and a Hindu from Meerut trying to pass themselves off as Chinese and Polynesian, respectively, after having gotten out of Berlin just ahead of the Red Army.

"My present command consists of about three hundred officers and men and a few civilians and WAACs. Hell, I'll take anybody I can sink my claws into who can cut the fucking mustard—male or female, commissioned or warranted or enlisted, white or black or yellow or polka-dot, Christian or Jew or Moslem of Buddhist or atheist, military or civilian. My work is vitally important, Milo, that's why I'm so powerful just now. When I found out that you'd come through the war in one piece, I knew just how valuable a linguist like you would be to me, and I put things in motion to get you for my team. You can do your country and yourself a hell of a lot more fucking good working under mee, here, than you could going up against the Japs in the invasion of their home islands.

"Just how many languages do you speak, anyhow? We were only able to test you out on ten or twelve, as I recall from Holabird."

Milo shrugged. "I really don't know, Colonel Barstow, not for sure. It's always only when I'm confronted with a person whose speech I can understand or a foreign book I can read that I come to know that I own yet another language. Maybe twenty, I'd say, of present knowledge."

Barstow just grinned and rubbed his palms together in glee, saying, "Good, good, Milo, you're an answer to prayers. I'm going to put in the paperwork on your majority today. You won't ever be sorry you came back to work for me, I promise you."

After so long wearing uniforms and nothing but uniforms, the civilian clothing issued by Colonel Barstow's operation felt odd and sloppy to Milo. He was assigned an office equipped with an OD GI steel desk, a dark-oak swivel chair, a straight armless chair for interviewees, a four-drawer steel filing cabinet and three-sided length of wood on which was lettered: "MILO MORAY, CAPTAIN INF., USA."

But he had not been a week on the job when Barstow gave him a handful of similar wooden name blocks with vastly dissimilar names. "I'll let you know when and if to use these, Milo. Just stow them away somewhere convenient, for now. Sometimes it's better that they don't know they're talking to military officers."

During the course of the six weeks that followed, Milo had pass before his desk a broad cross section of the flotsam and jetsam of the war now concluded in Europe, and he determined the most of them to be nothing more or less than just what they were purported to be: frightened, confused, often demoralized, malnourished displaced persons, frequently neurotic, sometimes psychotic. But now and then he was able to unmask a ringer, too. No big fish, just lower-ranking SS, mostly, clumsily essaying to fob themselves off as former political prisoners or nationals of other countries, all of these seemingly desirous of instant repatriation.

His majority came through. Barstow presented him with a pair of gold oak leaves and jokingly pinned them on the shoulders of his gray tweed civilian coat, before he poured them each a glass of Scotch and sat down behind his desk, waving Milo to another chair.

"Once all this is done and most of the Army has gone back home, what are your plans, Milo? Mean to stay in the Army, do you? You could do a lot worse, you know."

"I don't know, colonel," said Milo honestly. "My permanent rank is tech sergeant, and that, or at most master, is probably the best I could hope for in a reduced army of Regulars. I've promised to care as best I can for a dead buddy's widow and four children, and I can't see trying to do that on a sergeant's pay. I might do better in the civilian world—I could hardly do worse, pay-wise."

Barstow shook his head emphatically. "You've obviously been talking to old soldiers who stayed in after the last war. Things are going to be very different for America and for her armed forces, once this thing is done, you know. The Powers That Be have, I think, learned a hard lesson well; I doubt that the defense establishment will ever again be allowed to wither and rot away into the near-uselessness of long neglect that it was become by the late thirties and early forties. There won't be millions of men mantained under arms, naturally, but the defense forces will be substantial, and I'm certain that the draft is going to be maintained, which will mean a continuing recruit-training establishment and a ready-if-needed force of trained civilian reserves always on tap for any real emergency. Yes, there will probably be some reductions in rank, but nowhere nearly so many as the old soldiers think. So you really should think about staying in."

Milo savored the Scotch, thinking that poor Jethro's taste in whisky had been far superior. "But colonel, I don't think that the American people are militaristic enough to put up with an Army and Navy of any real size squatting around the country."

"Not that many will stay in the States, Milo," replied Barstow. "Think about it a little. We're going to have garrisons here in Germany, in Japan and probably too on the assorted chunks of real estate we've taken from Japan, back in the Philippine Islands, in Italy, in North Africa and other places too numerous to mention. A virtual empire has fallen into our laps, Milo, a worldwide sphere of influence, a power vacuum, as it were; if we as a nation handle things properly, act with the force we now possess, we can have peace—real peace, long-lasting peace—through our strength. If we fail to use what we have to quickly gain what we want, there are other forces waiting to fill the void, and we'll be dragged into another war or two or three every succeeding generation forever.

"But win, lose or draw, as regards the world and power, Milo, our armed forces are going to be in need of good, intelligent, combat-proven Regular officers for a long, long time yet to come. A man with a record like yours should strongly consider a peacetime military career."

"Do you intend to stay in after the war, colonel?" asked Milo.

Barstow laughed. "*Touché!* You're direct enough, aren't you, major? In answer: yes, for a while, at least, until I've made brigadier, anyway. Then I might retire to teach, maybe to go into politics. I think I'd like being a state governor or a U.S. senator, and with the right backing, who knows how much higher I might go?"

As the months rolled on, the endless parade of inter-

viewees passed before Milo's desk—the loud, the uncom-
municative, the cowed, the arrogant, men of honor and
others who never knew the meaning of the word in any
language. No one of them would freely admit to ever
having been Nazis, Fascists or anything approaching
extreme right-wing politics, but there were adherents of
virtually every other hue of the political spectrum, which
often made for a difficult time in maintaining order in
the displaced persons camps.

Barstow's "command" were at best an odd bunch. As
most of them—and every one of the interviewers—
rambled around in civilian clothes, Milo never knew a
man's or woman's military rank, if any. They seemed to
number among them almost as many differing national
origins as the populations of the DP camps. Most of them
proved friendly enough to Milo; those who were not, it
developed, were not friendly to any of their coworkers.
They all seemed to go by first names or nicknames—
Ed, Henry, Bart, Judy, Red, Mac, Tex, Bob, Ned, Baldy,
Padre, Tony, Betty, Buck, Earl, Dick and so on.

The office abutting Milo's office on the left side was
that of a short, swarthy, black-haired man who, despite
his name, Kelly, was clearly no Irishman of any description. The office on the right was that of a vaguely
familiar, patently Germanic, serious-seeming young man
called Padre. When he had time, Milo racked his brain in
vain attempts to recall just where he had seen Padre
before, and all that he could dredge up was the thought
that it had not been within a military setting, but the
when and the where always seemed to elude him.

Finally, one evening, when late interviews had seen
both Milo and Padre arrive very late at the command
mess hall, Milo seated himself across from the fair-
skinned young man with the close-cropped blond hair
and gray eyes. When he had eaten his food and was
puffing at a cigarette while he stirred his coffee, he spoke.

"Padre, why are you called that? You're no Spaniard,
are you?"

Setting down his own china mug carefully, the young
man said, "No, not a Spaniard, Milo, but truly a padre. I
am a Roman Catholic priest, a chaplain in the U.S.
Army. And yes, to anticipate your next question, you

have seen me before. It was in Chicago. Do you recall Father Rüstung?"

Milo nodded. Now he remembered. "You're the younger priest, then, Father Karl, wasn't it? Someone wrote me that you'd joined the Army after Rüstung was arrested for his Bund activities."

The blond man sighed. "Yes, the bishop felt that, under the understandable suspicion that I then was, it would be better for both me and Holy Mother Church if I indicated where lay my true loyalties by making this martial gesture. I acquiesced, of course. But the military is not my true vocation, I fear; I never have risen above the rank of first lieutenant, and I doubt that I ever will, either."

"Hmmph," grunted Milo. "You lucked into the right outfit, then. Tell Barstow you want rank and you'll be a captain practically overnight, Padre. He hands out promotions as if they were candy bars, that man does."

Padre smiled coolly. "No, I think not, Milo, though I thank you for thinking of me. But rank should be the reward of service and dedication to the military; I am definitely not dedicated to the Army, nor have I, I admit, served it very well in this war.

"But how have you fared, Milo, since Father Rüstung forced you to leave Illinois?"

"Well enough, Padre, well enough, thank you. I joined the Army within a couple of days after I left Chicago, of course, and I had risen pretty far—I was a senior NCO— by the time the U.S. entered the war."

The priest nodded. "So then they made you an officer."

"Not quite," Milo answered him. "I still was a tech sergeant when we landed in Normandy on D-Day. My promotions all were of the battlefield variety up until I joined Colonel Barstow. I was a captain of infantry when I came here; now, lo and behold, Barstow has waved his magic wand and I'm a major."

Padre looked sympathetic. "And you feel a bit guilty, eh? You feel that, unlike your earlier advancements in rank, this present one was not fairly earned? Disabuse yourself of so silly a notion, Milo. Aside from the fact that because you fought and no doubt bled on occasion across a third of France and half of Germany you fully earned what little the military has grudgingly given you, were your talents not of inestimable value to Colonel Eustace Barstow, he would not have dragooned you from the infantry and installed you here and given you higher rank."

"Well, if that's the case, Padre," demanded Milo, "then how is it you're still a first john? You've been with Barstow longer than I have."

A silent DP mess orderly approached and refilled their cups from a steaming two-quart stainless-steel pitcher. He was closely followed by another, who took away their trays, and Padre did not answer until they again were alone at their table.

"Colonel Barstow only bestows rank and perquisites upon those who serve him and his ends well, that or those he feels he may in future be able to use. He is a devious and, quite possibly, a very evil man, Milo. Moreover, I am firmly convinced that there is a great deal more to what he is doing here than appears on the surface, so I do my job and no more, flatly refusing to involve myself in any scheme that is not fully explained to me in advance. This attitude does not please Colonel Barstow.

"In addition, our two philosophies are diametrically opposed. Barstow envisions a worldwide empire controlled by the United States of America and policed by a huge American Army. He sees the seas and the oceans commanded by fleets of American warships, all bristling with guns, while vast aerodromes full of warplanes lie as an ever-present threat to any who would in any way resist American hegemony. He sees the entire earth, eventually, ruled under the blade of a 'Made in USA' sword. I find the entire premise obscene, and I have so informed him on more than one occasion, for should so capitalistic, so blantantly materialistic a nation as America seize and wield so much undeserved raw power over others for as long a time as he envisions, there would be only a long succession of nationalistically motivated wars and rebellions, uprisings and partisan activity in every part of the world for generations to come."

"Then what is the answer, Padre? Should we just sit back and let the Russians have the rest of Europe, with

maybe China and India thrown in? D'you think Pope
Pius will enjoy taking orders from a Red commissar?"
questioned Milo.

The priest smiled knowingly; patronizingly, he
replied, "Milo, you have clearly been propagandized by
the capitalist Red-baiters. There is not and there never
has been any real conflict between the Church and the
enlightened rulers of Russia, nor are churchmen and laity
persecuted in Russia so long as they devote their religions
and churches to God and remain apolitical.

"The cold facts are these, Milo: this must be absolutely
the last war fought in the world. Love of God and love of
mankind must in future rule the world, not Barstow's
American sword. I am not a Communist, but I recognize
that Russia at least fought this war for nobler motives
than did America and is, therefore, more deserving of
world rule than is the United States, morally speaking.
America's obsession with making obscene amounts of
profit for greedy merchants and businessmen and indus-
trialists at any activity damns the nation and its people.
On the other hand, were it properly and fairly presented
to them, I feel certain that the vast majority of the
world's common people would prefer the rule of a secular
government of their fellow common people like Premier
Josef Stalin and a true—rather than a distorted or deriva-
tive—religion to spiritually sustain them in a world of
peace and order. Barstow, of course, does not agree, but
he is a self-serving lackey of the Washington power-
hungry, profit-hungry, war-mongering, capitalist Jews
and Protestants. You can see the truth of my words, can't
you, Milo? Of course, you can—you're an intelligent
man."

Milo stubbed out his cigarette, drank down the last of
the coffee, then leaned forward and said, "What I can see
is that you, Padre, are as nutty as the proverbial fruit-
cake. Your old mentor, Father Rüstung, was a hellish
mixture of religious fanaticism, anti-Semitism and
Nazism. Well, you saw what happened to him, and it
scared the shit out of you, so you went to the opposite
extreme. You have become an equally hellish mixture
of Catholic fanaticism, anti-Americanism and Com-
munism. I can't imagine why Barstow keeps a nut like

you around. In his place, I'd ship you off to a room with soft walls. If you really, truly believe in this internationalist shit, Padre, you'd better keep your mouth shut around anybody with two brain cells to rub together, because your presentation of the wonderful world tomorrow and what it will be like will drive them straight into the arms of Colonel Barstow's variety of American supernationalist."

After that late-evening exchange, Milo took pains to avoid further one-on-ones with Father Karl, nor did the priest ever again try to speak with him alone. When, years later, he saw Padre again, Milo was to wish he had found a way to kill him quietly in Munich. But more than two decades was to trickle away before that meeting.

In August of 1945, the world entered into the Atomic Age, a deeply shocked, stunned, terrified Japanese Empire surrendered unconditionally, and the main event of what history was to call by the name of World War Two was concluded. That is to say, the real fighting was concluded, but not the vengeance-taking against the prostrate, disarmed and helpless Germans, Japanese, Italians, Austrians, Hungarians, Rumanians, Vichy French, anti-Communist Russians, Ukrainians and Albanians. Many heinous injustices were perpetrated in that brief spate of quasi-legal revenge, but those nations who came to be known as Western Powers were not to realize just how unjust they had been, just how much they had been misled by certain of their own leftist leaders and by the self-serving Russians until it was far too late.

On an icy January morning of 1946, Barstow called Milo to his office and said without preamble, "You've done good work for me, and this is reward time. Think you can get back to wearing uniforms again, Major Moray?"

"You're sending me back to my unit, then, colonel?" asked Milo.

Barstow's burgeoning potbelly jiggled as he laughed. "Not a bit of it, old bean. No, I've just been given my first star—Brigadier General Eustace Barstow now sits before you. Raaay!—and an immediate reassignment to

Holabird. I'll be taking along some of the personnel. Would you like to be one of my jolly crew?"

"You're goddamn right I would, col . . . uhh, general, but I don't want to accept under false pretenses, either. For reasons I explained to you shortly after I arrived here and for others as well, there is an even chance that I won't stay in the Army at all, whenever the Powers That May Be decide that my hitch is up," Milo told Barstow in complete sincerity. The new-made general's reply almost floored him.

"Aside from your desire to fulfill your pledge to the late General Stiles and take care of his widow and their children, which pledge I assume you have translated into marriage to her and the Stiles fortune, what other pressing reasons have you to leave the Army, Milo?"

Milo just stared at the pudgy officer across the desk from him. Then, finally, he demanded, "General, are you some kind of fucking telepath? Have you been reading my mind? I've never once so much as mentioned Mrs. Stiles to you or to anyone else here in Munich, and to damned few back in my battalion."

Barstow showed several gold dental inlays in a broad grin. "Heh, heh, heh, Milo, you forget, this is an intelligence operation, and I feel the need to know everything I can dig up about everyone connected with it and me. Not that I had to go any further than to certain files to find out about you and your rich widow lady."

"What is that supposed to mean, general? Why should there have been a file on me? I was nothing more or less than a simple captain of infantry before you had me transferred in here," said Milo in obvious puzzlement.

In place of an immediate answer, Barstow just looked at Milo in silence for a long moment, nodded brusquely, then got up and strode to the office door and opened it. To the uniformed first lieutenant behind the desk in the outer office, he said only, "Condition Four-Oh."

In silence, the junior officer opened a drawer of his desk to reveal an array of buttons. He pressed one of them and a succession of metallic slamming noises from the direction of the door to the reception office told of a number of bolts now in place. The pressing of another button brought forth a deep-toned humming noise that pervaded the room. Then the lieutenant opened the cabinet behind him, took out a civilian-model Thompson with no shoulder stock and a drum rather than the military box magazine, armed it and laid it on the desktop before him. Then and only then he spoke.

"Condition Four-Oh, sir."

When once more Barstow had closed and, this time, multiply bolted his office door and resumed his seat, Milo said, "Jesus fucking Christ, general, what are you expecting? The survivors of the Das Reich SS-Panzer Division to assault this place?"

"As I said earlier, Milo, you forget that this is a counterintelligence operation, but you can bet your bottom dollar on the fact that the NKVD and Red Army intelligence don't forget just what we have here. And the real pity of it all is that certain persons in very highly placed offices in Washington have allowed our armed services to become so infiltrated with Uncle Joe Stalin's agents that it sometimes is difficult to be sure of the motives of anyone. But, for now, let's get your question out of the way. I can't maintain Condition Four-Oh for any length of time without arousing comment.

"Why were your name and other facts about you in a certain file? For this reason, Milo: your involvement with Brigadier General Jethro Stiles, deceased."

"Oh, come on, general, I knew Jethro from my basic training days on. He was no fucking spy for the Red Army, the Nazis or any fucking body else, and you're not going to convince me that he was!" Milo exploded with heat.

"Please keep your voice down," said Barstow mildly. "The device we activated only mutes out normal, conversational speech. You are quite correct, Milo, Stiles was not a spy, not in the ordinary sense of that word. But still we felt it well advised to keep an eye on him and any of his friends who spent time alone with him. We also had in his quarters microphones connected to a listening post and a wire-recording instrument."

"Well, you're sweet, trusting bastards, aren't you?" Milo said bitterly. "And why all of this shit, just because he was buying a few things from Nazis who were due to lose everything soon anyway?"

Barstow smiled thinly. "That operation was nothing more than what we in the intelligence community call a cover, Milo. It gave him a reason for being in touch with the still-unconquered portions of Germany, a reason even for occasional trips behind German lines. The few who knew aught about his clandestine 'purchasing trips' were of the consensus that he was representing and given protection by a clique of greedy general officers at corps or possibly army level, and he himself enhanced that impression by allowing the commander of your division to buy in on the operation.

"In reality, of course, General Stiles was performing something of inestimable importance for the United States and the future. It was something that is still too highly classified to tell you about. But we are certain that sudden realization of the truth, the real purposes of his activities, was what got General Stiles and Captain Wesley killed that day in Delitzsch."

"General, I was there, remember? Jethro was killed by three Hitler Youth amateur snipers. And who the hell is Captain Wesley?" Milo tersely informed and demanded.

"Wesley? Oh, you knew him as Sergeant Webber, his cover name for that operation. He was a loan from another agency. And yes, the shootings were very cut-and-dried, but only on the surface, Milo. And I cannot impart any more information on that subject to you, not now. Should you decide to remain in the Army and should you be cleared to work for me in my new assignment, I might be able to tell you more, someday.

"But for now, Milo, the war is over. You've done all that you can in Europe, so why not take this opportunity to go home?"

Epilogue

As Milo closed his memories and ceased to speak, there was a ripple of movement around the ranks of seated boys and girls and men and prairiecats who had gathered about the main Skaht firepit to be entertained by his tale of long ago.

While others rubbed at arms and legs and sleepy eyes or began to gather up tools and handiworks to stow them away for another night, two of the Skaht girls kept to what they had been doing. Myrah Skaht cracked nuts from a pile, separated the meats and tossed the shells down into the bed of dying-out coals in the firepit. Karee Skaht then took up the nutmeats and fed them to Gy Linsee, who sat between them. From time to time, Myrah stopped her nut-cracking to take from its place in a nest of coals a small long-handled pot with which she refilled the horn cup for Gy with a heated mixture of herb tea laced with fermented honey.

Milo communicated on a tight, highly personal beaming to Tchuk Skaht. "Look at those three, would you? I believe that the first thing we are going to witness upon our return is a wedding—Gy Linsee and not just one but two of your Skaht girls, Karee and Myrah. What do you think your chief will say to that?"

The hunt chief grinned and said, "He will say just what he has said since she first saw Sacred Sun: 'Anything that my Myrah wants, she is to have.' That's what he'll say, Uncle Milo."

Milo grinned, beaming on, "Well, considering what I brought you all here for, I can think of much worse results than marriage of a son of a Clan Linsee bard to a brace of Clan Skaht females, one of them the favorite daughter of the Skaht of Skaht himself.

"Yes, I think that my purpose here is beginning to see accomplishment, Tchuk, Wind and Sacred Sun be thanked. A few more such ties made between your nubile young people and I think that we will have seen the last of any bloodletting, on any large scale, at least. What true Kindred father would ride to raid against his own children and grandchildren, after all, and what Kindred son would ride against the camp of his parents or in-laws?"

Tchuk grinned, beaming, "Have you met *my* in-laws, Uncle Milo? But, no, you're right, of course, as you have always been, so I am told. Those of us who for so long have desired to see an end to this ruinous conflict should have thought of something like this, but then we lacked your vast store of knowledge and experience, too. We soon will start back to the clan camps, then?"

"Not hardly," replied Milo. "For all else I intended this hunt to be, it still is an autumn hunt, just like any other save for the fact that few warriors and no matrons are taking part in it. When we have loaded down the pack-horses with smoked game and fish and dried plant foods, that is when we'll head back to the camps, not before then."

"Well, that boar that Gy Linsee speared will help mightily in that regard, Uncle Milo. Even without the hide and the guts and the bones, there must be three hundred pounds of flesh and hard fat in that carcass."

"True," Milo agreed, "and the rest of the pigs are still out there, awaiting our arrows and spears, too. But what I'd like to find now is a salt lick, for I dislike curing pigmeat without salt. Let's give that task to the foragers tomorrow, eh? They'll be frequenting the vicinities of springs, anyway, in their search for edible plants and roots. You might try mindspeaking the more intelligent and communicative of the horses, too—sometimes they can scent deposits on the prairie.

"Now, I suggest we all get some sleep, for the dawn will come early, as always."

To the seemingly bemused Linsee boy, he beamed,

"Come, Gy, it is late, and I am going back to your clan's fires, this night. We can walk together and converse."

While he waited, Gy arose and was soundly, lingeringly kissed first by Karee Skaht, then by Myrah Skaht, then by Karee once more, then by Myrah yet again. Finally, Milo strode over and tore the two girls away from the tall, dark-haired boy, admonishing them and him.

"If I didn't know better, I'd think Gy Linsee bound outward for a journey from which he might never return. You two will see him no later than dawn tomorrow, you have my word on the matter."

As the ageless man and the adult-sized boy strolled in the bright moonlight along the bank of the riverlet, Gy beamed hesitantly, "I . . . uh, Uncle Milo, if still you wish to take me with you and the Tribe Bard, I . . . that is, you had said that I might bring a wife with me. Might I . . . I mean, would I . . . could I . . ."

Milo chuckled, beaming back, "Two wives will be acceptable, Gy—another set of hands never hurts when setting up camp or breaking camp or loading or unloading horses. If you and they both are in agreement on the matter, I say, fine. They'll learn a lot, as will you, my boy, traveling from one far-flung clan camp to the next. You'll meet Kindred you'd never see if you lived long enough to go to a dozen Fifth-Year Tribal Councils. I'll teach the three of you how to read and to write more than just your name, and you'll help me in preparing a series of maps of the land as it now lies. We will explore ruins as we come across them, seeking out metals and ancient jewels and any artifacts still usable after so long in the earth; some, the best, of these, we will keep, others will be guest gifts to clans we visit, the rest we will sell to roving traders or bring up to the next Fifth-Year Camp.

"We may live or migrate with this clan or that for months, and then again we may go it alone in good weather for just as many months, only seeking out a clan with which to winter when the cold begins to nip at us. Perhaps we will winter one year in a friendly Dirtman settlement. Yes, Gy, there are a very few such places, although they are scattered most widely and most lie far to the south of where we now are.

"And of course, all the while, Bard Herbuht will be teaching you the history of the various clans and of the tribe itself—the facts, the legends, the heroes, the great chiefs, significant raids, battles, victories, defeats, genealogies of clans and septs, and so much, much more that a Bard of the Tribe must know and recall when the need arises. He and I will also school you in the proper use of your mindspeak, and I am convinced that you possess already great untapped powers of the various types and levels of mindspeak, Gy. I am anxious to see you develop those powers, for a Tribal Bard is more than that title might seem to imply. At times he must be a mediator, a peacemaker between clans or factions within clans, and on those occasions, in those ticklish situations, an ability to soothe the minds of angry, blood-hungry men as well as frightened horses is a necessity owned by few. Herbuht is one such, I am another, and I believe that you can be, too, once your mind is awakened and becomes aware of its true talents and potentials.

"But back to the very near future, Gy. In the morning, my hunt will be riding back to where we were today, after the rest of those pigs—they're just too much meat in one place to pass them up. I'll be wanting you along and any other good spearmen you know of, too."

"But . . . but please, Uncle Milo," beamed Gy from a roiling mind, "I . . . we . . . it was my section's day to fish. Karee and Myrah said—"

Milo clapped the big boy on his thick shoulder, laughing. "Oh, don't fret, Gy. I'll ask for your two intendeds on this hunt with us tomorrow, and I doubt that Hunt Chief Tchuk will voice any really strenuous objections to the rearrangement of schedules."

At the Linsee area, Milo shooed Gy off to his lean-to, but he himself did not immediately retire. Instead he sent out a mindcall for Hwaltuh Linsee.

"On the council rock by the water, Uncle Milo," came beaming the silent reply. "Come and join me."

Milo climbed the flat-topped, mossy rock and squatted beside the Linsee subchief, one of the few adult warriors along on this very unusual hunt. Below them lay one of the backwater pools of the riverlet, and in its near-stillness, the silver disk of the moon was reflected. Now and again at intervals, something splashed in the pool and sent ripples out to break that silvery radiance into wavering shards that slowly recoalesced as the agitation of the water decreased to near-stillness again. It all looked so quiet, so peaceful, but Milo well knew that it was not. It was anything but peaceful, night in the wilds; night was the time of death as the night hunters prowled with growling, empty bellies in search of their natural prey.

"Were you at my tale-telling this night?" beamed Milo.

"Yes, for the first part only, though," Subchief Hwaltuh beamed in reply. "Snowbelly mindcalled me from up above. Crooktail had found a strange scent out a few score yards from the area of short grasses, where the horse herd is biding this night."

"And you found . . . ?" inquired Milo.

The Linsee warrior shrugged and shook his head, his braided hair flopping. "No tracks that I could see in the moonlight or feel with my fingers. I couldn't smell anything, either, except a trace of skunk or weasel musk in a couple of places. Nonetheless, I told the cats that I'll bed down up there tonight, close to the herd. With a strong bow and a ready spear and a few darts, I'll be ready for whatever may befall, I think."

Milo nodded. "A wise decision, that one. Now make another one, Hwaltuh. When we return to the Tribe Council Camp, Gy Linsee will announce his intent to wed Karee Skaht and Myrah Skaht. I ask that you not only not oppose this match but give it your full support should your chief object."

"Oppose it, Uncle Milo?" The Linsee warrior grinned. "Why should I oppose it? Those two Skaht chits show taste and intelligence rare in Skahts. Besides, they both look healthy and strong enough, and that Myrah Skaht has a fine eye for archery. Certainly I'll favor the match should the Linsee object to it for some reason, but I don't see why he would. How does this matter sit, though, with Tchuk Skaht?"

"He is of the mind that it will be a good thing for both clans," Milo replied. "And he has offered unasked to intervene with his chief, the girl Myrah's sire, on the matter.

"But that is not all on which I want your help, your voice, Hwaltuh," Milo went on after a brief pause. "After the hunt is done and Gy is married to his two wives, I mean to take him with me and Tribe Bard Herbuht Bain of Muhnroh for a few years. The Linsee may object to it, the boy's sire is almost certain to do so, and a few words in favor of the idea from you would be at least helpful."

"Why in the world would you want to take a fledgling warrior with two young wives who are both certain to be rendered gravid in a very short time with you and the Tribe Bard, Uncle Milo? If it's bows and swords behind you you want, I can think of a goodly number of Linsee men who could and would ride with you for a couple of years for a reasonable figure, just as warriors hire out as guards for the trader wagons now and then."

"No," beamed Milo, "you misunderstand me. Bard Herbuht and I and our party carry very little of value with us, we both are ourselves proven warriors and our women too, so we need no hired guards. Look you, Hwaltuh, Gy has a rare gift of a voice and of a memory and of improvisation; he should rightly be a bard, he longs to be a bard, yet you know as does he that he never will be allowed by his sire to become the Clan Linsee bard, in favor of his elder brother. Not so?

"Well, I hate to see natural talent of any sort or description wasted needlessly, and Bard Herbuht is of like mind. I want Gy to wend with us for long enough for Herbuht and me to fully test him and make a determination as to whether or not he will be suitable material for the next Tribal Bard."

"A Tribal Bard? A boy of Clan Linsee to be Tribal Bard?" Hwaltuh Linsee was so shocked that he spoke aloud, in a hushed tone. "That is so great an honor for the clan that I feel safe in saying that you'll get no single objection from the chief, and any that the clan bard might voice will be overridden by the chief and the Linsee Council. The Song of Linsee tells of right many mighty warriors, brave and wise chiefs, skillful hunters and the like, but nowhere of a Tribal Bard of our blood.

"You tell the Linsee your plans for our Gy . . . or better yet, let me have the time to tell him before you come to the chief's yurt. I feel free to promise that there will be no slightest objection or condition to Gy going off with you and Bard Herbuht."

When, the next morning, half the horses were mind-called down from the prairie above to be saddled for the hunting and foraging parties, Hwaltuh Linsee came down astride the bare back of one of them, not looking as if he had slept well, if at all.

"There's some something nosing around up there, right enough, Uncle Milo," he reported. "It's never gotten really close to the herd, and it's canny enough to stay downwind so that neither the horses nor the cats can scent it properly, but it's there, anyway.

"You take half of my hunt with you, today. I'm going to keep the other half of them and both of the prairiecats with me here, and I mean to find out just what is up there and whether or not it represents a danger to the horses."

Milo shook his head. "Hwaltuh, recall if you will, these aren't grown warriors we're dealing with, this hunt. If whatever is up there is at all dangerous or very big or there's more than just one of them, you're going to be hard pressed with only a handful of boys and girls to back you, with or without the cats and a few stallions. Keep your entire hunt here today. I know exactly where I'm taking mine, for a change, and immediately we've harvested those pigs, I'll bring them back with the meat. We've done a lot of butchering down here in the last week, and who knows what sorts of predators or scavengers we might have attracted."

Once up on the prairie level, Milo rode close enough to the now-reduced horse herd to mindspeak the two prairiecats, Snowbelly and Crooktail.

"Uncle Milo," Snowbelly informed him, "I have never smelled this scent before. It is a little like a big weasel or a skunk, but also it is a little like an average-sized wild cat or a tree cat or even one of the cats of the high plains."

"Does it smell at all like one of your kind?" queried Milo, thinking that they still occasionally came across a wild prairiecat, though such occurrences were getting rarer and rarer.

"No, Uncle Milo, not one of our kind," the cat's

beaming assured him. "Whatever it is is as big as a full-grown wolf, but it is no wolf—no wolf ever smelled like that."

"Well," Milo beamed, "Subchief Hwaltuh is staying behind with all of his hunt today, and he means to find it, whatever it is."

Aided by the exceptionally keen-nosed Snowbelly, Subchief Hwaltuh Linsee with a half-dozen members of his hunting party had backtracked one of the creatures that had been prowling around the vulnerable horse herd. Now he and the youngsters were squatting on the muddy bank of a small stream, some mile or more from the campsite. Strange tracks, big tracks, were all about them, and the odor which had so bothered the cats was here strong enough for even the humans to catch its powerful, musky reek.

Wrinkling up his nose in clear distaste, the big prairie-cat beamed, "There are nine of the beasts, at least in this pack, and they made a kill in this spot last night. The smell of deer blood still is strong in this mud, despite the other stench overlying it. They killed it here and ate it here."

"Then where are the bones?" beamed Hwaltuh puzzledly. "What became of the hooves, the skull, the antlers, if any? Foxes?"

"No, Subchief," Snowbelly's powerful telepathy replied. "No recent smell of foxes or any other kind of small scavenger is here. Those strange beasts must have eaten the entire carcass—meat, guts, hide, bones, hooves and all. And I find this most odd, for this was no small deer they killed, Subchief Hwaltuh, and they did not lie up here and gnaw away at those bones like normal beasts, but seem to have eaten them as quickly and as easily as they ate the softer parts. No wolf could do such —or would so do in a country so full of game—yet you can see by the size and the depth of the spoor, these smelly beasts are none of them larger than an average prairie wolf."

The Linsee subchief frowned. "It is something beyond my ken or experience, Snowbelly. Can you range the hunt chief? Or Uncle Milo?"

"This cat will try," beamed Snowbelly, then, after a moment, "No, Subchief, both of them are out of my distance."

The warrior stood up then, saying, "All right. Let's see if we can trail them from this place to wherever they went next. Strung bows, everyone, with one shaft nocked and two more ready. Any beast that can carelessly munch the bones of a big deer could just as easily shear through the leg of a horse or any part of one of us. Only a fool would trail such a beast all unready."

The trail of the smelly beasts wound on down the stream bank for a quarter mile or so, then struck out across the prairie, angling back more or less in the direction of the horse herd and the campsite. This bothered Hwaltuh, and he ordered the pace increased accordingly, for in his absence, there now were no adult humans in the camp, only some bare dozen youngsters— one of them lying burned and helpless—and Crooktail, the other prairiecat.

Nearer to the herd and campsite, Crooktail had perceived the emanations of a large feline, not one of his own kind, but in many ways similar, and, even as Subchief Hwaltuh and his band rode for the camp, the prairiecat was in silent converse with the spotted, short-fanged cat (Milo would have called her a jaguar, while the far-southern clans would have used the Mekikahn word, *teegrai*, to describe her).

A young cat, without a clearly defined personal territory as yet, she had followed the migrating herds north in the spring, and she now was headed south again as the weather became colder. She was roughly of a size with Crooktail, though finer-boned and less beefy of body. She seemed fascinated to learn that twolegs and a variety of cat not only lived together in harmony but even shared the hunt and the protection of grass-eaters from other beasts.

When Crooktail "described" the scent of the strange prowlers, the spotted cat replied, "Yes, the skunk-wolves. There are not many of them anywhere, though they are more common farther south than here. They will eat anything living or dead, and although they often kill their own food, they will still take a kill from any other they can find or catch. They themselves are inedible, even the young ones. But tell this cat more of these strange twolegs you claim as brothers and sisters and who keep you fed even when you cannot hunt, in the times of the cold-white."

Far from Crooktail and his wild feline companion-of-the-moment, away over on the other side of the horse herd, near to the edge of the bluffs, a mare had just dropped a foal. Her dark-bay flanks still trembling with strain, she was licking the infant horseling clean when her heightened senses told her of the imminence of deadly danger to her and her foal.

Two brownish, striped meat-eaters were stalking her in the open in a series of short, sidling rushes. They both stood as tall as or taller than a prairiecat—as much as six hands at the withers, though their bodies sloped sharply back toward the crupper. An erect crest of stiff hair stood up along their withers and thick necks, and their opened mouths were all big, gleaming teeth.

The mare screamed a terrified warning, then moved herself to take a stand between the threatening predators and her helpless foal. Warned by her hearing more than her sight, she lashed out with a two-hoofed kick to the rear and received the brief satisfaction of feeling her hooves make contact with a hairy something that gasped a whining scream and then thudded to the ground some distance away and made no other sounds of any sort. But even as she fought so well, so victoriously, against one of her stalkers, she realized that at least one other had gotten to, and sunk its fearsome fangs into and was dragging off her newborn foal. And even as a snarling prairiecat arrived on the scene at a dead run, the valiant mare felt rending fangs tear through her near hind leg as, simultaneously, still another set of crushing toothshod jaws clamped down on her throat and windpipe.

One glance at the huge jaws and bulging forequarter muscles of these beasts the spotted cat had called skunk-wolves and Crooktail recognized that this fight must be one of movement, rapid movement, slash and withdraw to slash and withdraw again, for to try to close would mean being held and eaten alive by the dog-shaped things. Beaming out a wide-spreading call for aid from the clansfolk and the herd stallions, the cat dashed in to claw open the flank of an attacker that had just messily hamstrung the doomed mare.

The creature turned its head on its misproportioned neck to snap bloody jaws at its own claw-torn flesh once, before returning to its attack on the mare, hunger and bloodthirst driving it harder than pain.

Crooktail drove in yet again, this time at one of the brown, striped beasts that was wrenching loose great bloody mouthfuls of flesh and entrails from the body of the feebly thrashing, piteously screaming foal. As the cat turned to leap away after laying open the back and off ham of the skunk-wolf, he collided full on with another that had been charging down on him; the impact sent both cat and beast rolling to sprawl on the hard ground, winded. Even as Crooktail fought to breathe and regain enough control of his battered body to arise and keep moving, he saw his nemesis bearing down fast upon him in the form of one of the largest of the huge-jawed skunk-wolves.

At fourteen summers, Daiv Kripin of Linsee was big for his age and race, accurately drew a bow of adult weight, possessed a rare eye for casting darts and was developing rapidly into one of the best hands with saber and lance in the clan. He was sure of himself, as a good leader must always be (or, at least, project the appearance of being). All of his clansfolk recognized that if he lived to adulthood, Daiv would one day be a sub-chief, and Subchief Hwaltuh had felt no qualms at placing the boy in charge of the camp and the herd in the absence of adults.

Daiv had the ability to think ahead, to foresee possible dangers and prepare for them, and he had therefore ordered that a fast and veteran hunter be saddled and accoutered and kept on a picketline in camp for each of the half-dozen boys and girls left to him. Therefore, when the mare's scream alerted him, he and the rest were already tightening cinches and mounting even as Crooktail's mindcall reached them.

"Wait!" he cautioned those who would have immediately turned their mounts and essayed the steep trail up to the bluff top. "First string your bows and nock an arrow—there may be no time to do so above in whatever is going on up there."

As the little party leaned well forward in their saddles to aid their mounts in balancing on the steep, narrow ascent, they all could feel the vibration of the milling, stamping herd, could hear the whickerings and snortings, and could sense the plethora of mindspeaking and mind-callings among the restive, disturbed equines. Horses, even the rare breed of Horseclans stock, possessed nowhere near the intelligence of cats or twolegs, of course; Daiv was of the private opinion that even cattle and sheep were smarter, and he prayed Sun and Wind that this herd would not take it into their empty heads to panic and stampede out into the vast prairie. Not only would that mean many long, wasted hunting days of running the brainless creatures down, as many as had not by then fallen prey to predators, or broken legs caused by their headlong flight, but it would reflect ill on him, since the camp and the herd had been in his keeping this day.

Daiv's hunter crested the bluff almost atop the spot where a badly clawed doglike beast was gorging itself on chunks of flesh and bone torn from the flopping, twitching carcass of what had recently been a new-dropped foal. Without pause or even thought, the boy drove a stone-tipped arrow fletchings-deep in the side of the singular glutton, just behind the hunched shoulder. And the well-aimed shaft had but barely left the powerful hornbow when another had been nocked and readied for use.

Some dozen yards or so away from the riders, they could see a fast and furious and bloody running fight being waged between six more of the big, ugly beasts, Crooktail and, surprisingly enough, a short-fanged cat about of a size with the prairiecat but of a very odd color —a base coat of golden yellow thickly interspersed with large black near-circular blotches.

A momentary contact with Crooktail's mind assured him of the verity of his original surmise, and he both shouted and mindspoke the other boys and girls, "Don't shoot that spotted cat. She's fighting for us against these smelly things." Then he felt it wise to broadbeam the same instructions to the scattered herd guards who were frantically galloping around the herd or trying to force a way through it.

Fearsome as were the skunk-wolves as predators and fighters against other beasts, the pack proved no match for seven mounted, bow-armed boys and girls of the Horseclans, and shortly they were become only seven arrow-quilled lumps of bleeding flesh and bone covered over with matted, stinking hair. That was when Subchief Hwaltuh Linsee and his six riders arrived with Snow-belly.

Dismounting, the warrior examined each of the dead creatures at some length and detail, wrinkling his nose against their hideous reek. "Hmmph. The skunk part of their name is apt enough, but I don't think they're really wolves. For one thing, no wolf has ever had ears like that, and, look you all closely here, the creatures all completely lack dewclaws, and their toe pads are of a very different arrangement than a wolf's are. They—"

A high, wavering scream bore up to them from the camp below the bluffs. There was a cackle of inhuman-sounding laughter and a second scream . . . or rather half of one, chopped off into sudden silence.

"Sun and Wind!" exclaimed Hwaltuh. "What . . . who was that?"

Daiv Kripin of Linsee paled under his weather-darkened tan. "The burned Skaht boy, Subchief . . . he's lying down there alone, no one to tend him or defend him. Could there be . . . do you think there may be more of these . . . these *things*?"

Hwaltuh flung himself into his saddle. "Yes, Daiv, there're more. We've been tracking at least nine of them across the prairie, and you lot only killed seven up here. Come on. Half of us down the center path, half down the upstream route. Snowbelly, you cats go ahead and try to hold them until we get down. You herd guards, stay up here on your posts. Mindspeak the stallions and any other horses you know well—try to get this herd calmed down."

Milo Morai needed but a glance at the nine holed, bloody and stiffening carcasses laid out at the edge of the stream to make positive identification of the late marauders. "Hyenas, Hwaltuh, beasts that look like dogs and behave a great deal like them, too, but are more closely related to cats or weasels, actually. They aren't native to this continent any more than are a number of other beasts now living here, but some must have been imported before the Great Dyings. Probably the many-times-great-grandparents of these lived in a zoo or a theme park and must have lived well on all the cadavers lying everywhere during that long-ago time. I'd never before come across any of them, never even heard tell of them on the prairies, before this. I hope we never again come across any of them, either. In Africa, I've seen packs of them literally eat animals alive."

"Uncle Milo," said Hwaltuh earnestly and solemnly, "I am very sorry about the death of that boy, Rahjuh Vawn of Skaht, and poor young Daiv Kripin of Linsee, conscientious as he is, goes absolutely crushed that he did not think in the excitement of the moment to see that at least one boy or girl remained down here to see to the helpless lad. He feels that he has failed in discharge of his assigned responsibilities this day, fears that the losses of a Skaht boy, a Skaht mare and her foal may recommence the feud and that that too will be his fault. What can I say to him?"

Milo looked at the other warrior, who now stood beside him and Hwaltuh. "What would you say to such a lad in such a case, Hunt Chief Tchuk?"

Tchuk Skaht shook his head sadly. "It's not that poor, brave lad's fault, not any of it, not the deaths of mare or foal or . . . or Rahjuh. Part of the fault for his death rests squarely upon my shoulders, for I flung him into that firepit and burned him. But the larger part of that fault lay upon Rahjuh himself, for had he not been danger-ously insubordinate, there would have been no reason for me to so harshly discipline him. Nor do any of my younger Skahts seem to hold this Daiv Kripin of Linsee culpable—they only seem to regret that they were not here to share in the battle against these whatever-you-called-thems."

"Then," said Milo, "I think that you and Hwaltuh and a couple of your young Skahts should seek Daiv out and tell him what you just told me. Make certain that one of the young Skahts you take along is a pretty, unattached girl, eh?"

Tchuk Skaht nodded, with a broad grin and a wink.

As Milo and his hunt lay upon the large, flat-topped rock drying their bodies and hair in the sun, the three cats crouched around a heaping pile of pig offal, gorging on the rich, fatty fare, while Milo and Gy Linsee mindspoke them.

"We all are in your debt, cat sister," Milo informed the stray jaguar female. "But for your ferocity, Crooktail feels that he would surely have been killed or at least seriously injured by the skunk-wolves. And Subchief Hwaltuh still is amazed at how you dashed in and, at great risk to yourself, bit clean through the spine of that skunk-wolf that was savaging the body of the boy. What can we do to repay you?"

Tilting up her neat head, her eyes closed, her gleaming carnassials scissoring off a tasty section of pig gut, the spotted cat beamed, "Crooktail has told this cat that if a cat helps you twolegs to hunt and to guard your fourleg grasseaters from wolves and bears and other cats, you will always provide meat and a warm, dry place to sleep with safety for kittens and cubs until they are big enough to protect themselves. Is this true?"

"Yes," beamed Milo simply.

She swallowed the piece of pig gut and immediately went to work detaching another length, sublimely unheeding of the metallic-hued flies buzzing and crawling upon her bloody face and the bloodier feast that lay before her. "It sounds a better, more secure life than following the herds of horned beasts and trying to find and claim a hunting ground where no big cat now lives, and being always fearful of dying of hunger in the long, white-cold. Could this cat become such a cat as Crooktail, twoleg brother of cats?"

"Crooktail's clan will be honored to include so valiant a new cat sister amongst its fighters," Milo assured her. "But by what name is our cat sister called?"

"Why not call her Spotted One?" beamed Snowbelly, in friendly fashion.

As he lay back and relaxed in the warm sunlight, Milo wondered if the prairiecats and the jaguar were closely enough related to produce fertile kittens or any kittens at all, then mentally shrugged. Only time would tell, in that matter.

But in a closer matter, there was no slightest doubt as to the speedy outcome. In the midst of the gathering of nude, damp boys and girls on the rock, Karee Skaht, Myrah Skaht and Gy Linsee now were thoroughly occupied with one another, completely ignoring the others around them.

Karee half sat on the supine boy's upper chest, presenting her wet blond pudenda to his eager lips and darting tongue. Gasping her pleasure, her small hands twisted through his dark, loosened hair while his larger hands kneaded and pinched and caressed her small, pointy breasts.

Myrah was astride Gy's loins, her knees and shins pressed to the rockface, head thrown back, eyes scewed tightly shut, spine arched, hands clenched, every line and muscle showing tension as she rocked slowly back and forth, back and forth.

Milo reflected that, in company with Gy Linsee and his two hot-blooded young wives, the next few years of traveling should be anything but boring.

ABOUT THE AUTHOR

ROBERT ADAMS lives in Seminole County, Florida. Like the characters in his books, he is partial to fencing and fancy swordplay, hunting and riding, good food and drink. At one time Robert could be found slaving over a hot forge, making a new sword or busily reconstructing a historically accurate military costume, but, unfortunately, he no longer has time for this as he's far too busy writing.

**Buy them at your local
bookstore or use coupon
on next page for ordering.**